"I'm a little co..." "why did you claim me?"

"Your spirit intrigued me. You speak our language well, and I have some interest in the human perspective. Perhaps you can provide me with a new one."

Trinity looked at him as if he were slightly mad. As he would be, in most Opiri's eyes.

She rubbed her arms as if she were cold, though nearly all of Erebus was kept warmer than most of her kind preferred. "I know I have no rights. But I am...glad you won me."

Yet her eyes were soft, her lips parted, her face flushed as if with desire. The unmistakable scent of sexual arousal rose from her body.

Ares grabbed her by the shoulders, lifted her face to his level and kissed her. His teeth grazed her lower lip, giving him the smallest taste of her sweet blood.

SUSAN KRINARD

has been writing paranormal romance for nearly twenty years. With *Daysider* she began a series of vampire paranormal romances, the Nightsiders series, for Harlequin Nocturne.

Sue lives in Albuquerque, New Mexico, with her husband, Serge, her dogs, Freya, Nahla and Cagney, and her cats, Agatha and Rocky. She loves her garden, nature, painting and chocolate...not necessarily in that order.

NIGHTMASTER

—

SUSAN KRINARD

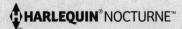

Recycling programs
for this product may
not exist in your area.

ISBN-13: 978-0-373-88584-8

NIGHTMASTER

Copyright © 2013 by Susan Krinard

Printed in U.S.A.

www.Harlequin.com

Dear Reader,

It's a time of peace between vampires—Opiri—and humans. But according to the Treaty, convicted criminals of the human Enclave must be sent as "serfs" to the vampire Citadel of Erebus, there to become the property of a Bloodmaster or Bloodlord.

Trinity is sent to Erebus with a shipment of so-called criminals...but as a spy, not a slave. And soon she finds herself belonging to one of the most powerful and dangerous Opiri in the Citadel: Ares, who is incapable of love. Or is he?

I hope you enjoy the second book in my Nightsiders series.

Susan Krinard

As always, with thanks to Lucienne Diver
and Leslie Wainger.

Chapter 1

Trinity Ward waited with the other dozen convicts, her wrists aching from the grip of the padded cuffs that kept her hands locked together at her waist.

Not that she would have fought to escape. This was where she was supposed to be, among these poor, lost souls whose punishment was to be more terrible than mere imprisonment. Or even death.

They were condemned to a life of blood slavery to some Nightsider master in the Opir city of Erebus—an existence of unending servitude—until they were too old to provide blood or serve in any other capacity.

But these living offerings around Trinity, men and women who had committed only the most minor crimes, were not old. Some were in their late teens; the eldest couldn't have been more than fifty. If not for the Treaty and the need to maintain the Armistice, they might have lived normal lives, sentenced by the Courts to jail time, probation and reparations.

Except that there were only two jails in the Enclave, and they were nearly empty. Crime had dropped to levels unknown in all of human history. Dropped so far that the bloodsuckers were growing restless.

"What did you do?" a young woman standing next to Trinity asked in a surprisingly calm voice.

Trinity met her gaze. She knew what the woman saw: normal human eyes, not the catlike pupils of a half human, half Nightsider dhampir. In a way, the contact lenses were like shields, not only concealing Trinity's identity, but also helping her keep her distance from those around her.

Distance, Trinity thought, shouldn't be a problem. She had been chosen for this assignment because she was known as the most unflappable, most controlled operative in all of Aegis. The one without close friends or lovers, because she wanted it that way.

Still, it was hard looking at this woman's face, knowing she hadn't earned the fate that awaited her. None of these people had.

"I didn't pay my taxes," Trinity whispered. "You?"

The woman's brown eyes filled with tears. "I stole a pair of earrings. They weren't expensive at all, but I hadn't had something pretty like that in—" She broke off, her calm dissolving in grief and fear.

"I'm sorry," Trinity said, awkwardly touching the woman's arm.

"It wouldn't be so bad if it weren't for my daughter," the woman said, wiping her eyes on her forearm. "She's going to stay with my parents now. They'll take good care of her. But I—"

She didn't have to finish. Trinity knew what it was like to lose family. Not that she'd ever really had one. Her Nightsider father, whom she didn't remember, had been killed at the end of the War when Enclave soldiers had found him in possession of Trinity's mother and their daughter, treating both as prisoners rather than anything a human would call a "family."

Trinity's mother had taken her back to the Enclave. But there had never been another father. And Trinity had grown up half vampire in a world of humans who feared and hated the part of her that made her so different, so much faster and stronger and keener of vision, able to see in the dark and with teeth made for drinking blood.

Something most dhampires would rather die than sink to.

"My name is Trinity," she said to her companion.

"Rachel," the woman said, raising her bound wrists. "I can't shake your hand."

Suddenly they both laughed, the laughter of people without hope. Trinity wasn't completely faking it. She knew her odds of coming out of this alive and free were minimal, but that wasn't what she feared. She *had* to obtain the necessary information and get word out of Erebus. If this was to be her last assignment, she intended to make it count.

"Attention," the soldier at the front of the column shouted, his helmet reflecting the sunlight. "You'll be boarding the ferry now. When we reach the Larkspur Ferry Terminal, you will board a transport to the border of the Zone, where we will proceed on foot to the transfer point." He scanned the small gathering, his eyes—and his feelings—hidden behind his visor. "Any disruption or attempt to escape will be met with force."

He glanced at his fellow soldiers flanking the crooked line of dozen convicts and moved closer. "Stay alive," he said in a soft voice obviously meant only for the prisoners. "There's always a chance things will change. If we ever beat the bloodsuckers—"

"Sergeant!" one of the other soldiers said. "Ferry's ready to board."

The sergeant stepped back and nodded brusquely, gesturing with his rifle. The convicts walked onto the boat and moved to the center of the deck, heads down and shoulders slumped. The soldiers instructed them to sit on the hard benches under the canvas canopy and then clipped the prisoner's ankles to rings fixed to the deck at their feet.

Trinity watched the soldiers patrolling the deck, far more than were needed to escort a dozen petty offenders. Did any of them have relatives or friends who'd been deported? She knew that the kin of politicians and higher-ups in the government were usually spared this punishment, including the board of directors of Aegis itself.

It wasn't fair. But neither was the fact that the bloodsuckers had devastated the earth before the attrition of their own numbers had forced them into a truce. These men and women were soldiers, and sometimes soldiers did what they didn't want to do.

You can never forget you're only a slave from now on, she told herself. *You have to make sure you're chosen by the right Bloodmaster or Bloodlord. And then you have to make yourself indispensable to him.*

That meant playing the part of a proper serf—and, if necessary, revealing her dhampir nature. Because, in spite of the supposed rarity of half-breed captives among the Nightsiders, it was believed that the leeches found nothing more delectable than dhampir blood.

Or more addictive. Some Nightsiders were highly prone to physical dependence on that same blood. And that was Trinity's most powerful secret weapon. A dependent Nightsider was one she could manipulate.

But she intended to keep her true nature hidden as long as possible. In addition to the contacts, she wore caps over her front teeth to conceal her longer incisors, and no Nightsider she encountered would immediately be able to detect the difference in the smell and unique taste of her blood.

The experimental drugs she'd been given—drugs whose antidote had been inserted into one of her molars—would mask those differences until she didn't need to hide them. They would also counter the addictive qualities of her blood until she required them. But just as important were the injections that were supposed to lessen the risk of Conversion or pregnancy.

Of course, no one was completely sure what happened when a dhampir was converted, in spite of the many times Aegis operatives had come into contact with Opir agents in the field. If any dhampir had become a Nightsider, he or she had never returned to the Enclave. And no one had ever seen the child of a dhampir and a Nightsider.

The engine of the ferry rumbled beneath Trinity's feet, drawing her out of her thoughts, and soon the vessel was pulling away from the pier. No one spoke until they reached the Terminal in the old county of Marin. One boy of about eighteen let out a yell of sheer terror and then went silent when one of the soldiers turned his way.

After that, there was only more silence as the soldiers herded the prisoners to the truck.

The ride was jolting and uncomfortable, the truck carrying its unwilling passengers over roads left to weeds and weather, across fallow and overgrown fields, past empty towns and small cities that seemed to echo with ghostly voices.

Trinity stared straight ahead as the truck cut north toward the transfer point in the abandoned city of Santa Rosa. It was dusk when the truck reached its destination. The soldiers helped the exhausted prisoners climb down from the vehicle, unfastened the cuffs and offered them dinner rations and water. Some ate as if they were starving; others ignored the food completely.

Trinity ate. She needed all her strength, and because she was one of the sixty percent of dhampires who didn't require drugs to digest solid food, she was free to eat whatever she wanted. Once she was finished, she listened to the hoot of an owl and the nearly silent footfalls of a coyote in the hills—sounds none of the humans could detect.

By sunset, as the human soldiers watched with guns raised and night visors glowing, the Nightsiders, anonymous behind their own visors, emerged from the fringe of oak woods at the base of the hills to the west.

In minutes the formal exchange had been made. The Enclave soldiers stepped back, and the Nightsiders closed in around the exiles.

No one put up a struggle. The Nightsiders spoke no more than was strictly necessary. The prisoners climbed into the hills and walked along narrow roads that wound through the Mayacamas mountains, wreathed in darkness lit only by the sweeping beams of the Opir soldiers' headlamps. Halfway up to the pass, the Nightsiders made camp and allowed their charges to eat and sleep.

Trinity remained awake, listening and observing as the bloodsuckers spoke among themselves in their ancient language, hoping that one of them would be careless enough to reveal something that might be of use to her.

But none said anything she didn't already know. After a while, the soldiers and their prisoners continued up the mountain, making camp again with the rising of the sun. The Nightsiders set up a shelter of heavy canvas, and two rested while the other two kept watch.

Near the end of the second night, they saw Erebus.

The vampire city was all black crystal spires and obsidian facets, a vast hive surrounded by pastures and fields of grain that produced food to keep the serfs alive and healthy. Trinity knew that Erebus housed some five thousand Opiri—and three times as many humans. Below the Citadel's foundations lay countless chambers occupied by the lowest-ranked free Opiri and public serfs who served the city as a whole.

In the spires, the Towers, lived those of highest rank: the Bloodmasters and Bloodlords with their Households of vassals, serfs and client Freebloods. In their feudal society, rank and power were everything.

One of the prisoners began to weep and collapsed to her knees. A wiry man in his twenties helped her up with quiet words of comfort. Then they were moving again at a faster pace as the Opir raced the sunrise, descending out of the hills.

When the exiles were within a quarter mile of their new "home," three of the soldiers picked up the slowest prisoners and flung the humans over their shoulders like sacks of grain. The rest, including Trinity, crept closer and closer to the Citadel until they were at its foot, gathering under the stares of the Freeblood guards along the sheltered battlements.

Trinity gazed up at the tall, heavy gates, obsidian black like the rest of the Citadel, and watched them swing inward. More Opir soldiers waited inside to take charge of the prisoners.

The humans stood inside a wide, enclosed area between the curtain wall and the Citadel proper. Heavy material that seemed to be a combination of canvas and plastic stretched across the open space several yards above Trinity's head, protecting the Opiri within. Bright lights, harmless to the Nightsiders, shone from niches in the walls, obviously installed for the benefit of the human serfs, who were hard at work performing various tasks. The towers, visible through a slight gap in the canopy, pierced the lightening sky and the scudding, orange clouds.

The second set of soldiers uncuffed the prisoners' wrists and gestured with their rifles toward a second gate on the other side of the courtyard. Moments later they entered a

wide, dimly lit corridor, elaborately etched and painted
with baroque designs and stylized figures in different hues.
The corridor led to another and yet another, a maze humans
might negotiate only with the aid of the changing colors
and designs on each wall. Trinity could feel the passages
descending into the bowels of the city, smelling of damp-
ness and a taint of old blood.

The final corridor ended in a row of holding cells. Two
by two the new serfs were ushered into the cells, and Trinity found herself housed with Rachel. The cell itself contained only two narrow cots, a toilet and a sink with towels.

"Are we supposed to clean up in here?" Rachel asked
in a dull voice.

"I don't know," Trinity said, examining the sink. "There's
some kind of soap dispenser, but I can't believe they expect
us to do much with it."

Nevertheless, she wet one of the towels, squirted a little
soap on it and washed the grime off her face. She undid
her hair from its rough ponytail and shook it out.

"You've got pretty hair," Rachel said.

"Thanks," Trinity muttered, hardly knowing how to
react to the compliment. She wasn't good at that even under
the best of circumstances.

As Rachel washed her own face and sat on the edge of
one of the cots, slumping in exhaustion. Trinity lay face up
on hers, pillowing her head on her arms, and tried to clear
her mind.

She knew what was coming: the Claiming, where the
highest-ranked Opiri were given a chance to bid on the new
serfs. Considering the process from an entirely intellectual
perspective, Trinity knew the experience was going to be
unpleasant. But her only goal was to catch herself a Bloodlord or Bloodmaster who would unwittingly help her achieve
her goals. The higher the rank of her owner, the more free-

dom she was likely to have within the Citadel. And such freedom was what she needed to carry out her mission.

Trinity woke to the sound of the door to the cell swinging open. She jumped to her feet in a single motion, forgetting that she had to blend in with the untrained serfs. Rachel got up more slowly, shrinking behind Trinity as if she knew her cell mate was capable of much more than her ordinary appearance indicated.

In the doorway stood a Freeblood, white haired and pale skinned, no soldier but some kind of functionary in plain black robes. He gestured to Trinity and Rachel.

"You are to be prepared," he said in a voice that told Trinity that he had little interest in the proceedings. "Come with me."

She assumed her role as a subjugated human and walked out of the cell, Rachel on her heels. The other female prisoners were huddled in the corridor under the supervision of several black-robed Opiri. The Nightsiders herded the new serfs to the door of a much larger room, fitted with open showers, a row of curtained booths and three female attendants.

As Trinity and the other convicts entered the room, two of the attendants, wearing shapeless white shifts, smiled encouragingly. The third woman, dressed in a white tunic and trousers, was considerably more severe.

"You have to be examined," she said without preamble.

Trinity stiffened and then forced herself to relax. She'd been thoroughly briefed, after all. The bloodsuckers had to know what they were bidding on.

The new serfs were instructed to undress, shower and then enter the booths. A few minutes later the examiner swept aside the curtain and entered Trinity's cell. With practiced efficiency, the women examined Trinity's body, looking for scars, disease or other defects.

She frowned as she finished. "Something different about you," she said.

Trinity laughed to hide her unease. "I don't know if that's an insult or a compliment."

The examiner sighed. "Are you a virgin?"

"No," Trinity said, releasing her breath. "Is that important?"

"It doesn't really matter," the other woman said. "Not to most of them." She made a notation on her pad. "You'll do."

The examiner instructed Trinity to dress, and then swept out of the booth. Trinity followed, and the attendant waiting outside gestured her to a seat facing a row of mirrors.

"The more attractive you appear," she said, smoothing her fingers over Trinity's damp hair, "the greater the chance that you will be claimed by an Opir of high rank and live a life of relative ease." She selected a brush from among the items on the nearby shelf. "You have lovely hair. I think we'll leave it loose."

When the attendant had finished brushing Trinity's hair to a glossy, chestnut sheen, she produced a shift similar to her own but much shorter and sheerer. It would do little to disguise the body beneath.

That, too, was no surprise.

The other prisoners were put through the same ordeal, and when the attendants were finished even the older women, dressed in more modest shifts, seemed nearly incandescent. Only their grim and frightened faces spoiled the effect.

"Be brave," the elder attendant advised them. "Remember, your fate is at least partly in your own hands."

The prisoners were led into the corridor where they met the equally dazed men, who were dressed in longer tunics and groomed to their greatest possible advantage. With the black-robed escorts around them, the humans were ushered into a large elevator, which swiftly ascended several floors.

When they arrived at their destination, the humans stepped into an entirely different world—not dark like the lower levels, but gleaming with saturated color like rich velvet and painted with golden symbols.

Trinity observed carefully as she was shown to a private cell, this one with a transparent front wall and no furnishings at all—the "display case" for the serfs to be claimed. Through the slightly opaque sidewalls she could make out the boy who had panicked earlier, though his face was only a blur.

Outside the clear wall was a semicircular room, a kind of covered amphitheater with rows of richly upholstered seats. Within minutes the first of the Opiri arrived, male and female, some dressed in embroidered robes that reached nearly to the floor, others in thigh-length tunics and loose pants tucked into handmade leather boots. Jewels cascaded from long white hair, at throats and belts; the men were as regally clothed as the women. Each and every one could pass as a king or queen of his or her own realm.

But one stood out from all the others. A silence fell among the murmuring Nightsiders as a tall lord wearing a long tunic, wide embroidered belt and trousers of deep blue entered the room. He appeared to be in his early thirties, but Trinity knew he could be anywhere from one hundred to ten thousand years old.

This man's age wasn't what interested her. He had raven-black hair. No Opiri except vassals, who retained their human coloring for some time, had anything but white hair. And this one's skin, instead of being bonewhite, was a very fair gold. His face was lean and handsome, and his eyes…

As if he sensed her stare, he looked directly at Trinity. His eyes were not the deep purple or maroon of a normal

Opir's; they were a pale tint of violet that would have been extraordinary in any human. Trinity could feel that gaze stripping her shift from her body.

Without taking his eyes from her, the Nightsider gestured to the young human male behind him. The attendant held a tall staff capped with what looked like an ancient Corinthian helmet cast of gold. He handed the staff to his master, and the Nightsider held it firmly planted on the floor beside his chair as if he were staking a claim to territory no one dared dispute.

He was powerful. Trinity didn't need anything but simple observation to make that very clear. The other Bloodlords and Bloodladies kept their distance from him, and several seemed to regard his presence with surprise.

Trinity knew then that he was the one. She couldn't have explained it rationally, but instinct told her she was right. Dhampir instinct. And she intended to trust what her half-vampire nature told her.

Even if it told her that she was feeling things she had no right or reason to feel. That suddenly she didn't look upon surrendering her body and blood to a Nightsider as a terrible sacrifice.

And that feeling, unfamiliar and insane as it was, held far more danger than fear. Especially if her instincts were wrong, and this man was the cruelest, most barbaric bloodsucker in the Citadel of Night.

Chapter 2

Ares had expected nothing like the woman in the center cell.

It wasn't only that she was beautiful. That was clear at first glance. The display at the top of the cell marked her as a healthy female of twenty-nine years, free of disease or obvious defect. Further description indicated that she was well educated in her own Enclave, fluent in the Opir tongue and several ancient human languages. Her hair, a rich coppery-brown, fell just past her shoulders. Her striking eyes were brown rimmed with green.

Those eyes gazed at him unflinchingly, as if she thought nothing of her near nudity and her pitiful situation. That was unusual in a new serf put up for Claiming. They were usually frightened and confused, rarely defiant.

Not this one.

Ares rested his chin on his fist, suddenly aware of all the sounds and scents and small movements in the room. He had come to the Claiming because Lady Roxana had

convinced him that it was well past time for him to reinforce his rank as a Bloodmaster. He preferred keeping to
himself and appeared in society only as often as maintaining his status made necessary.

But suddenly this ritual seemed far less pointless than
he had expected.

He signaled to Daniel, who stood attentively behind
his chair. Most of the other Bloodmasters and Bloodlords
in the room had brought several servants, some merely as
decorative accessories, some to provide fresh blood should
their masters develop a thirst during the Claiming. Ares
had far better control, and he believed in self-discipline,
like the philosophers he admired.

"Wine," he said. Daniel stepped away and returned with
a cabernet bottled at Ares's own vineyards to the north of
the Citadel. The serf poured it into a crystal glass and offered it to his master.

"What do you think of her, Daniel?" Ares asked.

"Beautiful, my lord. Will you bid?"

The other Bloodmasters and high-ranking Bloodlords
around Ares studied each serf with varying degrees of calculation, determining which might be an asset to his or her
Household. But most Opiri were eager to claim the most
attractive humans, and Ares could see that the woman had
captured their attention as much as she had his.

Shifting in his seat, he realized his body was respond-
ing to the subtle curves of her figure and the warm scent
that escaped through the ventilators in her cell. The blood
beating just under the surface of her skin smelled of wine
and wildflowers, sparking a need that surprised him.

Daniel knew him far too well. Ares was aroused as he
had not been for some time, in spite of the excellent ser-
vices provided by his Favorite. He took Cassandra's blood
and body because his physical needs had to be met. But it
was never like this.

For the first time in years, Ares found himself considering making a claim.

That didn't mean he would do so. It was one thing to admire the female, and quite another to let lust and hunger lead him around by the teeth.

So he waited, observing silently as the first of his prospective rivals rose to examine the serfs more closely.

"Palemon," Daniel whispered.

Lord Palemon, Bloodmaster, Ares's equal in wealth and status. Like Ares, he had walked the earth for centuries before the Awakening. He was a vicious killer and one of the leaders of the Expansionists, the Citadel's war party, allied with equally malicious Opiri who scampered at his heels like hyenas after a lion.

Dripping with jewels and furs, the Opir lord moved casually toward the female's cell. He paused to look over the serf in the cell next to hers, a boy just entering manhood as humans reckoned such things. The boy trembled and refused to look up from the floor.

Palemon turned his attention to the woman, who met his gaze through the transparent barrier without a hint of submissiveness. Palemon looked her up and down with careless disdain, as if he had no interest in her at all.

No one, least of all Ares, was deceived by his playacting. Palemon's mouth twisted in a smile of haughty amusement. "This claims you are a scholar of some kind," he said to the woman, briefly gesturing at the display above her. "A historian, well versed in the arts and sciences of previous eras." He glanced back at Ares with deliberate mockery. "How extremely dull." His smile vanished, and he turned to the woman again. "Remove your shift."

The female heard him well enough, but she didn't move. Almost immediately one of the black-robed Freeblood attendants entered the cell from the door behind and repeated

Palemon's command. She pulled on the ties at her neck and waist and the shift fell around her shapely ankles.

Several Bloodlords moved up behind Palemon, careful to keep their distance from him. Ares rose, handed his staff to Daniel and made his way through the gathering. There was no need for aggression; the others retreated to either side of his path, unwilling to Challenge one they were unlikely to defeat.

"She is a beauty, is she not?" Palemon remarked without turning. "Full breasts, hips made to fill an Opir's hands and a neck begging to be bitten. And such a face, such bold eyes…"

"Why should she interest you?" Ares asked with a semblance of indifference. "All Erebus knows you hold more serfs than any other Opir in the Citadel. This one—" he waved a dismissive hand at the female "—if she is some kind of intellectual, she can hardly be your type."

Palemon chuckled. "You must know how much I enjoy the challenge of a rebellious serf."

Ares knew, and so did every other lord in the Citadel. Palemon acquired not only the most attractive humans for his Household, but also bid extremely high sums for those who seemed to require the most breaking. And when they were broken and he was weary of them…

"What makes you think she will be rebellious?" Ares asked.

"Look at her," Palemon said. "She cannot hide it."

Palemon, Ares thought, was perfectly correct.

As if she had heard his thoughts, the female looked directly into Ares's eyes. He beckoned to the attendant.

"Let her dress," he said.

Palemon eyed him with exaggerated surprise. "Is that pity, Ares?" he asked. "But of course every ranking Opir in Erebus knows how you indulge your serfs."

"I find I receive better service if my humans do not live in constant fear of me," Ares said.

"Ah, yes. And now, after years without a new serf, you finally found one worth claiming. It seems you have changed since we last had dealings with each other."

"*You* have not. Or have you given up campaigning for war?"

"Still against us, I see."

"I have seen nothing to change my opinion of your politics, Palemon."

"Your politics are those of fear, Ares."

"Fear of humans?" Ares smiled. "I merely wish to avoid any disturbance to my preferred way of life. If I were afraid of my serfs, I would treat them as you do. And I still wonder, Palemon, why you bother with Claimings when you can illegally breed humans to behave exactly as you wish."

He and Palemon locked stares. The attendant in the cell bent to retrieve the female's shift, but she snatched it out of his hands and held it loosely in front of her body. Her gaze darted from Palemon to Ares with an intensity Ares couldn't interpret. It almost appeared as if she was pleading with Ares, and that hardly seemed in keeping with her demeanor.

But Ares didn't doubt her intelligence. It shone in her bright eyes. She had certainly realized that Palemon would be a harsh, even brutal, master. And that Ares would be a far better one.

She was too young to have attained much wisdom, Ares thought. Still, she might provide him with the different perspective he had been seeking....

Oh, yes, he thought with a silent, cynical laugh. He could find many excuses for claiming this female. His blood was running hotter than it had in years, and he found it easy to envision her gratitude for her rescue from

Palemon…imagine her in his bed, offering her neck and her body to him.

No act was more exhilarating to an Opir than taking a serf's blood in the act of sex. Until, as with Cassandra, it became a matter of routine.

Routine that had perfectly satisfied him until today. And that made him wonder, with some bewilderment, how he could move from curiosity to calculation to surging lust in a matter of minutes—uncontrolled thoughts and emotions that tested the rationality and control he valued above all else.

He could think of no better trail of his discipline than taking this female as his serf.

"Where is the staid philosopher now, Ares?" Palemon asked, leading Ares to wonder just how obvious his reaction had been. "Have you discovered that you, too, have weaknesses of the flesh?" He lifted his head slightly, addressing the attendants who waited out of sight, prepared to record the offers. "Ten thousand bloodmarks and three prime serfs."

Ares stiffened. It was a very high bid. "Twelve thousand," he said.

Palemon raised a pale brow. "No serfs?"

"I am not required to offer any of my humans as part of my bid."

"You are sentimental, Ares. A trait I think you will one day have cause to regret." He waved his hand. "Fifteen thousand and five prime serfs, including two produced from my best breeding stock."

Now he was openly defiant, advertising his "forbidden" activities. Ares glanced at the woman again. She was still looking at him, her skin pale but her gaze as direct as ever.

"Twenty thousand," he said.

A deep hush fell over the room. It was an amount only

the most wealthy Bloodmasters could afford to offer for a single serf.

"Twenty-five thousand and twenty prime serfs," Palemon said, looking at Ares inquiringly. The silence pressed down on Ares as if all the weight of the Citadel were driving him deep into the earth from which the Opiri had arisen more than two decades ago.

He knew that if he exceeded Palemon's final bid, he would be leaving himself dangerously vulnerable. His income was considerable, but he required it to provide for his serfs, maintain several client Freebloods and put on the occasional ostentatious display of wealth and power.

Any failure to uphold appearances put the elite of Erebus in constant danger of Challenge by a fellow Bloodmaster or ambitious Bloodlord, and if he impoverished himself, he would have to fight one foolish duel after another simply to maintain his status.

"She is not worth so much to me," he said, turning away before he could observe the woman's face again.

He retrieved his staff and started for the door, but some unfathomable compulsion made him stop and listen, his back to the rows of seats and the Opir lords and ladies awaiting their chance to claim the remaining humans. Daniel, carrying the wine and glass in their case, moved quietly out of his way.

The attendants were opening the woman's cell. Ares could hear her sharp intake of breath as she fully understood her fate.

"My pretty little serf," Palemon said. "I believe I shall enjoy you for some time. If you behave."

Ares heard a scuffle, a gasp and a thump as a body fell heavily to the ground. He swung around. The serf, her shift torn away, was trying to rise from the floor. Her mouth was smeared with blood.

Primitive rage flared in Ares's gut as Palemon jerked

the serf to her feet and seized her mouth with his, licking up the blood as he thrust his tongue between her lips.

Ares strode back to Palemon and grabbed his rival's shoulder.

"Stop," he said, his voice sounding ragged to his own ears.

There were shocked exclamations among the observing Opiri. Palemon pushed the female away and jerked free of Ares's grip.

"You dare?" he asked softly.

Ares held the other Bloodmaster's stare, taking dangerous pleasure in Palemon's astonishment. No Opir ever touched another without risking a violent reaction. It was considered one of the gravest insults one Bloodlord or Bloodmaster could give an Opir who was not demonstrably his inferior.

Ares glanced at the woman, who was wiping her mouth with the back of her hand in an obvious gesture of disgust. He knew then that Palemon would have to kill her in order to break her. She showed little emotion, but Ares could almost feel the banked fire inside her, just waiting to be released.

"Are you offering Challenge?" Palemon demanded.

If Ares had been thinking clearly, he would have realized that Palemon would be compelled to call for an accounting. If he failed to do so, he would lose status, inevitably leading to a catastrophic decline in fortune and, ultimately, death. Palemon himself hadn't lost a Challenge since the founding of the Citadel, but he knew that Ares hadn't lost one in centuries.

Even a victory would bring unwelcome disruptions to Ares's life. But if he didn't respond appropriately, it would be even worse.

Palemon had calculated very well indeed.

"I offer Challenge for the serf," Ares said, "to disability."

Palemon looked Ares up and down as if *he* were a human up for claiming. "You are badly out of practice, Ares," he said, more confident now that he knew his life was not at risk. "I confess I am at a loss to understand why there have not been many more Challenges called against you. You are a freak of nature, an affront to our species. You should have been eliminated long ago."

It was not the first time Ares had heard such threats. To the contrary, he had become accustomed to them more than two thousand years ago, after the most ancient and powerful Opiri had gathered to arrange the details of the Long Sleep.

"Do you intend to hurl insults," he said, "or accept the Challenge?"

Palemon's pale face turned grim. "I accept. And I will accept nothing less than my personal choice of half your serfs when I win."

Ares was almost driven to laughter. But Palemon was still a deadly fighter, and it was conceivable that he might fulfill his boast.

"You will have nothing of mine," Ares said.

Fury flared in Palemon's eyes, though his expression remained unchanged. "We shall see," he spat.

In the tense silence that followed, the attendants pulled the female away and gestured for the other Opiri and their serfs to clear the open area at the front of the theater. The unclaimed serfs huddled in their cells, as far from the observation windows as they could get.

The Bloodlords and Bloodmasters watching from the sidelines made no sound, but Ares felt the other Opiri's poorly concealed eagerness, their bloodlust, their hunger to be entertained by the spectacle of two Bloodmasters locked in combat.

For the female it was no game. When Ares glanced at her one last time, he knew from the rigidity in her naked body and the way her fists clenched that she understood what was at stake.

Daniel came up beside Ares. "My lord," he said, his voice strained with worry as he offered the staff to his master. "Is there anything you require?"

Blood, he meant. Palemon was already availing himself of one of his serfs, sloppily feeding with no regard to the comfort of the female he abused.

Ares shook his head. He shed his overtunic and shirt, tossed them to Daniel and ordered the human to the side of the room.

Wiping his mouth, Palemon allowed his other attendant to remove his tunic and strutted to his side of the area allotted for the fight. He banged the head of his staff against the floor, sending an echoing crack around the room. Ares did the same with his own staff and passed it to one of the attendants.

Then he abandoned the last vestiges of detachment and let the thrill of battle rise from within, his muscles tightening, his heart speeding. Palemon grinned, his teeth still stained with blood, and flexed his fingers. His nails, kept long as most Opiri preferred, were almost as deadly as claws.

The fight was swift and vicious. The only weapons permitted were strength, swiftness and the tearing bite of long, razor-sharp incisors. Twice Ares pinned Palemon to the ground, his teeth inches from the other Bloodmaster's throat. But each time Palemon threw him off, and soon both of them were panting and dripping blood from numerous small wounds on their arms and chests. Three times Ares heard the female human gasp, once more giving the lie to her formerly dispassionate demeanor.

The thought of her naked body under his distracted him

for one vital moment. Palemon lunged and drove Ares down, sinking his teeth into his enemy's neck.

"No!"

The female ran toward them, as fearless as a humming-bird protecting its egg from a hungry crow. She struck Palemon on the shoulder. He reared back, lashing out at her, and she danced out of range.

Ares didn't hesitate. He flung himself on Palemon, banged his head against the floor several times and bit down hard on the other Opir's jugular. Blood gurgled in Palemon's throat, and he gave up the struggle.

Rising to his feet, Ares stared down at his enemy and caught his breath. Palemon would recover from the bite; all Opiri healed as quickly in an hour as a human might over many days, or even weeks.

But Palemon was in no condition to move now, and Ares had no desire to gloat over his victory. He looked around the room at the other Opiri. None would meet his gaze.

That was as it should be. Ares had gone far to reinforce his status, and without seriously maiming his opponent as he could have done. Palemon was within his rights to demand a rematch because of the female's unprecedented interference, but he would look the fool for seeming to suggest a serf had made a difference in the outcome.

No, Ares thought. When next Palemon Challenged him, it would be to the death.

As Daniel cautiously approached to return Ares's clothes, the female stood with her arms wrapped around her chest and stared at Palemon with obvious shock at what she had done. It seemed incredible that she had put herself between two Opiri who could have torn her apart in an instant. But had her actions been born of ignorance, desperation…or almost unimaginable courage?

Now that she was unquestionably his, such questions would be answered in due time.

"Find another shift for the female," Ares said to the nearest attendant. The Freeblood hurried off to fulfill his task and returned quickly with a slightly longer shift, less transparent than the first.

"Dress yourself," Ares ordered the woman. Moving slowly, she held his gaze as she slipped the shift over her head and tied the belt around her waist. It was the most unattractive garment in all Erebus, one assigned to City serfs, yet she was still beautiful, her hair falling about her shoulders and the curves of her body very much in evidence.

"Would you have her bound, my lord?" the attendant asked.

"Should I bind you?" Ares asked the woman harshly in the Opir language, his blood still thick with the dregs of violence. "Or will you come with me of your own will?"

Chapter 3

Ares heard the shifting and barely audible murmurs of the other Opiri. They knew he would not address a serf in such a way before his peers if he were not utterly secure in his power.

The female seemed to know it, too. "I'll come," she said, lifting her chin.

Turning to the attendant, Ares pressed his ring seal onto the tablet the Freeblood presented. He became aware once more of the silent audience, waiting for him to complete his claim with the serf's blood.

"Bend back your head," he told her.

She did as he commanded, baring her throat. Hunger flooded Ares's mouth and desire hardened his body. He took her by the shoulders, and she didn't resist.

Most Opiri would be satisfied with physical submission. But that wasn't enough for Ares. He sensed that she had accepted his power over her because she had no choice— and, perhaps, because she *was* grateful.

But he still smelled her defiance, saw it in her posture, in the clenching of her fists and the set of her jaw. He would never attempt to break her as Palemon would have done, so it was quite likely that she would always keep some part of herself away from him.

That would be a mixed blessing for what he had in mind. He wanted her thoughts free enough so that she would be of use to him in his study of human behavior and emotion, but at the same time he recognized that part of him craved another kind of challenge.

It would be a kind of game he played with himself, keeping that uncommon lust for her in check and rising above his species' predatory nature. He would call upon the discipline, persistence and resolve that had kept him alive over the centuries and allowed him to fend off every Opir who would take what was his.

"Daniel," he said, releasing the female's shoulders, "take the staff and return to the Household. Have them prepare for a new arrival."

After the servant left to do his bidding, Ares nodded to the woman and walked out of the Claiming room. She fell in step behind him, and he could smell her arousing human scent. Once they were out of the Claiming room and in the lobby, she abruptly stopped.

"Why didn't you bite me?" she asked.

Ares continued on without looking back. "I chose not to."

"What about the others?" she asked, changing subjects so quickly that it took him a moment to realize she was referring to the remaining serfs.

"They will all be claimed," he said, slowing his pace. "You are said to be a female of some intelligence. Were you unaware of what would happen to every human in your party when you arrived in Erebus?"

"I was aware," she said. "But Palemon…"

Ares stopped and turned to face her. "Palemon will be in no condition to claim any serf today."

Her shoulders slumped in relief. Ares knew she had been deeply worried about her fellow *Homo sapiens,* afraid they would fall to a cruel master as she almost had.

"Why do you care?" he asked. "Did you know these humans before you were sent here?"

"No," she said. "But maybe that's something you wouldn't understand."

"Perhaps I wish to learn."

She blinked, clearly surprised. "You wish to—"

"What is your name?" he asked.

"Trinity," she said in a husky voice. "I know you can change my name if you want to. But I'm hoping you'll let me keep one thing that still belongs to me."

"You very nearly lost your life," he said, absurdly angry when he had no cause to be. "You interfered in a Challenge."

"I thought you were about to lose."

"I would not have lost."

"It looked bad to me," she said. "I knew what Palemon would do to me if you didn't win."

That was exactly the motive Ares had expected. "You made a grave error," he said, holding fast to his temper. He turned away again. "Come."

Her hand darted out to touch his arm. An instant later he had her by the throat. She dropped her hand from his sleeve and coughed, but her gaze never left his.

"There is something *you* must understand," he said, releasing her almost instantly. "You saw what happened during the Claiming when I touched Palemon. No serf touches an Opir unless she is commanded to do so."

"Commanded?" she whispered, rubbing her throat. "Is that what you plan to do to me?"

"No," he said. "That is not how I handle my humans."

"You mean by the throat, or are there other ways?"

It was hardly possible for an Opir to feel shame over the treatment of a serf, but Ares knew he had behaved no better than Palemon by giving way to his instinctive rage at her unexpected touch. He had hurt her, though he should never have expected her to fully grasp the taboo against unwanted physical contact when humans were so drawn, even compelled, to initiate it.

And her touch had done more than enrage him. It had aroused him to such an extent that he would gladly have dragged her into one of the private rooms off the lobby and taken her then and there.

He would not fall prey to such primitive urges again.

"Are you in pain?" he asked more gently. "Do you require medical assistance?"

She touched her throat again. "I know you could have broken my neck. But you didn't. I don't think you plan to kill me anytime soon."

Ares couldn't help but admire the courage that allowed her to behave with such composure when she had twice come so close to death. He pulled her hand away from her throat and bent close to examine her skin. The marks were nearly gone, but her pulse still beat very fast in the hollow of her neck.

She did not need healing. But still he felt...

Regret. That was the proper word. Regret for touching her in anger, for marking that delicate flesh. And there was a small, hard knot in his stomach, like the grain of sand that becomes a pearl within an oyster's mantle.

His gaze fell to her parted lips and the small cut where Palemon had struck her. The soft, pink skin still held a trace of blood.

He glanced down at her chest, rising and falling with each harsh breath, her erect nipples pushing against the shift's thin material. He stiffened, imagining those breasts in his hands, those sweet, rosy nipples in his mouth.

Then he remembered the vow he had made to himself. He would not take her in any way, body or blood; she must come to him of her own will. She was an intellectual puzzle to be solved, her bewitching essence a challenge to his self-control. A challenge he intended to win.

"You must understand," he said, "for your own safety. You are my property. Step outside of the boundaries set for a serf when we are in public, and you must suffer for it."

"Because of your pride?" she asked.

"Pride, as humans understand it, is not a factor."

"Of course. It's because you have to maintain the respect of those who would be happy to take you down."

"You understand our culture, then."

"I've studied it," she said. "But I still don't understand it."

"Perhaps you will come to, in time."

She gazed into his eyes. "I'm a little confused," she said. "Why did you claim me, if you're not going to use me the way most of your kind use humans?"

"Your spirit intrigued me. You speak our language well, and I have some interest in the human perspective. Perhaps you can provide me with a new one."

She looked at him as if he were mad. "Will Palemon Challenge you again?" she asked.

"Perhaps. But that will not be your concern."

She rubbed her arms as if she were cold, though nearly all of Erebus was kept warmer than most of her kind preferred. "I know I have no rights," she said. "I know you can kill me on a whim and no one will care. But I am... glad you won me. And not just because you saved me from *him*."

Ares wondered if she was confessing to some kind of attraction. It seemed very sudden, but then so was his lust for her. Perhaps, in a way, her admission allowed her to keep some dignity, some small control over her situation, even though she would never again set foot outside the Citadel.

Yet her eyes were half-closed, her lips parted, her face flushed as if with desire. The unmistakable scent of sexual arousal rose from her body.

Ares grabbed her by the shoulders, lifted her face and kissed her. His teeth grazed her lower lip, giving him the smallest taste of her sweet blood. She struggled for a moment and then went limp in his hold, her eyes losing all expression.

Disgusted again at his own behavior, Ares altered the composition of his saliva and took her lower lip into his mouth. The bleeding stopped instantly. Soon there would be no trace at all of what he had done.

Not on her body. But frightening her, making her believe he would use her whenever he liked, was not at all what he wished.

"I…did not intend—" he began. He hesitated, knowing he could never apologize to a serf, and yet wanting her to know he regretted his actions. "It was not my intention to harm you."

Her eyes focused on him again. "I know," she said softly.

He nodded and continued along the corridor. She followed, her footsteps a little slower than before.

Ares knew curses so ancient that no human remembered them. He must… He *would* conquer this savagery within himself. As he would conquer Trinity—without ever again touching her against her will.

It had not gone quite as Trinity had expected.

Ares strode ahead of her without once looking back to make sure she followed. He wouldn't have had to worry even if she hadn't promised to go with him willingly. Getting to this point had been difficult enough, and she wasn't going to ruin what she'd managed to achieve against all the odds.

She watched the play of Ares's muscles under his clothes, the grace of his long stride, and marveled at her luck for the dozenth time. She never would have expected that her new master would ask her if she should be bound, as if she were free to make the decision. That he wouldn't bite her after he'd won his Challenge, when she knew Opir custom demanded that he complete his claim. He'd only tasted her blood when he'd—

She probed at her lower lip and then at her throat. It felt as if Ares had never touched her. She couldn't hate him for half choking her; it was as much her fault as his.

More her fault. She'd done it deliberately, as a kind of test, to see just how far she could push him. She'd discovered his limits the hard way.

Ares had simply acted out of sheer Nightsider instinct. Vicious, animal instinct that ran in all Opir blood like a poison. A poison she'd known must be hidden under the skin of the black-haired Nightsider, even when she had chosen him as the master she must win.

Walking obediently behind him, Trinity could still remember how she had felt when she had first met his gaze. She remembered her inexplicable emotions, the way her whole body had lit up inside like a Fourth of July sparkler even while he had been assessing her as he would a broodmare, his surprisingly light eyes taking her in with unnerving interest. Unnerving because there was no naked lust in his that gaze, not at first. Only remote curiosity.

Not like Palemon's greedy stare, his undisguised hunger when he had forced her to strip and had seen only a female to service him, a human to break with casual cruelty.

Until that moment, she hadn't been ashamed...not of her

nudity or her vulnerability. She had always thought she was ready for anything that might occur during the Claiming.

But she hadn't been prepared for Palemon. When he had begun to show interest in her, she had fully realized how much she could lose if the black-haired Nightsider didn't choose to claim her. She could still feel the crack of Palemon's hand against her face, sending her to the floor with the taste of blood in her mouth.

Trinity stumbled, though the floor of the corridor was smooth as glass. She knew now that she should have worked more diligently to appear submissive, even frightened—the kind of serf that would bore a creature like Palemon. But when she'd seen Ares's interest, she knew that ploy wouldn't work with him. She needed to arouse more than his lust; she had to intrigue him, engage his intellect and admiration as well as his desire.

But she'd also have to "negotiate" with that dark, animal side. The side that had reacted so violently to the touch of a human hand.

Yet *his* hand had caressed her so gently afterward, and she'd felt his regret. "Sentimental," Palemon had said. Ares had come as close to an apology as any Opir could.

Trinity smiled grimly as she put one foot in front of the other, careful of her strangely uncertain balance. Most humans believed that Nightsiders couldn't experience emotions that weren't directly related to survival or protecting their status in the Citadel. Perhaps it would be easier to manipulate Ares than she'd had any right to hope.

But she knew she'd be lying to herself if she denied her own loss of emotional discipline. And it wasn't getting any better with time. She was reminded of her unwilling attraction every instant she was in Ares's presence. He smelled not of blood but of wholly masculine scents she couldn't quite name. His uncommon black hair, drawn into a simple queue at the back of his head, framed his starkly handsome face like raven's wings, making her ache with the need to bury her fingers in it. His nearly human eyes had an almost metallic sheen that reminded her of a dagger's blade, yet she could imagine she saw warmth in them.

And his body... Under his loose clothes his physique had been a mystery, but once he had removed his shirt she had seen a chest, shoulders and arms hard with muscle and honed for battle. She remembered how powerful he had been, how graceful and deadly his every move as he'd fought for her.

She could so easily imagine herself in those strong arms, her nails raking his back as he entered her, as she cried out in pleasure and...

A sudden wave of nausea made her stumble again, and she fell against the nearest wall. Ares stopped immediately and turned to grasp her arm.

"You are ill," he said.

That *was* concern she heard in his voice, though his speech was harsh and clipped. He caught her chin in his hand and tilted her face to his.

"Are you still in pain?" he demanded. He brushed her lips with the pad of his thumb, and she shivered violently.

Ares scooped her up into his arms. Hovering on the edge of consciousness, Trinity only became aware of her surroundings again when she heard the hum of the elevator hurtling upward into the highest levels of the Citadel. Ares had set her on her feet, but his arm around her shoulders prevented her from falling.

She breathed in his scent, her cheek resting against the velvety fabric of his tunic, aware of the slow thump of his heartbeat. The elevator came to a smooth stop, and Ares held her tighter against him.

"Can you walk?" he asked.

Bracing herself against the wall, she pulled away from him. "Yes," she said. "I...don't know what happened."

He frowned. "I will have my human physician examine you."

"Please," she said. "I'm all right. I...I'm grateful for all you've done."

"You will be given every opportunity to display your gratitude."

And she was ready to show it, to play the part, to become whatever Ares wanted her to be.

Play the part, she thought. Nothing more....

The elevator door opened onto a grand lobby faced with black marble and punctuated with alabaster busts of presumably important Opiri, each one a stylized depiction carved of planes and angles that she guessed were representatives of Nightsider "art." Ares urged her down the hall to another set of elevators—three this time, each one marked with an Opir name and an emblem that represented the Household of the Bloodlord to whom it belonged.

Ares helped her into the one identified with the design of a Corinthian helmet. Its interior was padded and gilded like something out of a grand nineteenth-century hotel. It began to rise without any move on Ares's part and opened to yet another lobby. But this one was not decorated with busts, and it wasn't empty.

Three humans, two men and a woman—all dressed in deep blue tunics and pants belted with tooled leather— were waiting as if they had expected their master's arrival. The younger man was missing one eye, and the elder was scarred across the face but standing foursquare against the pull of his years. The woman was middle-aged with a round, pleasant face.

The three serfs bowed, and the scarred man offered a large silver goblet of liquid as fresh and red as the petals of a newly opened rose. Ares accepted the cup and sipped, barely wetting his lips, and then returned it.

Neither of the men paid any visible attention to Trinity,

but she could feel them observing her out of the corners of their eyes. She took the opportunity to study them, wondering if any of the three might be connected to the Underground. There was no guarantee that a member of the Underground lived within this Household, but it was her task to find out as quickly as possible.

After introducing Trinity, Ares glanced at the older woman. "Elizabeth, she is unwell," he said. "Take her to Levi and see that she is cared for. Send Abbie to find suitable clothes."

"Yes, my lord," Elizabeth said, bowing again.

"Diego," he said to the man with the cup, "I will have your report in two hours."

"Yes, my lord."

"Jonathan," Ares said, turning to the scarred man. "Ask Cassandra to attend me in my rooms."

The serf responded with a bow, and all three retreated, Elizabeth supporting Trinity toward a door at the end of the hall. Trinity balked, looking over her shoulder at Ares. He looked back at her, his light eyes unreadable, and disappeared through the double doors.

"Do you need more assistance?" the middle-aged woman asked in a gentle voice.

"I'm all right," Trinity said, touching her pounding temples. "I'm just a little dizzy, and I have a headache. If you have any pain relievers…"

"Of course," Elizabeth said with a slight smile. "The Opiri don't need them, of course, but we do."

"Who were those men?" Trinity asked as they reached the door.

"Two of the senior serfs. Diego—the young gentleman— is the majordomo of the Household, and Jonathan is the Master of Serfs."

"Wouldn't those jobs usually go to vassals?"

"Ares hasn't any vassals," she said.

Surprised at Ares's flouting of Opir custom, Trinity raised a brow. "And what are *your* duties in the House-hold?" she asked.

"I guess you could say I look after the women's matters. You've been through a lot today, and there'll be plenty of time to learn after—"

She didn't finish, but Trinity knew what she meant. After Ares had done what he'd failed to do at the Claiming. After she'd shared his bed, and he had marked her as his.

No emotion, she reminded herself. No fear, no desire, no admiration. Nothing existed but the mission.

And that mission had well and truly begun.

Chapter 4

They descended a staircase to what Elizabeth referred to as the serf's quarters and entered a brightly lit corridor. "This is where we live and where Household operations are located," the older woman said. "Everything above belongs to the Opiri—Ares and his few Freeblood clients."

Casing the layout of the Household was one of the first things Trinity needed to do. "Is there another way up the tower besides the elevator?" she asked.

Elizabeth threw her an amused glance. "There's a staircase off the other side of the lobby, but we prefer to avoid climbing all those steps."

"How big *is* this place?"

"Ares shares this tower with two other Bloodmasters," Elizabeth said, tightening her grip on Trinity's arm. "*Are* you able to walk?"

"I'm all right," Trinity said, though she hadn't been faking either her dizziness or sudden exhaustion. Where had it come from? She knew it wasn't just because she'd had a rough couple of days—she had far more stamina than any normal human.

Could it have been because Ares had drawn a tiny bit of her blood when he'd kissed her? Could he have done something to her in spite of her injections?

"You'll soon learn your way around," Elizabeth said, oblivious to her thoughts. "Right now I'm taking you to Levi, our physician."

"The serfs' doctor?"

"Naturally. There are no Opiri physicians."

Of course not, Trinity thought. Certain diseases were unique to Nightsiders, however rare, but their injuries from Challenge or accident either healed on their own or killed the Nightsider, and Opiri had no sympathy for the weak among their kind.

"I heard that Ares hasn't claimed a serf in quite a long time," she said.

"That's right. I heard he actually Challenged for you." Elizabeth hesitated. "In all the time I've been here, he's never done that. He despises Challenges."

"He seemed to like my 'spirit,'" Trinity said with a brief laugh.

"You are quite beautiful," Elizabeth said. "But physical beauty has never seemed to matter to him when it comes to serfs. In fact, he has a tendency to pick up the ones no one else wants, as you might have noticed with Diego and Jonathan." She came to a stop in front of one of the many doors along the corridor, her expression relaxing. "Here we are."

The door slid open, and they entered a large, pristine infirmary. A man in his forties with neatly cropped salt-and-pepper hair sat behind a desk situated on one side of the room, his gaze fixed on a monitor. He rose quickly, gazing at Trinity with distracted surprise.

Once Elizabeth explained the situation, Levi put her

through the paces of a typical physical exam and declared her suffering from exhaustion.

"She needs to rest," he said to Elizabeth. "What can Ares have been thinking?"

"He brought her back himself," the older woman said. "What does that suggest to you?"

Levi gave Trinity a second, far less professionally detached look. "Is he tired of Cassandra?" he asked.

"I'm sitting right here," Trinity said. "We may be slaves, but I refuse to become an object to be discussed like an expensive piece of jewelry."

Levi and Elizabeth exchanged knowing glances. "I can't believe that pure lust would be enough," Levi said. "There must be something special for her to be treated like—"

"I was under the impression that he treats all his serfs well," Trinity interrupted.

"He's always been a good master," Elizabeth said. "We need to get her into bed, Levi. Abbie will be coming to measure her when she's rested."

"And then Ares is going to send for me, isn't he?" Trinity asked.

"When you were brought here, you must have known what to expect," Levi said, not quite meeting her gaze.

"I didn't deserve to be sent here at all," Trinity said, injecting resentment into her voice. "Why were *you* deported?"

"We don't speak of such things in this Household," Elizabeth said with a pained smile. "Unless you want to offend your fellow humans, and no one wants to be alone among enemies."

Interesting, Trinity thought, that Elizabeth would come right out and say the word "enemy." It was something a member of the Underground might say, especially if she'd forgotten she couldn't trust everyone around her.

"Come along now," Levi said, taking one of Trinity's

arms as Elizabeth took the other. They half carried her to a bed and helped her climb onto it. "I think we'll give you an IV drip. You look more than a little dehydrated."

Trinity didn't object, and soon she was resting comfortably while Levi worked away at his desk. She badly wanted to jump out of bed and take a good look at the serfs' area of the Household, check out every possible exit and search for likely hiding places.

But all too soon a very tall young woman, who introduced herself as Abbie, arrived with Elizabeth and walked around the bed, cocking her head as she studied Trinity from all angles.

"Very promising," she said. "When does Ares want her?"

"He only said to let him know when she was feeling better," Elizabeth said, talking over Trinity the way she had before.

"I'll put together something simple for now," Abbie said. "I know just the thing…"

"Do you always talk about new serfs as if they were animals?" Trinity said, looking at each of the three in turn. "Or is this your way of making your lives more bearable?"

Abbie looked at her blankly, and then blinked as if she had snapped out of a dream. "I'm sorry," she said, her long face crumpling in remorse.

"Sometimes we forget the things we most need to remember," Elizabeth said. "You're handling this better than anyone I've ever met."

Trinity wondered if she could pry a little more information out of Elizabeth. "Earlier, you mentioned that Ares seemed to be acting out of character…."

"I made too much of it," Elizabeth said, flushing a little. "I meant it when I said he was a good master. He very seldom interferes with the running of the Household."

"He never gets angry, almost never even impatient,"

Abbie said, jotting a note in the pad she kept in her wide front pocket. "He's never sold any of us or given us away as gifts to other Opiri."

"Everything runs like clockwork in this Household," Levi said, checking Trinity's pulse against the watch he wore on his wrist. "Ares likes peace and quiet. We're rather used to it."

A Household that ran like clockwork, where everyone knew their places and no one caused trouble. The perfect cover for members of the Underground.

"Who is Cassandra?" she asked.

"Oh, dear," Elizabeth said, masking her obvious relief with a look of chagrin. "Didn't I tell you? Cassandra is the master's Favorite. Whatever blood he took from you at the Claiming wouldn't have been enough to satisfy his needs."

"But he didn't bite me," Trinity said.

"He didn't?" Levi asked, his unflappable demeanor giving way to genuine surprise.

Trinity touched her lip again. She didn't know if she was telling the full truth or not, but she wanted to gauge the others' reactions.

"When he does," Abbie said, "he won't hurt you. He's very careful about that."

"Have *you* ever been with him?" Trinity asked.

Abbie almost jumped. She recovered quickly and wrote out another note. "He has Cassandra for that," she said, "though technically he can take blood, or anything else, from any of us whenever he wants to."

"But he doesn't," Elizabeth said. "He doesn't even keep a harem for variety."

That was unusual, Trinity knew. Almost unheard of. A Bloodmaster relying on only one human for his blood? He must drink very sparingly, yet he showed no signs of weakness.

"Don't worry about anything for now," Elizabeth said.

"You have the potential to rise high in this Household. Make the most of it."

She and Abbie left the room, and Trinity closed her eyes for a while. When she opened them again, Levi was standing at the foot of her bed.

"You can shower now," the physician said, indicating a door inside the room. "And you must be hungry. I'll have someone bring you a tray."

"Thank you," Trinity said.

"I'm stepping out for a few minutes," Levi said. "If you need anything, use the buzzer just inside the front door and someone will come."

In a moment he was gone. Trinity sat on the edge of the bed, repeating Elizabeth's final words in her mind.

Make the most of it. Could that possibly be some kind of code, letting her know that Elizabeth suspected her true purpose here?

That, too, she would learn in time. She was just heading for the shower when a stunning young woman walked into the room.

She wore a deep red gown of a fabric that caught the corridor lights and accented every lush curve of her figure, the neckline plunging in folds that opened just above her nipples. Her face was striking, her blond hair falling in glorious waves around her shoulders.

"So you're the new one," the woman said, smiling as she draped herself against the doorframe. "Elizabeth tells me you've been a little sick. The Claiming can be difficult for novice serfs."

"Thanks for your concern," Trinity said, keeping her expression neutral. "I'm fine now." She offered her hand. "You must be Cassandra."

The other woman ignored Trinity's friendly overture. "How did you know?" she asked.

"You're too beautiful to be anyone else."

Cassandra's smile flickered as if she suspected Trinity of a backhanded compliment. "I've heard a great deal about you, too," she said. "You're as lovely as they said. Or you will be, once you're cleaned up."

"Thank you. I didn't expect to be so…warmly welcomed."

"We're all family here," Cassandra said, her body relaxing. "But your arrival has created quite a stir, what with Ares Challenging for you and all."

"So I gathered," Trinity muttered.

"Well, I'm sure everyone will get used to the change. You are fortunate to have been claimed by Ares, but here's a friendly word of advice—don't expect too much."

"Why should I expect anything?" Trinity asked.

Cassandra tossed back her hair. "You tell me."

"You were just with him, weren't you?" Trinity asked, feigning naive curiosity. "Was he different than usual?"

Ares's Favorite almost permitted a scowl to twist her full red lips, but she covered her anger quickly. "He was… very energetic, shall we say," she said. "Hot-blooded, to use a human expression."

"I always heard Nightsiders were insatiable," Trinity said, swallowing nervously for effect.

"Ares is a good lover. Very considerate for an Opir. Enjoy it while you can."

Elizabeth had said nearly the same thing earlier, but somehow Trinity didn't think that Cassandra meant it in quite the same way.

"You mean he'll get tired of me?" she asked.

"It depends on what he wants you for. I've been his Favorite for three years." She smiled unpleasantly. "I don't expect that to change anytime soon."

"Then why are you worried about me?"

"Worried?" Cassandra stroked her long, graceful neck, running her perfectly manicured nails over a set of small red marks that had almost healed. "Did I give you that impression?"

Trinity knew she'd made a mistake in resorting to sarcasm. "No," she said. "Not at all."

"I'm sure things will settle down again very soon," Cassandra said, favoring Trinity with another false smile, "and once Ares is done with you, you'll be given some task in the Household that will make you content, like everyone else here."

"I hope so," Trinity said. She gazed up at Cassandra like a lost puppy. "Maybe you could show me around when you're not busy."

Cassandra yawned behind her hand. "I'd love to help you, Trinity, but I'm on call twenty-four hours a day. I doubt I'll have the energy."

In spite of herself, Trinity felt a little sorry for the woman. She suspected that Cassandra's sense of self came entirely from being the Favorite of Ares's Household.

But pity couldn't distract Trinity from her mission, and she quickly brushed it aside. "I understand," she mumbled, looking down at the floor.

Cassandra placed a slender hand on Trinity's shoulder. "Just give yourself a little time to adjust, and don't be too hard on yourself."

"Thank you," Trinity said, laying her hand on top of Cassandra's. "I think I won't find it quite as difficult now."

"I'm glad my little visit was of some help to you." Cassandra glided to the door and turned around again. "Just remember, Trinity…it's very important to remember your place. It won't be so easy if you make enemies of your fellow servants."

"Yes," Trinity said. "Elizabeth said—"

"Cassandra."

The voice was unmistakably Ares's, and he was standing somewhere very close to the door. Cassandra started, and her confident attitude changed to one of uncertainty and fear.

Not of Ares, Trinity was sure. It was the fear that came from being caught doing something forbidden.

"Why are you here?" Ares asked, still out of Trinity's sight.

"I only came to welcome the new serf, my lord," Cassandra said, moving from the doorway.

"She was to rest," Ares said, a trace of anger in his voice. "Go to your room."

"Yes, my lord."

Trinity heard Cassandra's soft footsteps retreating, and then Ares was filling the doorframe, a dark silhouette with eyes that seemed to pin Trinity to the spot. He wore a long, deep blue tunic, and his hair was loose around his broad shoulders.

He entered the room and strode to her side. "Are you well now?" he asked.

"Yes," she said, averting her gaze. "Much better. Thank you, my lord."

He took her chin in his hand and drew her head up. "What is this new humility? It doesn't suit you."

Trinity shivered at the touch of his hand, the nearness of his body, the clear evidence that he was very much aroused. He'd just been "served" by Cassandra, but it was obvious that he was far from satisfied.

His desire still seemed at odds with his normally cool, controlled demeanor, but she'd seen just how much he could change from one moment to the next.

"*Should* I resist you, my lord?" she said, meeting his gaze. "Is that what you want me to do?"

He released her chin and stepped back. "When you have bathed and receive proper attire," he said, "you will join me in my apartments. I shall see if you are worth the trouble it took to win you."

Chapter 5

Trinity struggled to contain her sudden rush of desire, the moist heat between her thighs, the pounding of her heart.

She kept her face averted, praying Ares couldn't detect her inner thoughts. It seemed impossible that she should welcome his touch, especially because such feelings on her part went well beyond the scope of her mission.

Still, she couldn't keep pretending these feelings didn't exist. Fighting them would only expend energy she couldn't afford to waste.

And she needed him to trust her, to talk with her, to allow her freedom in the Household. When she "surrendered" to Ares, her attraction would seem all the more genuine. She'd be able to concentrate on the work that was of the utmost importance.

She met his gaze. "I will be honored to serve you in any way, my lord," she said.

"Will you? Even after what I did to you?"

He meant the kiss, she thought. As if he still felt badly about it. Even guilty.

Surely that wasn't possible.

"What must I do to prove myself?" she asked.

With a sharp, almost clumsy motion, he turned away. "Have you eaten?"

"I was told a tray would be brought here for me."

"And clothing?"

"The same."

"Then I will leave you." He walked out the door with a single, smoldering glance over his shoulder.

Trinity's mouth was dry, and her breath seemed to burn in her lungs. She quickly found the shower and removed her shift, intensely aware of her body, even more so than when Palemon had forced her to strip. Her breasts were tender, her nipples hard, her legs trembling.

She turned on the water, adjusting it to the coldest setting. But as soon as she began to lather her body with the sweet-smelling liquid in the dispenser, her imagination began to kick into overdrive. She felt hands caressing her breasts, teasing her nipples, working the soap into her stomach and lower regions. She felt the hand slip between her thighs, sliding into her natural wetness.

Ares's hands. And his lips grazing her neck. His teeth…

Trinity half stumbled out of the shower and snatched at the towel hanging from a rack set into the wall. She rubbed herself furiously, removing every last drop of moisture from her body. Then she dragged on her shift and sat on the bed, closing her eyes and focusing on regaining her equilibrium.

When a young serf knocked on her door to deliver a tray of fresh, fragrant food, Trinity ate it as if she had an appetite. Soon afterward, Abbie arrived with a gown: a simple, floor-length, amethyst silk slit to the thigh and cut low in the neckline, though not as low as Cassandra's. Trinity allowed the tailor to help her put it on. There were no undergarments to mar the clean lines of the gown or disturb the liquid caress of the silk gliding over her skin.

Elizabeth arrived just as Abbie was leaving. The two women exchanged a few brief words in the hall, and then the older woman came into the room. She looked Trinity over with obvious appreciation.

"I don't know what to say," she said. "Abbie has out-done herself this time…." She hesitated. "Are you all right, Trinity?"

"I'm fine," she said with a look of carefully constructed tranquility. "I'm ready."

Elizabeth sat on the edge of the bed. "I'm afraid we really haven't been of much help to you," she said slowly. "But I want to make sure you aren't afraid of Ares. When I was quite a bit younger, I belonged to another Bloodmaster. It was not a pleasant experience. When I had grown too old to interest him, he offered me for open Claiming." She released a breath. "It's usually reserved for cast-off serfs, and most are only valuable for increasing the number of an Opir's staff, and his or her prestige."

"What happened to you?" Trinity asked.

"After the Bloodlords and Bloodmasters have chosen all those serfs that interest them and paid their former owners the pittance they are worth, the rest are available to House-less Freebloods. You understand what Freebloods are?"

"Former vassals converted into full Opiri."

"Made free to build their own destinies," Elizabeth said. "Some become clients either to their own Sires or other Bloodlords. But they can also choose to fight their way up the ladder and form their own Households. For them, acquiring serfs is not a simple matter of bidding. They fight for their property, and many die." She sighed. "Two very nasty Freebloods were fighting over me when Ares stepped in and claimed me. I have been here ever since."

"So he saved you. What would have happened if he hadn't?"

"Freebloods live on the edge. A serf's life under such circumstances is fragile. And often short. Now I have a comfortable home where I can be useful. And I'm not alone."

"Thank you for telling me this," Trinity said.

"No need to thank me." Elizabeth rose again, her eyes crinkling as she smiled. "I'm just saying that even if Ares doesn't keep you with him, you'll have a comfortable life. Cassandra deliberately sets herself apart from the rest of us. It won't be that way with you."

"No," Trinity said. "It won't." Suddenly self-conscious, she smoothed the silk over her thighs. "When do I—"

As if in answer to her unfinished question, the serf she'd seen with Ares in the Claiming room entered the infirmary. Daniel, she remembered Ares calling him—a young man of medium height, with sandy hair and light blue eyes. "Good afternoon," he said, the words as flat as his expression.

"Is it afternoon?" Trinity asked, glancing up at the ceiling as if she might see the sky.

"We keep clocks in the Household to remind us and help us keep to our routines." He looked her over appraisingly. "Are you ready? Ares said he'd wait if you needed more time."

"I'm as ready as I'll ever be," she said. "But I'm not afraid."

Daniel's eyes warmed slightly. "Ares chose you for more than just your looks." He gestured toward the door. "Come with me."

Keenly aware of her naked skin under the gown, Trinity followed Daniel through another series of corridors to a curved staircase ascending to the main floor. At the top of the stairs, a plain door opened onto a hall that could have been the throne room of a palace, elegant and imposing.

Daniel escorted Trinity between stately Grecian columns to a set of double doors. Behind the doors was an antechamber, one wall decorated in the style of ancient Athenian vase paintings. Yet another door, carved with images of ancient warriors in battle, stood at the end.

Daniel touched a panel to the right of the door. Beyond was a room unlike anything Trinity had ever seen. It stretched out in a vast semicircle, a huge, shuttered window taking up half of the curved wall at the back. The floor was strewn with embroidered cushions, and couches from many historical periods were scattered in groups around the room.

On the other half of the back wall hung nearly a dozen paintings, some of which Trinity recognized as well-known masterpieces lost in the War. Sculptures, most in the Greek and Roman style, stood on stands or in wall niches, interspersed with several shelves of old-fashioned books.

"Philosopher," Palemon had called Ares. But what kind of philosopher? How much of this was for show to his fellow Nightsiders? "The Great Room," Daniel said, unaware of her musings. He pointed to an arched entryway to the left. "That door leads to the harem chambers, unoccupied at the moment. That door—" he swept his hand toward the opposite side of the room "—leads to Ares's personal suite. Cassandra lives in rooms adjoining his, but with a separate entrance from the antechamber."

"I was told she's been his Favorite for three years," Trinity said, feeling breathless.

"Yes," Daniel said, his face turning cold. "Perhaps she won't retain her place for long."

He doesn't like Cassandra, Trinity thought. "Does Ares intend to make me his Favorite?" she asked.

"That's not for me to know. He has seemed content with Cassandra, taking her blood about once a day." He met her gaze. "If you feel any gratitude toward him, encourage him to take yours."

"I *am* grateful," she said. "Did he save you, too?"

Daniel look startled, as if she'd read his mind. "That's unimportant," he said, gesturing toward the door to Ares's suite. "Go right in. The master's waiting."

He retreated through the doors to the antechamber, leaving Trinity alone. She hesitated, staring at the door to the suite. This was not the time to lose her nerve. She was where she needed to be.

Lifting her head, she walked to the door. She caught Ares's scent, clean and masculine, but the room she entered was empty.

Once again she paused to get her bearings. His suite was just as comfortably appointed as the Great Room, if a little less elaborate in decoration. It had three interior doors, and one was open. More bookshelves lined the walls. A large desk stood to one side of the room, with a computer monitor facing a padded leather chair. A seventeenth-century map of the world hung behind it, and the dark wood and furnishings made it feel like a Victorian gentleman's office, his private domain in a world run by servants and women.

All so very "human," Trinity thought.

She looked to see if anyone was watching and went to the desk. The computer wasn't on, and Trinity assumed it was seldom used. The internet was a thing of the past, at least in a worldwide sense, but both humans and Opiri still kept electronic data and records. If she could get into those records in Erebus…

"Trinity."

A chill slid down Trinity's spine. Ares hadn't seen her yet, but he didn't have to. Just as she hadn't needed to see him to know he was there. Like her, he had other heightened senses at his command.

"I'm here," she said.

"Come in."

She followed the sound of his voice through the door farthest to the right. The first thing she saw was the bed, easily large enough to accommodate four people, heaped with pillows and covered with a spread embroidered with a nearly perfect reproduction of the famous Bayeux tapestry. A huge Persian carpet stretched across the floor.

The rest of the room was surprisingly spartan. Ares sat in a chair to the right of the bed, next to a small table set with a plate of delicacies, two glasses and a bottle of wine.

Wine was almost impossible to get in the Enclave. The Nightsiders had taken over most of the vineyards, and living on blood didn't mean they couldn't enjoy some human food and drink.

For a moment, Trinity felt only anger and disgust for what Ares's kind had stolen from humanity. She stopped just inside the door, and his gaze swept over her with seeming indifference.

"Abbie should not have dressed you this way," he said in the Opir language. "I brought you here to talk, not to serve me in bed."

Trinity had thought she was ready. But now, enduring his intense inspection, she found herself trembling.

And oddly disappointed.

"Are you afraid?" Ares asked, his voice almost gentle.

"Do I look afraid?" she asked in the same language.

"That's better," Ares said with a slight smile. He gestured to the thickly upholstered chair on the other side of the table. "Sit."

She glided toward him, lifting her skirts to lengthen her stride. She took the chair, feeling the silk tighten across her breasts and thighs. Ares seemed not to notice as he filled both glasses with wine.

"A very good year," he remarked, offering her one of the goblets. "I think you'll enjoy it."

"Can I refuse?"

"You have that choice," he said. He sipped from his glass, and then set it down. "For the time being, I want to know more about my newly acquired property."

"Wouldn't you prefer to start by tasting it? Isn't that why I'm here?"

He leaned back, steepling his fingers under his chin. "What did you do in the Enclave? You speak our language fluently, and you apparently know some history. Tell me."

Trinity could hardly believe he was genuinely interested in hearing about her work or her past. In fact, her background story was not entirely concocted. She had studied languages and history as her specialty at the Academy, and she was grateful she wouldn't have to fake it.

"I was one of the lucky citizens to be chosen for an advanced education," she said quietly. "I learned ancient Greek, Latin and modern languages. And Opir, of course."

"As I see. You have very little accent. Our tongue is not easy to master."

"Because it's a mishmash of ancient languages," she said, leaning toward him. "Greek, Latin, Babylonian and various ancient Indo-European languages we have yet to decipher."

"A mishmash," he said drily. "I am certain our own experts in human languages would find that description less than amusing, especially because they believe all ancient human languages derive from ours."

She held his gaze. "Did I offend you?"

"I wouldn't have asked if I didn't want your opinion."

"Why would the opinion of a serf matter to you?"

He smiled slightly, and she felt a deeper stirring of interest that went well beyond helpless sexual attraction.

He was treating her almost as an equal, and she doubted that this was his ordinary way of dealing with new serfs.

"You intrigue me," he said. "You're clearly intelligent, and your spirit has not been broken by your deportation from your city."

"And so that's the reason I'm here. That and your interest in the human perspective. But on what?"

He nodded at her glass of wine. "Drink."

Reluctantly she picked up her goblet and sipped. The wine, as expected, was glorious.

"I don't suppose you share your wine with your serfs as a rule," she said, setting the glass down again.

"Not as a rule." He stared intently into her eyes. "What crime did you commit to be sent here?"

She hesitated, as if it were a painful memory. "I didn't pay my taxes."

"Such a small thing," he said.

"They're finding it more and more difficult to gather criminals to send to you as serfs, and they don't want to break the Treaty."

Ares was silent for a while, perhaps brooding over her insolent behavior. But he didn't chastise her. To the contrary, he appeared more intrigued than ever.

"And why weren't you able to find a protector to clear you of these charges?" he asked. "You are a beautiful woman. Surely some powerful male would have been prepared to spare you exile in return for—"

"Is that what you think of human women?" she interrupted. "That we give ourselves to men so they'll protect us from the consequences of our actions?"

"Trinity," Ares said in a soft voice. "Do not speak to me in that manner again."

All at once, without warning, he was master and she his slave, utterly subject to his will. She was reminded that, in spite of his mild manner now, taking liberties with him too quickly might result in her being punished, or even sent away.

Or perhaps it would arouse his sexual interest again. The kind that had gripped him—and her—just after the Claiming.

"I'm…I'm sorry, my lord," she said meekly.

He picked up his glass and set it down again without tasting the contents. "I warned you before that you should consider the consequences of your behavior, Trinity. In Erebus, those consequences can be much worse than mere exile."

"I know," she said. "But if you'll allow me to explain…"

When he waved his hand to grant her permission, she continued more carefully. "The women of the Enclave aren't like that," she said. "Most would never think of seeking that kind of protection from a man. All people, regardless of gender, are equal."

"But it was not always so," he said, relaxing again. "I remember. Among my kind—through all the ages—there has never been any significant distinction between male and female Opiri in terms of power or status. You've come far since the days when you were merely the extensions of your mates."

"That's right," Trinity said. "But I don't understand why you don't already know this, my lord. Opiri faced plenty of female soldiers during the War."

"Yes," he said. "I was merely interested in your experiences." He smiled slightly. "I can imagine you as a soldier."

Trinity tried not to let him see her alarm. "I'm not brave enough for that."

Ares leaned over the table and touched her cheek. "I think you are. But that is of no consequence now. That life is over."

"I know."

"I don't think you'll find it displeasing," he said, stroking her face.

"I'm ready."

He jerked his hand back. "You speak as though you must brace yourself for some unspeakable torment."

Now that she had reached the crucial moment, Trinity lost her resolve to acquiesce so easily. "I owe you so much, my lord," she murmured.

Ares bolted from his chair. "I don't want your gratitude," he said. "I want—"

He broke off, and Trinity held very still, aware that he had begun to lose his grip on the calm and rationality he seemed to value so highly. He strode to the other side of the bed and punched his finger on a keypad set in the wall. Wide shutters slid open, revealing another window.

"Come here," he said.

Trinity rose and joined him. She looked out the window. The dome of the city curved below—smoky-gray rather than black from this angle—shielding Erebus from the sun.

Beyond the dome and the towers on the opposite side of the Citadel stretched the muted sky, the fields and the mountains, robbed of their color and vividness by the protective glass. Ares touched the keypad again, and suddenly they were looking directly into the interior of the city, thousands of roofs and open plazas and strange gardens under artificial lights. It was frighteningly beautiful.

"Nothing can touch you in this city," he said. "No one can harm you. Not as long as you belong to me." He turned to look at her. "And I intend to keep you, Trinity. Make no mistake."

He pressed on the pad, closing the panel, and then returned to the table, slopping more wine into the glass.

"I will know everything about you," he said, capturing her gaze. "Your mind, your soul, your body. You will never hold any secrets from me. But when you come to me, you will do it because you wish to."

Trinity realized how vulnerable Ares had just made himself, vulnerable in a way that was almost human. She felt an uncertainty in him, bewilderment that he should treat any serf as he treated her…as if she mattered to him as a woman, not merely a slave. "I wish it now, my lord," she whispered. And she did. More than was practical. Or sane.

"No," he said, dropping into his chair. "You will sleep in the harem quarters tonight."

It wasn't going to work. Not now, not for Ares. For some reason he was holding himself back. She bowed and retreated.

"Trinity," he said, stopping her as she moved to the door.

"Yes, my lord?"

"My name is Ares. You may use it when we are alone."

"Thank you…Ares," she said, bowing her head.

He made a sound very like a snort. "I told you before that such humility doesn't suit you. Don't play games with me. You can't win." He caressed the stem of his wineglass. "I do want to know your thoughts, Trinity. Your true and honest thoughts. I have had long experience with humanity. I walked the earth while most of my kind slept under it. But now I require a human of the Enclave to share her views and understanding of our people, and to explain her world to me."

"Why?" she asked. "I will never give you information you could use against the Enclave, even if I'd ever had access to it."

"I have no interest in acting against the Enclave. My life is as I wish it to be, and any disruption such as a new war would only disturb it."

"An excellent reason for opposing the deaths of thousands of humans and Opiri."

"Trinity—"

"Forgive me, my lord. I'm sorry for speaking out of turn."

Suddenly he was on his feet again and striding toward her, and it was all she could do to hold her ground. He loomed over her, staring down at her like a hungry panther.

"Do not mock my liberality," he said, his voice a deep rumble. "I can withdraw it in an instant. I can still take from you whatever I wish."

"What I offered already," she said, tipping her head back to give him easy access to her throat.

He leaned toward her, and she could feel his warm breath fanning over her flesh. Once again she imagined his teeth grazing her neck, puncturing her skin on that big bed, while he…

Oh, God, she thought. She couldn't let it happen. No matter how decent, how reasonable…how sexually attractive and potent he was to her. She couldn't let herself *feel.*

"Go," he said, stepping back as if he didn't trust himself any more than she did her own mind and body.

Stumbling out of the room, Trinity half ran through the office and into the Great Room. His abrupt dismissal didn't matter. He wanted to probe her mind and absorb her knowledge—though she didn't trust his reasons in the slightest—and was clearly fighting his own desire to take her. He'd given her a kind of power over him she could use to her own advantage.

She would learn everything she could about the workings of the Household. She would make friends of even the lowliest serfs. She would use any method necessary to find members of the Underground in Ares's Household and contact those outside it.

And she'd become invaluable to Ares. So indispensable, so trustworthy and useful that she'd make it impossible for him to resist her.

He's only the means to an end, she reminded herself. And she was a soldier of the Enclave who hated everything he stood for.

And always would.

Chapter 6

Ares summoned Cassandra six hours later, after Trinity had retired to rest. He ordinarily avoided taking blood from his Favorite more than once a day, but his body's other hungers had become too demanding to ignore, and he knew that Cassandra would never object.

He had spent those six hours pacing his room, trying to concentrate on ancient human texts, receiving his client Freebloods, taking reports and drinking wine until he could drink no more.

Every hour he had considered calling Trinity to him. His entire body throbbed with wanting her. She moved him not only physically, but also emotionally, and that made no sense to him.

He had told her the truth: he wanted to know her thoughts, to hear her views of things about which he could not be objective. But, above all, he needed to understand why she could be so unwillingly attracted to an Opir, especially when he owned her very life. She had every reason to hate him, like any of the humans in Erebus. But he had smelled her arousal, heard the rapid thrum of her pulse when he came near. She seemed to be giving way to some primal urge within herself that had little to do with gratitude.

He wondered if she was drawn to him because he was different.

From the beginning of human civilization, when the first Opiri had begun to gather in groups and hunting parties, Ares had been branded an outsider. The earliest Bloodmasters had declared that he could not be full-blooded because of his hair and eyes—that he was, as Palemon had called him, a "freak of nature" and a throwback to some ancient, more primitive species no Opir wanted to remember.

Many had tried to kill him, but he was strong, and he had fought all the harder to prove himself. Fought to show he was more a true Opir than any of them, in every way that implied. He had fought and killed until no one dared Challenge him again, and he had remained awake while the vast majority of other Opiri had taken the Long Sleep.

In all those years, weary of bloodshed and battle, he had lived alone, making no contact with the other Bloodmasters still roaming the earth. Since the Awakening, he had maintained a solitary existence within the Citadel, devoting himself to study and intellectual pursuits.

That had directly led to his choice to treat his property with decency and avoid unnecessary conflict. It was simple logic that one's life ran more smoothly without such complications, and he despised any alteration of the Household routine.

Now, merely because of her arrival, Trinity had completely unsettled it. "My lord?"

Cassandra, dressed in a sheer sleeping shift, her eyes

heavy and her hair tousled, stood in the doorway to his bedchamber. She had never looked more beautiful.

"Come in," he said. "Wine?"

"Please." Cassandra glided toward him, the diaphanous fabric sliding over the lush curves of her body, concealing and revealing naked flesh with every step. Smiling seductively, she lifted the glass of wine he poured and watched him over the rim of the goblet.

"How may I serve you, my lord?" she asked, her full lips stained red with the wine.

Before she could answer, she set down her glass, undid a tie at her neck and let the shift fall into a foamy puddle at her feet. As he had expected, she clearly had no objection to sharing his bed again after only six hours.

He had never asked her why she had been Deported, but she had been both experienced and unafraid when he had claimed her. She had told him more than once, when they were entangled in the bed and the barriers had fallen, that he was a superb lover.

Without waiting for his suggestion, she climbed onto the bed. She seldom required any foreplay, and she seemed far more eager than usual.

Because of Trinity, he thought. She believed she had a rival.

Refusing to think on it further, Ares began to shed his clothes, hardly aware of what he was doing. When he joined Cassandra on the bed, he wasn't thinking of her at all. It was not *her* hips he caressed as he positioned himself behind her, not *her* lovely back or the elegant lines of her neck.

"My lord," she said, squirming to entice him. "Please."

He rolled off the bed, leaving her looking after him in confusion. He dressed with his back to her.

"I have no need of you now," he said, more roughly than he had intended.

"My lord?" she said. "How have I displeased you?"

He forced himself to look at her. She seemed very small, very vulnerable, all her sophistication and provocative manner gone as if she had shed it along with her shift.

"It is not your fault," he said, belting his tunic. "Go to your room, Cassandra. I have asked enough of you today."

Cassandra stared up at him, tears leaking from her eyes. Ares had never seen her cry.

"How long will it *be* my room?" she asked, clutching the sheets tightly above her breasts. "I knew this was going to happen ever since I saw her. *She'll* have my place, won't she? You'll send me to the harem, and I—"

"Silence," Ares snapped. "You will do as I tell you. Go to your room."

She climbed down from the bed, dragging the sheets with her. "I *know* you," she said, her voice trembling. "She can only cause trouble here. Why did you fight for her?"

"You would be wise to hold your tongue, Cassandra," he said.

"I know she excites you, but she'll never let you have her the way you want her."

"She is a serf. She will obey me."

"But you don't want it that way, do you?" she laughed bitterly. "She isn't afraid of you. She's not afraid of anything. You could take her if you wanted, but you expect her to come crawling to you and beg. You never had to do that with me." She took a step toward him. "There is something wrong about her, Ares. If you can't see it…"

All the tension in Ares's body seemed to explode out of his skin. He strode to Cassandra and grabbed her wrist. The sheets fell to the floor.

"I have given you every privilege," he said. "Every comfort, the highest status a serf can possess. But you will not speak to me this way, Cassandra. You will never challenge or question my decisions again."

She stared down at his hand on her wrist. He let her go, sickened by the look of despair on her face.

"I have no wish to cause you pain," he said as gently as he could. "Trinity will live in the harem quarters. Her value to me is in her knowledge."

"You are generous, my lord," Cassandra said, bending to pick up the sheets. Ares got to them first and stood holding them in his hands until she took them and covered herself again. "I shall never forget your kindness. May you always find what you seek."

She walked through the door to her room, the sheets sweeping behind her like a train. Her parting words rang in Ares's ears.

They made no sense to him. Had he not just told her that Trinity would never fill her role in his life? Yes, he wanted his new serf, and badly. But it was all part of the experiment to test Trinity…and himself.

Wasn't it?

The next morning—or what passed for morning in this city of perpetual darkness—Trinity woke to the sense that she had been asleep far too long. She kicked the sheets away and rolled off the bed, instinctively ready to fight.

But there was no one here to be afraid of, not even Ares. She was already in a position that would make it much easier to do her work, as long as she didn't goad Ares into the kind of jealous possessiveness he'd briefly displayed when he'd shown her the city.

I intend to keep you, Trinity, he had said. *You will never hold any secrets from me.*

Little did he know just how well she was keeping them.

She yawned, sat down on the edge of the bed and glanced at the ornate clock on her bedside table. It was just past 5:00 a.m. She'd fallen into a fitful sleep not long after

Ares had dismissed her, though it had still been early in the evening and only ten hours since Ares had claimed her.

Just before Trinity had given into exhaustion, Elizabeth had brought a selection of sleeping shifts, loose tunics and pants and another gown from Abbie. She had informed Trinity that she was to remain in her room until Ares summoned her, but had seemed relieved that Trinity appeared well and unafraid in her new surroundings.

As if for the first time, she glanced around the room. It was luxurious, with attractive paintings above the bed, a small Persian carpet and furniture that might really be Louis XVI. Several dozen books stood on a small shelf against one wall. A dresser, supplied with various kinds of makeup and skin lotions, supported a large mirror. A side door led to a private bathroom.

Fully awake, Trinity went to shower and prepare herself for her second day as Ares's serf. She sat in front of the mirror and, ignoring the facial enhancers, combed out her hair and pulled it behind her head. She didn't intend to make herself look seductive; she had to play this out carefully, because Ares was bound to make the next move in their "game." The one he'd told her she couldn't win.

She put on the serf's tunic, pants and slipper-like shoes, tying the tunic with a colorful sash that marked her "uniform" as slightly different from the ones she'd seen most of the other serfs wearing. The neckline of the tunic was low, exposing her throat,

All the better to bite you with, my dear, she thought, still dizzy in the midst of such contradictory feelings. She thought she might actually have to lie down again.

Someone knocked on the door and Trinity shot to her feet. Daniel stood in the doorway.

"I've been told to escort you to breakfast," he said.

"Am I…dressed properly to meet Ares again?" she asked, pretending unease.

"You're not going to Ares," Daniel said. "He's ordered that I take you down to the serf's dining area."

For a moment Trinity was completely startled. Was it really going to be that easy for her to make contact with the other serfs and scope out the Household?

"Is he dismissing me?" she asked as she joined Daniel at the door.

"I told you I don't know his mind," Daniel said stiffly, leading her toward a side entrance within the empty harem quarters. "He didn't take your blood, did he?"

"No, but—"

"Did you refuse?"

"No. I offered. He still wouldn't take it."

Daniel snorted. She stopped him with a touch on his shoulder.

"You don't want me here, do you?" she asked.

"Not if you disturb his peace and give him nothing in return. He's been happy as he is."

"Are Opiri ever happy?" she asked.

He began to walk again. "Until you know him," he said, "you can't understand him."

"Then *help* me know him," she said, catching up. "I have to live here, and I don't know what I—"

"I'll help you enough so that you don't make too many stupid mistakes," he said, "like interfering in a Challenge."

"Ares already warned me about that," she said. "You care about him, don't you?"

"We'd all be much worse off in any other Household."

Which wasn't much of an answer, Trinity thought, but she'd begun to realize that she might learn a great deal about Ares from Daniel. If he was willing to tell her.

Still, she remained silent until they entered one of the narrow side corridors reserved for servants. Soon they reached a back staircase that descended to the floor below. Trinity memorized their path.

Instinctively she turned toward the delicious scents she knew must lead to the kitchen, but Daniel hung back.

"I have other duties," he said. "The mess is through that door. Try not to make any trouble."

Then he was gone, and she was left angry and frustrated by his unwarranted hostility. He was clearly very protective of Ares, and for some reason he thought she would be a detriment to the master's life. The question was…why would he jump to such a conclusion?

But until she'd been in the Household for a while, Trinity knew she wasn't likely to find the answers she sought. And anger wasn't going to get her anywhere.

She entered the mess hall quietly and cautiously, poised to observe every detail and listen in on every conversation she could get close enough to hear.

And hope she stumbled onto something that would help her learn what she badly needed to know.

Chapter 7

No one noticed her at first, but soon most of the faces were turned toward her—some friendly, a few wary, the majority only curious as to why Ares had broken an apparently long-standing tradition to claim her.

Wandering through the room with a deliberately vague smile on her face, Trinity made the rounds. She immediately noticed a pattern in the appearance of many of the serfs; about half of those she saw would have been considered "cast-offs," as Elizabeth had described them. Some had suffered injuries or illness that had marked or changed parts of their bodies or faces. Many were older like Elizabeth or Jonathan, past the "prime" that Nightsiders valued. There were very few serfs of the kind Trinity knew many Opiri liked to collect—the graceful, the striking, the beautiful.

Trinity exchanged polite greetings and light conversation with the friendly serfs and left the hostile-looking ones alone. In general, she received a cautiously positive reception. But she overheard only the most banal conversations about various Household romances, a new shipment of books for the common room and—behind her back— speculation about the new serf.

But no one showed any sign that they might suspect who or what she really was, or behaved in any way that might suggest they were members of the Underground. Of course, if they had been, it would have been extremely foolish to talk about it in public.

The meal was generous and wholesome, and Trinity knew it had come out of the hard work of field serfs outside the city. Aegis's unnamed contact, the one who had warned them about the Council's possible plans for war, had come from the fields. And it was to him or her that Aegis's return messages had been sent…until all response had stopped.

If she could get into the fields soon, she might find out what had happened to their contact. But that would depend on Ares, and if she could persuade him to take her outside.

The breakfast crowd began to break up within an hour of Trinity's arrival. She was about to set off to explore the other servants' areas when she caught sight of a young man and woman being crowded against the wall outside the mess by three large, imposing serfs. They were taunting the couple, trying to force them farther into the hallway with threats of violence.

Without thinking, Trinity stepped in. She punched the biggest man in the jaw and sent him staggering against the opposite wall. By the time she was facing the second thug, a small crowd had gathered. She took the second man down with a kick to his knee, and he fell with a sharp cry.

The third man turned and fled. The crowd was silent, obviously startled and confused by Trinity's speed and strength. Even the couple she had "rescued" stared at her in astonishment.

While Trinity was cursing herself for her idiocy and considering a strategic retreat, Jonathan appeared. His gaze swept over the men Trinity had disabled and settled on Trinity. He wasn't smiling.

"What the hell is going on here?" he demanded.

Trinity noticed that the young couple had disappeared, and others she recognized had arrived with the Master of Serfs. Elizabeth was there, looking worried, and so was Daniel.

"These men were behaving aggressively toward other serfs," Trinity said calmly. "I stopped them."

The second man, who appeared to have a broken knee, groaned loudly. Jonathan ordered four of the serfs to carry him and the unconscious man to the infirmary.

"Violence is not permitted in this Household," Jonathan said.

"You do realize that those men were already committing violence," Trinity snapped, refusing to be cowed by the older man's stare.

"They didn't touch Erin and Vijay," one of the serfs said. "She just attacked Novak and the others without warning."

"So bullying and threats are just fine," Trinity said, "as long as no one tries to stop the bullies."

"You should have sent someone to inform me at once," Jonathan said, narrowing his eyes. "The master will not be disturbed with petty quarrels." He looked around at the observers. "Do any of you have something to say about this?"

No one spoke. Even Elizabeth hung back, eyes wide with concern. And the other serfs were either too afraid to speak up or considered her a "troublemaker" not worth defending.

Did the bullying come from a twisted desire to hurt others, or could it be part of some internal system of corruption, the kind that could happen in any large organization? Extortion, perhaps? That would get you Deported from the Enclave, and some criminals might bring their "skills" with them into Erebus.

But extortion over what? The Household had plenty of food and clothing, all the necessities of life. Certainly there were black markets for valuable goods, even in the Enclave. But why here? Did the young couple have access to stores that could be sold to the serfs of less "comfortable" Households, and the outside connections to move them?

Trinity knew she'd have to track down the couple and see what she could learn. But at the moment she had a more pressing issue: Jonathan looked as though he'd have thrown her into a dungeon if he dared.

"I'm sorry," she said, trying for some semblance of contrition. "I shouldn't have done that. If something like this happens again—"

"It won't," Jonathan said. "You're new here, and Ares favors you. But he will have to be told of this." He grunted and ordered the others to disperse. "Daniel, you take charge of her."

With a scowl of disgust, Daniel dragged her out of sight of the others.

"What are you?" he demanded in a harsh whisper.

Trinity tried not to show any physical response to his question. "I don't understand what you mean," she said.

"You brought two large men down without any real effort." He looked her up and down. "You're supposed to be an academic of some kind. Does the Enclave teach its ordinary citizens to fight like that?"

"Let me by," she said.

He thrust his arm out, blocking her way. "Ares is a good man by any measure," he said. "But maybe you still don't understand that in Challenging for you, he has attracted unwelcome attention and put himself in grave danger."

"I know how Opiri Bloodlords and Bloodmasters extend their power," she said. "Palemon is dangerous. But Ares won the fight, and—"

Daniel cut her off with a short bark of laughter. "Ares has awakened a beast who will stop at nothing to take his revenge. Palemon has hated Ares for centuries. He will never let this rest until he has killed our master."

"What makes you think Ares is more at risk now than he ever was?" she asked. "It's obvious that other Opiri are afraid of him. I understand that he hasn't been Challenged in years."

"But he has lived too long apart from other Opiri," Daniel said. "He is not careful enough. Palemon has many allies who would be glad to help take him down."

"But I thought Challenges were always one-on-one."

"They are," he said. "But it isn't as simple as you think. If you don't adapt yourself quickly, you'll become a liability to all of us."

"Is that a threat?"

"I have no right to make such a threat," he said, "but I know you aren't what you pretend to be." He dropped his arm. "Watch yourself, Trinity. And don't believe for a second that Ares is hu—"

He broke off, looked around quickly and strode away. A prickle of instinctive awareness raised the hairs on the back of Trinity's neck, and she caught a familiar and riveting scent.

Ares was somewhere nearby. She followed her senses and found him with a visibly nervous Jonathan in the mess hall.

"No one had to tell me," Ares was saying. "Do you think I didn't sense it?"

"My lord—" Jonathan began.

"Who was involved?"

Jonathan's eyes darted about as if he were searching for escape. "Leonard, Dwayne and Novak."

Ares's face darkened. "Where are they?"

"Two are in the infirmary. We don't know where Novak went."

"Find him and confine him." Ares showed a flash of incisor. "Who injured them?"

The Master of Serfs continued to hesitate, clearly afraid to admit the truth. Trinity knew she had a decision to make.

Keeping her cover was more important than anything else. But Ares would find out what had transpired sooner or later, and if she didn't tell him herself she might lose whatever rapport they'd already developed between them.

And she couldn't afford to let the Household suffer because of her errors in judgment, or risk the hostility of every serf in the place.

"I did it," she said.

Ares turned to stare at her. "Is this true?" he asked Jonathan without looking away from Trinity.

"Yes, my lord," said the Master of Serfs.

"Report to me when you have Novak," Ares said, and strode toward Trinity. She braced herself, but he only walked past her with a flick of his hand, gesturing for her to follow.

He took the same servants' stairs by which she and Daniel had come and returned to his apartments. She followed him and paused in the Great Room, unsure of what to expect.

But instead of punishing her or demanding an explanation, Ares gave her a gruff command to return to her room. Trinity considered following him again, but decided on another strategy. It might be an utter disaster, but she needed to poke a stick in the hornet's nest to see how badly she was about to be stung.

She returned to her room, sat at the dresser and loosened her hair. She'd never used much makeup before, but now she rubbed a little blush into her cheeks and reddened her lips. The gown Abbie had given her was still hanging in the closet. She put it on, and then went to Ares's office.

He was sitting at his desk, a scattering of fine paper around him and a quill pen in his hand. He didn't look up when she entered the room.

"What are you doing here?" he asked.

"I hoped you would allow me to talk with you."

He wrote another line of script. "Dressed in that manner?"

This was going to backfire quickly, Trinity thought nervously. "I…hoped you might understand that I do recognize my position here, no matter what—"

He held up a hand to silence her. "You seem unaccountably eager to seduce me," he said. "But somehow, I do not believe you are entirely sincere."

Careful, she thought. "I've made mistakes, but it was never my intention to defy you. And as I seem to recall, you kissed me first."

"So you plan to win my approval with sex and thereby gain forgiveness? Or perhaps you wish to obtain some control over me?"

He had struck so close to the truth that she caught her breath. "You said you wanted me to come to you willingly."

Ares looked down at the paper, so neatly marked with script in the complex Opiri language. "Have you something else you wish to discuss?"

"I didn't get a chance to apologize," she said. "I really didn't set out to—"

"You frightened the other serfs," he said. "But so did I." He set the pen in its stand. "I have never done such a thing before."

"Never?" she asked. Without waiting for permission, Trinity moved to stand over the desk. "You own everyone in this place. Isn't it your right to determine what goes on in your Household and mete out punishment to those who displease you?"

He looked up at her, jaw set. "Are you mocking me, Trinity?"

"No. I understand that I created problems in an otherwise peaceful Household." She swallowed hard. "I know I owe you an explanation."

His chair creaked as he leaned back, and his eyes grew cold. "I am listening."

Glancing around awkwardly, Trinity spotted a chair on the other side of the room. "May I sit?"

At his brusque nod, she pulled the chair close to the desk and sat down.

She began by telling him what she had seen. "They were just a young couple, and from what I could see they weren't causing any trouble. These three men were attacking them, and no one was doing anything about it."

"So you felt it incumbent upon yourself to interfere."

"Should I have allowed three of your serfs to hurt two of your others?"

"Why were you so eager to protect humans you didn't know?

"It was the right thing to do," she said, leaning toward him, very much aware that the position emphasized the swell and curve of her breasts.

But Ares didn't seem to notice. "How is it that your papers did not include the vital information that you are a skilled and deadly fighter?" he asked.

"I don't know. I didn't write them. But my parents had sent me to martial arts schools from the time I was very young. Crime still exists in the Enclave, in spite of Deportation."

"And yet, with such skill, you became a scholar?"

"More of a student than a scholar. And I didn't want to be a soldier."

"I see." He rose and walked around the desk to stand over her. "Do you know why I sent you to the serf's mess?"

Her heart beginning to pound at the leashed strength and quiet ferocity looming so close, Trinity shook her head. "I thought you might be sending me away."

"Sending you away?" He caught a lock of her hair and twisted it gently around one of his long fingers. "I merely wanted you to see a little of the Household and meet other serfs. I wanted your judgment of them as an outsider."

Of course, Trinity thought. He'd said he "required a human of the Enclave" to share her views about *his* people. She'd assumed he meant the Opiri.

But he'd never mentioned wanting her to spy on his serfs. Why would that be necessary unless he needed to find out something he couldn't learn by any other method? And why *her?* Why not someone as devoted to him as Daniel so obviously was?

"I…didn't realize that was what you wanted," she stammered, allowing a little of her real surprise to show on her face.

"I did not expect you to insert yourself into matters that did not concern you." He dropped his hand. "If you had gone to Jonathan—"

"There wasn't time."

He moved around her and stalked across the room. "I can see no possible reason why any of my serfs would attack others when they are fully aware of the penalties for such transgressions." His voice deepened. "You asked if I 'mete out punishment.' I assure you, these men will face the consequences of their actions."

"You'll put them up for Claiming?"

"It is likely. Once I've learned why they acted as they did."

"Sometimes people act as they do simply because they enjoy hurting others," she said. "Like Palemon."

Ares returned to his desk and began to stack his papers neatly. "We are not speaking of Opiri."

"But humans believe violence is *your* natural state."

He met her gaze. "Do you believe that, Trinity?"

"I would say that not every Opir is like Palemon. Not if I'm to take you as an example."

"Ah. Then I meet with your approval," he said drily.

"If you want my honest opinion…"

"I have told you that I do."

"Then I would say that you and Palemon seem to be opposites in many ways, and that means there must be a whole range of Opir behaviors, as there are among humans."

"Were you, who have apparently studied history, unaware of this?"

"When you live in the Enclave and are fighting for survival, such distinctions don't seem to matter."

"Yes," he said. "The need for survival outweighs every other consideration."

She hesitated, wondering if she ought to ask him more about Palemon and their enmity, but decided to wait for a better time.

"You don't seem to be very angry with me," she said.

"Anger," he said, finishing at his desk, "would be pointless. Either I punish you, or I overlook this incident."

"How will you punish me, if you decide you want to keep me?"

Chapter 8

He rose again, disappeared into his bedroom and re-emerged with a new bottle of wine and a single glass.

"No wine for me?" she asked with a brash attempt at humor.

His glance was less quelling than bemused. "You know very well that I would neither send you away nor put you up for Claiming. And you did flush out three troublemakers—for which, in spite of your intemperate actions, I should be grateful."

Grateful, to a serf? Yet that, she thought, was no stranger than treating her almost as an equal and seeming so interested in her observations.

"Do you think I treat my serfs fairly, Trinity?" he asked.

"I haven't seen anything to indicate otherwise," she said.

The wine bottle was already open, so Ares pulled out the silver stopper and carefully poured himself a glass before he spoke again. "Are they content?"

"As content as slaves can be."

"Always truth from you," he said with a brief laugh. "You heard Palemon call me 'indulgent.'"

"And you said you found that you received better service if your humans didn't live in constant fear of you."

His eyes grew remote. "Do not make the mistake of thinking me kind, Trinity. Perhaps I have gone too far with this indulgence."

"Have you ever had any real trouble with any of your humans until now? You have serfs who were cast off for imperfections, what I guess some Opiri would call 'defects.' From what I've seen, most of them are grateful to have a second chance."

"Did anyone speak to you of this?"

Oh, no. She wasn't about to name names, not when she didn't yet know what exactly Ares was looking for. Or why.

"I could see it, just as I could see that they aren't unhappy here." She hesitated, weighing her next words. "Palemon obviously doesn't treat his serfs as anything but animals or disposable objects. That's one of the things that sets you two apart."

"And in what ways are we similar?"

Dangerous ground, she thought. But she *had* to understand him, and so she had to keep taking risks.

"Possessiveness," she said. "Pride. The desire to win. The instinct to master others. Anger."

"Yet, as you said, I am not angry with you now."

"No," She wet her lips. "You can obviously control it when you want to."

"Unlike Palemon?" He turned his glass in a circle. "You did not seem unduly afraid of him."

"Then I did a good job of concealing my feelings."

"You showed no fear of *me,* even when I attacked you."

"Considering how well you treated me when you first

claimed me, I've had no reason to believe you would hurt me out of desire to cause pain."

"In spite of your assessment of Opir emotions? In spite of my violence against Palemon?"

"I had a feeling." She bit her lip. "The same feeling that makes me—"

She broke off, suddenly afraid…not of him, but of the likelihood that she would reveal something she didn't want him to see. That she didn't want to see in herself.

"Makes you what?" he asked, cocking his head.

"Able to trust you."

"*Trust* me," he said, that bemused expression crossing his face again. "And if you did not?"

"It would be much harder for me to…accept my situation here."

"Sharing my bed and giving me your blood." His voice held a note of belated anger. "Again, you speak as though you believe I will insist on taking you against your will."

Trinity swallowed again, her mind suddenly crowded with vivid erotic images of Ares pulling her toward him, his muscles rippling under golden skin as he caressed her naked body, suckled her nipples, stroked and licked the tender lips between her thighs as he made her ready for him.…

"I don't think that," she said at last. "You wouldn't lie to me."

"You seem certain. Is that, too, a 'feeling'?" Easing himself into his chair, Ares took a sip of the wine. "Before I claimed you," he said, "I believed I understood human behavior, at least on an intellectual level. But I missed something important in failing to anticipate the actions of the serfs you fought. You have already helped me to reach beyond intellect."

Did he mean learning to think in terms of "feelings"? Emotion? Was he capable of the kind of empathy he seemed to be seeking?

"What more do want me to do?" she asked.

Ares set the glass down and pushed it away, a brooding look in his eyes. "If these men are the only troublemakers and their motive was simply to inflict pain, it should become evident quickly enough. If I sent you back down among the serfs and you observed more conduct of this nature, would you report back to me honestly?"

This, Trinity thought, was a situation fraught with both danger and opportunity. Mingling amongst the other serfs and getting to know them was essential if she was to find any Underground presence in the Household. But she couldn't expose them to Ares if she found them.

"You made clear that I would never hold any secrets from you," she said.

"But where does your loyalty lie, Trinity? Is it to me because you are grateful that I saved you from Palemon, or to your fellow humans?"

"You said you didn't *want* my gratitude."

His eyes flashed. "Somehow I find it difficult to believe you were sent to Erebus simply because you evaded paying your taxes. You are far too clever to make such a mistake."

Trinity kept her face expressionless in spite of her shock. Had he begun to guess the truth so quickly?

"Cleverness doesn't preclude stupidity," she said, adding a touch of bitterness to her voice. "It doesn't take much to become a convict. Your kind put us in that position."

Suddenly he laughed, as if he found her statement supremely amusing. "Come here," he said, rising again.

She left her chair to join him behind the desk. His shoulder brushed hers, sending shockwaves of sexual awareness jolting through her body. The desk was covered with a map, carefully protected under glass. Trinity estimated that it must be centuries old. Ares laid his fingertip on the strangely distorted coast of Spain and traced eastward.

"For thousands of years," he said, "*your* kind believed

one might fall off the edge of the world if one sailed too far in your primitive ships."

"It doesn't take a scholar to know any of that."

"No. But we who remained awake during the Long Sleep spent most of our time wandering among humans, observing the advancement of mankind's understanding of the world, the rise and fall of governments, cultures and religions. Waiting for the time when your population would be sufficient to accommodate not only all the Opiri who slept, but also the new society some dreamed of building."

"It seems you've succeeded," she said.

He glanced at her. His face was very close, and she almost forgot to breathe.

"You don't believe that, Trinity," he said. "Whatever you may have said, you believe we are savages."

"In all honesty, I can't accept a society based on the constant struggle to stay alive and an unending compulsion to elevate status by enslaving another intelligent species."

"And is yours so much better?" he asked softly. "Your various cultures have frequently employed slavery as a major source of labor and wealth, even so recently as your own former nation's nineteenth century. Your species has persecuted your own kind because of differences in gender and religious beliefs. You allowed your weakest to starve and die of curable illnesses."

"I never said—"

"And that is not all," Ares interrupted. "You wasted your resources. You abused this planet and came close to destroying it. Only the nearly total destruction of your own way of life taught you the value of what you had."

So much of what he said was true that she couldn't find a ready denial. But why was Ares bringing all this up now? What was he trying to tell her?

"You would have destroyed all humanity out of sheer, unbounded hunger," she said.

"But we did not," Ares said, his breath caressing her cheek. "If we had not risen when we did, this world would have been made uninhabitable by either of our species. We were almost too late."

"So then you brought war."

"We offered a bargain," he said, "an arrangement by which humans would give us what we required, and we would share this world in harmony."

"You mean you asked for what you ended up getting," she asked, edging away from him. "A constant supply of humans to provide you with all the blood and status you wanted."

"I am not referring to the terms of the current Armistice. I speak of what was offered before the War began. And it did not involve compulsion, Trinity."

"You mean you…would have allowed people to volunteer to give blood?"

"Not all of my people agreed, but the majority were in favor of the offer." His expression was grave, concealing nothing, and Trinity knew he wasn't lying. "Is it possible they didn't teach you this in your Enclave?" he asked, moving just enough to remain close to her.

Trinity's stomach tightened. Surely Aegis wouldn't let its agents operate without such information, and neither would the government.

Aegis *had* to know. But she had never been told. She, a dhampir, one of Aegis's top operatives, had been kept in the dark the whole time.

Was it some kind of cover-up, knowledge the Enclave wouldn't trust even with the agents who put their lives on the line every day to maintain the hard-won peace?

"I can see you weren't aware," Ares said. "Your government chose to keep it from you."

Trinity didn't trust herself to speak. She couldn't look at Ares, afraid her feelings might show all too clearly.

"Things might have been very different if both sides had been more willing to compromise," Ares said. "But the offer our leaders made was an outrage to yours, and there was little negotiation." He sighed. "Still, it was not entirely the fault of humanity. After negotiations failed, most Opiri believed war would be an easy path to victory over such weak animals."

"But it wasn't, was it?" she asked numbly.

"No. The Bloodmasters who met in council to determine the time of the Awakening underestimated the courage and determination of your kind."

"Because, like you—even after all these years—they understood humans only on an 'intellectual level.'"

"Blindness afflicts all creatures," Ares said. "Yet here we are, with the Enclaves sending humans to feed us and serve as units of value when there might have been some element of choice. We might truly have been equals, you and I."

"No. We'd always have been the inferiors. We're very good predators, but you're the only creatures better at it than we are."

"Perhaps."

She looked at him. His lips were so very close to hers. "Would you set your serfs free if you could?" she asked.

"The only freedom they might have would be to serve another lord, or starve in the wilds. Your Enclave would not welcome their return."

Trinity knew he was right. But she'd heard rumors of colonies in the Zone and beyond, where Nightsiders and humans were living together in peace.

A hope. A wish. A dream without substance.

To cover her agitation, Trinity moved away from Ares again and walked into the Great Room, pausing to examine the many works of art. His nearly silent footsteps came up behind her.

"Van Gogh," she said, stopping in front of a landscape with rich yellow fields of wheat and a whirling blue sky. Beside it hung a portrait of the artist, one she remembered seeing in art books at school.

"Remarkable," she said. "Did one of your serfs paint these reproductions?"

"None of these works are reproductions," he said, his breath stirring her hair. "During the war, many great human artifacts were nearly lost. I saved a number of them, as did others."

"You stole them, you mean."

"As we all have cause to know, war is no respecter of persons or art."

"Do other Opiri collect objects of beauty the way you do? Besides humans, I mean?"

"'Everything has its beauty, but not everyone sees it,'" he quoted.

"That doesn't sound like an Opir sentiment."

"It isn't." He moved around to face her, blocking her view of the painting. "It was written by your philosopher Kong Zi, also known as Confucius. But in answer to your question… Most of my people make a pretense of finding human art much too sentimental and primitive."

The expression in his eyes was suddenly so intensely sensual, so hungry, that she began to lose control of her arousal again.

"I perceive much about you now, Trinity," he murmured. "How many of your kind actually desire one of mine?"

"I…I don't understand," she said, hastily looking away.

"I have not been unaware of your body's responses to my proximity, even in the beginning."

Trinity's nipples pushed against her bodice, and she knew he couldn't miss the scent of her need, of the flood of warmth gathering between her thighs. Denial would be pointless, but she couldn't let him think…

"I don't know how many humans have desired Opiri," she said hoarsely, "but our women were abused by your kind during the War. That doesn't exactly engender those kinds of feelings. Neither does slavery."

He moved so close that his chest brushed her aching breasts, and she gasped. He smoothed her hair away from her forehead. "But how do *you* feel, Trinity?"

She realized that she was breathing much too fast and worked to steady herself. "Do you have any idea what this has been like for me, knowing how much…"

"You have not answered my question," he said, his lips hovering over hers. "Do you desire me?"

Chapter 9

Trinity shivered, even more aroused by his blunt question than she would have believed possible.

You speak as though you must brace yourself for some unspeakable torment, he had said when she'd first offered herself.

But he'd also said he would know everything about her. Her mind, her soul, her body. Had he been waiting to confirm that she harbored some desperate longing for him, a sexual attraction completely beyond her control?

Whatever his beliefs, Trinity reminded herself, this was what she wanted. No matter how uneasy she might feel at his candor, this was only another step closer to forging a bond he would be reluctant to break.

"Yes," she whispered. "I desire you."

"Where does it come from, Trinity?" he asked, caressing her cheek with his fingertips. "Is it my supposed kindness?"

She ignored his question. "What about Cassandra? She obviously feels the same attraction."

"There is a difference. I do not yet understand it, but I wish to." He cupped her chin in his hand. "Is it because I do not resemble an ordinary Opir?"

"I…I don't know," she said. "You're handsome, even by human standards. Your body is very attractive."

"As is yours." His gaze fell to her bodice, molded to her breasts like a second skin. He dropped his hand to run his finger across one of her nipples. She shuddered, barely containing a moan of excitement.

"Then it is simply due to my physical traits, this reaction," he said, "but no less intense than my need for blood."

"No," she said. "It's not that simple. I wish I could—"

"I fully understand my lust for *you*," he said, interrupting her. "Taking blood in the act of sex is particularly pleasant for us."

"But you haven't given in," Trinity said, quivering as he rubbed her other nipple with his fingertip.

"No," he said, his attention fully on the caressing motions of his hand. She wanted to cover herself, and at the same time she wanted to tear the gown from her body and let him see her, take her, get it over with so her mission could continue without all these complica—

"Do you want me?" he demanded, his hands stilling on her breasts. "I will have the truth, Trinity. Do you want me to take you now?"

From the time she had entered Erebus, Trinity had intended to feel nothing when this time came, but that resolve had fallen by the wayside. Now, she felt everything. Desire, excitement, glorious pleasure, yearning she had only experienced one time in her life.

But that had been a child's yearning to belong, to be like the other kids in school, to have a living mother and father. A *human* father.

There was nothing childlike about this.

"Yes," she sighed. "Oh, God, yes."

He grasped her arms in his hands before she could finish the thought, lifted her off her feet and kissed her. It wasn't quite like the first time, when he'd meant it to warn and punish. It wasn't gentle, either.

She accepted it without hesitation, opening her mouth to his tongue. It darted in and out, mimicking the motions of lovemaking, and she moaned again. He responded by deepening the kiss.

Risking his anger, she put her arms around him. He stiffened for a moment and then gave in to her touch, pulling her hard against him. His erection ground into her belly, straining against the fabric that confined it. He licked the side of her lips, her jawline, her neck. She closed her eyes, wondering if he would take her to his bed or bite her first.

She had to be prepared. She knew it was almost too soon to be making such a crucial decision, but she decided at that moment that she would test the possibility of addicting him. He might not be one of the vulnerable ones, but she couldn't dismiss the possibility that if she didn't take that chance, he could choose to cast her aside as soon as he'd satisfied himself with her. Addiction would bind him to her with a need he couldn't break.

She slid her hand down to his cock and ran her fingers along its length, at the same time biting down on her molar to break the tiny capsule containing the drug that kept the addictive qualities of her blood in check.

Abruptly Ares let her go, pulled her into his office, drew her to the chair at his desk and settled her on his lap. She let herself melt against him, gasping as he gripped her bottom and positioned her over his groin. Her gown ripped to the tops of her thighs on both sides. He drew back, tearing the skirts all the way to her waist. She whimpered as he undid his belt and pulled open his tunic, revealing the silk shirt underneath and the powerfully muscular chest, shoulders and arms she had seen during the Claiming.

He kissed her again, working at the fastening of his pants. She was so wet that she knew there would be no discomfort, even though it had been years since she'd taken a man into her body. Her thoughts blurred as she felt his cock slide against her, seeking its home. She wriggled to help him, straddling him with her thighs to either side of his waist. Suddenly all rationality was gone, and all she could think of, all she could feel was her need to feel him moving inside her.

Then, with no warning at all, he stopped. She reached for him, but he pushed her back, panting raggedly.

"No," he said. "Not this way."

He took her by the shoulders and lifted her off his lap, leaving her swollen and aching.

"Ares," she whispered.

Without a word he swept her into his arms and carried her to the bed. He set her face down on the embroidered bedspread, pulling the remains of her gown aside, lifting her hips, spreading her thighs.

Trinity had made a clinical study of Nightsider sexual practices, and she knew this was their preferred position. But there was nothing remotely clinical about this. She moaned again as he stroked his finger over her swollen flesh, exploring her wetness, easing his finger inside her. She moved against him and he withdrew, gripping her hips, positioning himself behind her. She felt the head of his cock graze her lips, teasing, penetrating only a fraction of an inch.

She gasped. Ares tensed, curling his body over her back. His breath was hot, and his cock burned her like a firebrand. His teeth grazed her neck.

And then he stopped. Again. Trinity cried out as he

withdrew, resting her forehead on the pillows. Ares rolled away and off the bed in one fluid motion. He strode out of the room, fastening his pants.

A moment later she heard Daniel's voice, and knew something had gone very wrong.

Ares found Daniel waiting in the office, standing stiff and alert as if he were bracing himself for immediate punishment.

He very nearly got what he expected.

"I didn't summon you," Ares growled. "Why are you here?"

The serf bowed his head briefly, but his gaze was determined. "You asked to be informed of further trouble in the Household, my lord," he said. "I have come to tell you—"

Ares heard quiet footsteps behind him. Trinity, wrapped in one of his robes and carrying herself with all the stateliness of an ancient human goddess, approached with a wary gaze that moved quickly from Ares's face to Daniel's.

"Return to my room, Trinity," Ares said.

"If this is about what happened downstairs," she said to Daniel, "I've already told Ares it was me."

Ares was very much inclined to take her by the arm and force her to return to her room in the harem, but that would entail a loss of dignity he was not prepared to surrender. It was difficult enough ignoring the persistent ache in his groin and the blood hunger that made his head pound as if a column of heavily armed human troops were marching through his head.

"If reporting on Trinity was your purpose in coming," he said to Daniel, "you may leave now."

Daniel flinched. Ares could smell the human's perspiration and the adrenaline pumping through his blood, and it angered him that Daniel, of all his serfs, was actually afraid. He deserved to be berated in no uncertain terms for bursting in without permission, but he had been Ares's valet and personal servant since he had been hardly more than a boy. Those years should have taught him that Ares would never harm him.

"Do not waste my time," Ares snapped. "What is it?"

The serf didn't move a muscle. "There has been a death, my lord."

Ares frowned. "Of what cause?"

"By serious injury." Daniel stared past Ares at Trinity. "If she told you—"

"Who was it?"

"Leonard, my lord."

One of the three men Trinity had fought, Ares remembered.

"How did he die?" she asked, more subdued than he had ever seen her.

"His skull was damaged," Daniel said. "He lapsed into a coma and never recovered."

Trinity covered her face with her hands. "It was an accident," she said. "I only meant to disable them."

"She is dangerous," Daniel said in such a sharp voice that Ares was genuinely startled. The serf had never spoken to him in such a tone before. "Please, my lord, consider what she has done."

"She acted to protect two of my serfs against aggressors," Ares said brusquely.

"She has brought violence into the Household."

"I didn't bring the violence," Trinity said, lifting her head. "It was already here."

Ares's temper was frayed almost beyond endurance. Daniel's report, and Trinity's confession, reminded him that he might have made a serious mistake in allowing the serfs to run their own lives largely without his interference.

"My lord—" Daniel began.

"I will not have my Household further disturbed," Ares said. "Has Novak been found?"

"Yes," Daniel said in a very low voice.

"Where is he?"

"In the holding cell. Dwayne is in the infirmary."

"Then I will speak to both of them myself. There will be no more injuries or deaths among my humans, even if I must personally confine every serf to quarters until all of them have been questioned. Tell Jonathan and Levi to expect me. You are dismissed."

The valet hesitated, bowed and left the room. Ares broke into a round of furious pacing, working off his anger step by step. He stopped before the Van Gogh Trinity had admired earlier and stared at the pattern of blue swirls in the Dutch painter's frantic sky, searching for some order in the chaos.

"I'm very sorry that man died," Trinity said behind him.

Ares didn't doubt her sincerity, but the damage was done. The penalty for maiming or murder, which he had never expected to see in his Household, was consignment to open Claiming. If he failed to punish Trinity...

She moved closer, the remains of the silk dress sliding erotically against her soft, sweet-smelling skin. "I would change it, if I could," she said. "If you have to punish me, I'll understand. I don't want to make things harder for anyone else or make them believe I—"

Lost to all sense and reason, Ares grabbed Trinity, spun her around so her back was to the wall and trapped her there with outstretched arms. He pressed his mouth to her neck, seeking the precise spot where her pulse was strongest. It leaped under his lips.

He wanted her blood. He was starving for it, and she had admitted she wanted him.

He closed his eyes, his teeth barely grazing her skin. He remembered how she had felt under him, wet, ready, hungry for him to fill her and take all he desired. Everything about her—the scent of her arousal, her moans of pleasure, even the chemicals in her blood—had been almost impossible to resist. It had seemed that no discipline could overcome his hunger.

But it had. Abruptly he drew back and walked away.

"Ares," Trinity called after him. "I've only been a cause of trouble for you. I didn't realize what would happen after you Challenged Palemon, that you'd put yourself in danger of future Challenges, maybe even to the death. Not only from him, but from his allies."

"Who told you this?" he said, keeping his back to her.

"It doesn't really matter, does it? I know what I've done."

"I chose this 'danger,' as I chose you. You had nothing to do with it." He spun around and stalked toward her again. "Perhaps you have also been told that I have not lost a Challenge in several of your centuries."

"You've faced him before?"

"Palemon and I have been enemies since before the Long Sleep," he said through clenched teeth. "He and I fought over territory during the most savage era of our kind, when Opiri were first gathering in groups instead of living lives of solitary hunters with a few bound vassals to serve them."

Trinity shivered. "Did you kill people then, Ares?"

He gave her his darkest frown, absurdly disappointed that she would think that of him. "To kill those who supplied me with blood would be to kill myself," he said, "even if I had been so inclined."

"But others did?"

"As they killed each other, in large numbers. The first writings say that the eldest realized that we were destroying too many of our own kind, as well as humans. They knew that there must be some means of controlling the struggles for dominance that occurred when solitary Opir crossed paths."

"But you were one of the eldest. You helped find a solution."

"I was not welcome among them then." The memories, he found, were still far from pleasant. "Once the first Bloodlords were chosen, I preferred to live apart. Palemon seemed intent on provoking me. In time, I convinced him to leave me alone."

"But that didn't quite work out."

"There was never more than a fragile truce between us. We avoided each other in the centuries following the inception of the Long Sleep. Until the War and the building of the Citadel."

"And you're still caught in the same struggle."

"You were merely the catalyst for the inevitable, final contest."

Trinity swallowed. "What would happen if he *did* win?"

He bit back his irritation. "The victor may claim all of the loser's property."

"If you got rid of me, would it make a difference? Would he leave you alone?"

The courage she continuously displayed usually elicited his admiration, but now it only angered him. "Not even if I offered him all my wealth and my serfs."

"I was afraid of that. But maybe, if you offered *me*—"

"*Give* you to him? Is that what you want for yourself?"

"No. Only to protect you."

"I have never required the protection of any serf." He circled her and backed her up against the wall again. "Palemon would use you in ways you cannot imagine. You are a fool if you think I could possibly—" He broke off in sudden confusion, the kind he hadn't felt since his first youth. "I do not understand you. Why would you offer to make such a sacrifice?"

She met his gaze as directly as ever. "You're already setting an example of decency and fair treatment that other Opiri may eventually follow. If there are enough like you, there might be some hope that—"

"Hope?" he said, searching her eyes. "Of a lasting peace? Have you ever been on the front lines, Trinity? Have you seen the level of barbarity on both sides, the senseless loss of—"

"You said you didn't believe I was cast out for tax evasion," she said, interrupting him. "You were right. I know what war is, even though I was only a few years old when the Armistice was signed. I saw what it did to those who *had* fought and survived. I would have been one of those people, if I'd been the right age then."

"What are you saying?"

"You wondered why I'm such a good fighter." She lifted her chin. "I *was* a soldier. And I would have been ready to fight against your kind if I hadn't made a mistake that cost me my freedom."

Trinity had never planned to admit even the smallest part of the truth about herself until she was completely certain of Ares's need for her. She'd almost had him— confessing that she *did* want him, that he could give in to his own hungers without compelling her in any way.

But the situation—not only Leonard's death, but also Daniel's involvement—had forced her hand. Ares had seen through her, even though he clearly hadn't guessed who or what she really was. She realized she was taking a terrible risk, but sometimes skimming near the truth would keep an enemy from searching further.

"A soldier?" Ares said in a flat voice. "A soldier deported to Erebus by the Enclave?"

"Military discipline in the Enclave is severe," she said,

holding his gaze. "A grunt who tries to kill a superior officer wouldn't be sent anywhere but to a firing squad."

"You attacked one of your own?"

"I was out of my mind with anger. I saw my friend beaten nearly to death by the officer's thugs."

"Why would discipline be so strict when the War ended twenty-seven years ago?"

"Because we might be called up anytime if a new war started."

"But they were unwilling to execute you?"

"I escaped by joining the shipment of convicts. None of the escorts bothered to search there, and I was careful to blend in."

For the first time since their lovemaking had been so rudely interrupted, Ares looked more intrigued than angry. "You preferred slavery in Erebus to death?"

"You have thousands of years of life, and you still fight for it just as desperately as we do for our paltry hundred years."

"You must have known your likely fate if your profession were discovered here," he said. "It would be assumed that you have some knowledge that could be of use to the Council. You would be interrogated, and if you refused to cooperate, your death would have been far more torturous than the Enclave would have given you."

"Then you can understand why I kept the truth from you until now."

"And yet you revealed your skills in spite of the risk."

"Am I right in believing you won't turn me over for questioning?"

"Do you think me so weakened by lust?" Ares countered heatedly. "Do you think you have some power over me I cannot break, that I would betray my own kind?"

"I've never thought that."

"Yet you *do* still feel loyalty to those who would have killed you."

"You've asked me twice before why I care about people I don't know," she said. "They're my fellow human beings in a very dangerous world. I would fight for the Enclave if your people broke the Armistice."

"Do you believe that is likely?" he asked.

"You tell me. You must have some idea about what your Council is planning."

"The Council is not all of one mind, and I have no interest in politics."

Easy, Trinity told herself. *Don't ask too many questions. Don't arouse any—*

"Would the Enclave allow you to return to fight?" he asked, cutting into her thoughts.

She shrugged, shifting the scraps of her dress. "If they don't, I'll remain a slave unless the humans win. And then…who knows?" She laughed. "I was always a troublemaker."

"I believe it," he said, a touch of amusement in his voice. He sobered quickly. "You never told me whom you left behind in the Enclave."

Trinity saw that she was entering perilous waters again, though Ares had apparently accepted her story. "My parents are dead, and I'm… I was estranged from my brother," she said. "No other family, really."

"That wasn't what I meant."

She glanced up, looking for some clue as to his emotions. Surely he couldn't be jealous of some phantom human lover when jealousy among Opiri seemed to revolve entirely around property and status.

Yet she'd seen confusion in him before, a kind of bewilderment such a powerful Opir should never feel. The same uncertainty was in his eyes now.

That meant she could still seal the deal. If she was very, very careful.

"A long time ago, I had a lover," she said. "I'd almost forgotten what it felt like, until you—"

"Do not lie to me again, Trinity." He backed away and strode to one of the marble busts on its tall pedestal, staring at it as if it held secrets he might unlock. "You have already deceived me. Should I forgive you for that?"

She moved cautiously up behind him, laying her hand ever so lightly on his shoulder. "You can still send me away. You can sell me to some other master. But before you do, let me know what it's like to feel you inside me."

Ares's shoulder was rigid under her hand, and she knew he might still react with Opiri instinct and toss her across the room for daring to touch him. But he turned, very slowly, and lifted her into his arms. She pressed her face into his chest as he carried her into his bedchamber and set her on her feet at the foot of the bed.

"Undress," he said, his gaze holding hers with absolute command. Palemon had given her the same order during the Claiming, but that had been meant to shame, to put her in her place. Ares also put her in her place, but it was a place she wanted to be.

A delicious shiver ran through her body. She was in his power.

And he was in *hers*.

The bodice was nearly the only intact part of her gown, but she intended to make the most of what was left. Slowly she pulled the left strap from her shoulder, never taking her eyes from his. She let the strap fall to her side as the neckline of the bodice sagged nearly to her nipple. She moved to the other strap, and when she pulled it down only her hand across her chest kept it from falling to her waist.

"Remove your hand," Ares said.

She did. Her nipples puckered not only from the exposure, but because of the way he seemed to devour her with his gaze.

"The rest," he said.

Moving her hips, Trinity dislodged what remained of the gown and felt it slide over her belly and thighs to pool around her ankles. She stepped free of the silken puddle and stood as straight as a soldier under inspection.

And what an inspection. Even with her few lovers, she had never felt so utterly naked. Ares didn't need to touch her to make her wet, to set off a throbbing ache between her thighs.

He covered the space between them with one step and cupped the weight of her breasts in his hands. She let her head fall back as his thumbs circled her nipples. That single touch alone brought her close to the edge.

His hands slid down her sides to her hips and then behind to her bottom, kneading her cheeks gently. He slid one hand between her thighs from behind and stroked her swollen flesh.

"You are not deceiving me now," he said, his voice husky with raw desire.

"No," she whispered. "God, no."

"Get on the bed."

It wasn't exactly the way she might have wanted, but she'd been more than ready to go through with the relative lack of foreplay before. She didn't think she could stand the wait, anyway. She got onto the bed and knelt facing away from him.

"Turn around," he said.

Her heart pounding in her throat, Trinity did as he told her. He had already removed his pants again. Like her, he wore nothing underneath. He was hard. Very hard and very large, his cock riding high against his flat belly. Trinity licked her lips, her entire body flushing.

"Tell me what you want," Ares said softly.

She knew what she wanted. She wanted him inside her, thrusting hard, making her gasp with pleasure at being possessed utterly.

"I want you," she said hoarsely.

"I will take your blood."

She closed her eyes. "Yes."

She heard him move toward the bed, felt his weight press down on the mattress, felt his hand stroking over her shoulders with astonishing gentleness. He tangled his fingers in her hair and pulled her head back.

Maybe there wouldn't be any lovemaking after all, she thought. Maybe he'd just go for the blood.

But she had underestimated him. He kissed the base of her neck, dipping his tongue into the hollow, but never so much as grazed her skin with his teeth. Instead, he eased her down and began exploring her lips with his, firm and tender at the same time.

Trinity returned the kiss, parting her lips to let his tongue in. His hand moved to her left breast, encircling it, lightly pinching her nipple between his fingers. She arched up against him, desperate to feel his mouth on her, his agile tongue stroking her breasts.

But he wouldn't be rushed. He kissed the sides of her mouth, her forehead, her chin, each move like that of the most experienced human lover intent on heightening his partner's arousal with every little caress. He ran his hand over her belly, resting it just above the nest of curls that were already damp with desire.

When she thought she couldn't bear another movement, his lips moved to her breast. She gasped as he took her nipple into his mouth and rolled his tongue over and around it. He ran his hand in slow circles over her stomach, never venturing lower, tormenting her.

Desperate to distract herself from the overwhelming sensations, she opened her eyes to look at his face. It had changed in some indefinable way, hungry and intent, but with no trace of suspicion or anger. He looked into her eyes, and she turned her face aside.

"Are you ashamed?" he asked, pausing to give due attention to her other breast.

"What?" she said, moaning under her breath as he teased her nipple with the tip of his tongue.

"Of being pleasured by an Opir."

He began to suckle again, and his fingers brushed the slick curls below her stomach.

"No," she said, her voice cracking as his finger slipped into the indentation of her vulva and stroked over the nub hidden within. She opened her thighs, inviting him to explore and discover every part of her in intimate detail. "I thought I made that—"

She gasped again as he slid his finger through the wetness, circling her entrance with the greatest delicacy. "I thought it was going to be like…the last time," she said.

"You expected that I would take you the Opir way?" he said, kissing the taut skin over her ribs.

"Why…aren't you?" she said as his mouth brushed over her belly button.

"Because when I take you, you will hold nothing back from me. And I will see it on your face."

Chapter 10

She never thought of a reply, for he had replaced his rov-
ing fingers with his hot mouth, and his tongue was sliding between her lips below, licking, drinking as she dug
her fingers into the sheets and clenched her teeth to keep
from crying aloud.

"Almost as sweet as blood," he said when he stopped
again. He licked the wetness from his lips with obvious
relish, and she nearly tore the sheets with her fingernails.
All she wanted to do was lace her fingers in his dark hair
and pull him back down again.

"Is it...okay if I touch you?" she asked thickly.

His low chuckle was muffled between her thighs. She
gasped as he thrust his tongue inside her and reached for
his thick, straight hair, tangling it between her fingers. "I...
can't stop," she said, quivering uncontrollably.

Abruptly he withdrew, and the blinding light of orgasm
receded. He stroked the inside of her thigh with his fingertips, easing the tension from her muscles.

"Not until I tell you," he said, his voice rough with unrequited lust.

She clenched her jaw and pulled her thighs together. But Ares was between them again, his body settling over hers, his cock nestled snugly against her belly as he supported himself on his arms.

"Look at me, Trinity," he said.

She met his gaze. His violet eyes were nearly all pupil, and the tips of his incisors showed just beneath his upper lip.

"Do you want this?" he asked.

"Yes," she said, feeling her neck begin to throb in time with the heat between her thighs. "I wouldn't be...if I didn't—"

"I still give you the choice. I will let you go if you ask me." He shifted, his cock sliding deeper between her legs, and she whimpered.

"What will you do if I want to stop?" she asked, hardly aware of the words she spoke. "Will you...call Cassandra?"

He didn't answer with words. He shifted again, and this time his cock was riding along the inside of her thigh, inches from entering her. Moving her own hips, she tried to urge him in.

His lips grazed her neck as he held himself above her with one arm and reached for her wrist with the other. He gathered both her wrists in one strong hand and trapped them above her head.

"Make your choice," he murmured against the hollow of her neck. "This is your last chance, Trinity. After this, you will be branded as mine."

But there had never been a choice, even before she had accepted her desire for him. She needed Ares inside her more than she'd ever needed anything in her life. She wanted him to master her. At this moment, she wanted to be his slave in every way.

"I'm yours," she said, tilting her head back to expose the entire length of her neck.

All at once he was inside her, the first thrust gentle, as if he expected her to break. She cried out a little, feeling him stretch her, move deeper, withdraw.

"Am I hurting you?" he said, his lips moving against her neck.

"No. Please, don't stop."

He didn't. As she wrapped her legs around his hips, he began a steady rhythm, rocking her a little with each thrust, holding her hands above her head so that she couldn't touch him, though she knew he'd release her instantly if she asked.

It was incredibly erotic, even if it was all a kind of game. Yet it was not a game at all. Because Ares meant what he'd said. He was branding her, and even when she did what she had to do, that indelible mark would never go away.

As he increased the pace of his movements, she could feel the pressure building inside her, her thighs tightening reflexively around his waist, drawing him in as deep as her body would allow. Then, abruptly, as she was about to come, he withdrew completely.

Trinity sucked in her breath. "Don't," she said. "Please."

He released her wrists, stroked her hair back over the pillow and kissed her. "Patience," he said.

"Is this my…punishment?" she said, unable to meet his burning gaze.

"Would it be punishment, my Trinity?"

"Yes. Damn you, yes!"

He settled back between her thighs and thrust again, deeper and harder until she was crying out without shame or inhibition. She lifted her hips and shuddered violently, gripping his cock an instant longer until the ecstasy took her completely.

Ares's heart drummed as if somehow it would burst

through his chest and enter hers. He remained within her for some time, his head bowed, his hair like a veil over their faces. As she came down from the heights, she realized what was wrong.

He hadn't finished. He hadn't reached his own completion, though his breath came harsh and his body trembled.

And he hadn't bitten her.

Trinity touched his face. He began to jerk away, but then let her graze his cheek with her fingertips.

"What's wrong?" she asked, feeling foolish tears gather in her eyes. "Why didn't... What did I do?"

Ares rolled to the side, his shoulder touching hers, and laid his forearm over his forehead. "Nothing," he said.

"You didn't bite me."

"I didn't choose to."

"Why?"

He pushed himself onto his elbow and stared into her eyes. "Did I make you suffer by not taking your blood?" he asked.

"You didn't finish," she said. "What good was making me want you, if—"

"How did I *make* you, Trinity?"

"I don't..."

He turned his back on her, and suddenly she understood.

"You can't finish if you don't take blood," she said, turning on her side. "Then why would you stop?"

Shaking off her hand, he stood and began to dress. Trinity sat up, drew the sheets tight around her body and huddled against the pillows. He had rejected her, endangering her mission, and had also made her doubt herself in the process.

"Ares," she said as he fastened his shirt, his gaze fixed on the wall. "What does this mean? Are you going to send me away after all?"

His fingers stilled in their work. "No," he said. "You will remain in the harem."

"And you'll keep calling on Cassandra."

"I never intended to do anything else."

"What do I need to do to please you?" she asked, struggling to contain all the emotions roiling inside her.

He finally turned to face her, his eyes empty of expression. "You will come with me to interrogate the instigators of the trouble in my Household. Go and put on something more appropriate."

"Ares—" She swallowed. "My lord…"

"Leave me."

Trinity climbed off the bed, feeling even more exposed than she had when she'd been stripped and groomed for the Claiming. Ares didn't seem to notice when she left the room.

She went straight to the harem, finding a fresh set of the usual tunic, pants and boots hanging in the closet.

Somehow, she thought, she'd failed. But this was only a temporary setback, and all that concerned her now was getting what she needed, regardless of how much she had to humble herself. *Before* Palemon had a chance to kill Ares.

Nothing else mattered.

Nothing at all.

Ares finished dressing and went to the door to the Great Room, gazing in the direction Trinity had gone.

His body ached, his breath came short and he could feel the undeniable stirrings of blood deprivation in his muscles and heart. He hadn't taken blood from Cassandra since the morning of the Claiming, more than thirty hours ago. And though he'd gone several days without nourishment in the past, to test both his stamina and his discipline, the consequences seemed worse this time.

He would need to call Cassandra again, and soon, though the mere thought filled him with revulsion.

There was only one human whose blood he wanted, and he had been afraid to take it. Afraid because he knew what would happen if he did.

He returned to his desk chair and sat, breathing deeply to calm his thoughts. If she knew anything about Opir culture, Trinity must also know about vassals and their part in Opir society. They were the lowest rank of Opiri, former serfs who relied on blood but maintained a largely human appearance, utterly bound to their Sires unless they were converted into Freebloods.

Trinity had never asked Ares about his lack of them, but surely she knew that changing serf to vassal was entirely a matter of choice for any lord. All he need do was alter the fluids he injected into a human's bloodstream with his bite, and that human would be bound to him forever.

A matter of choice. Ares laughed roughly. Not for him, not where Trinity was concerned. He had seen her surrender completely, yet he hadn't dared to do the same, though it had left him in torment.

He wouldn't be able to control himself when he lay with her again. He would make her his vassal, rob her of the last choice she had, no matter how small it was. Her pride, her dignity, everything he admired in her would be erased.

Remembering that he and Trinity still had work to do, he went to the harem. She was waiting quietly, wearing the blue tunic and pants of a common serf. It disguised much of her lovely figure but did nothing to dampen Ares's desire for her.

"It is time to question the men you injured," he said. "I want you to listen carefully and give me your observations afterward."

Her body stiffened ever so slightly, but she nodded and followed him downstairs to the serf's quarters. The humans he passed bowed and averted their gazes. He could feel their unease.

Their fear.

He went on to the infirmary, aware every moment of Trinity walking behind him. Jonathan, Diego, Elizabeth and several other serfs had already gathered in a nervous cluster in the center of the room. Their eyes darted from Ares to Trinity and back again.

Levi was standing over the bed, where Dwayne lay with his knee tightly bound and his face gray with pain. He saw Ares and shrank as deeply as he could into the mattress. When he noticed Trinity, he reacted as if he would leap out of the bed, injured knee or no.

Jonathan stepped forward. "These are the serfs who were attacked, my lord," he said, gesturing to a young man and woman who stood apart from the other humans. "Erin and Vijay."

The young woman met Ares's gaze with a stubborn expression that nearly matched Trinity's. The male's complexion was almost as gray as the skin of the man on the bed.

"Explain what occurred," Ares said.

The woman, Erin, kept her mouth firmly closed. In spite of her seeming defiance, Ares could smell her deep unease. He took Trinity aside.

"You will ask the questions," he said. "I want honest answers, not those compelled by fear of me."

Trinity nodded, her expression troubled, and returned to the witnesses. Ares kept his distance.

"I would be better if you told me the truth," Trinity said softly to Erin. "Lord Ares told me you won't be punished if you do."

Startled by her presumption, Ares stared at Trinity. She didn't look at him, though she must know that she had taken a grave responsibility on herself and risked his anger in doing so.

Speaking very slowly, Erin gave a surprisingly clear, precise account of the incident.

"Why did they attack you?" Trinity asked.

Her partner, Vijay, seemed close to collapse. "We don't know," he said.

"I think you do."

With a frightened glance at Ares, Vijay evidently thought better of his attempt to dissemble. "We were…we were being blackmailed," he said, "because we sold spare food to some serfs the last time we were given a pass to leave the Household." He stared at Trinity as if she could somehow save him from a terrible fate. "We only did it once, but those men wanted us to keep doing it and make us give them whatever we got for the food."

"What did you receive in return?" Trinity asked.

"Alcohol," Erin said. "Some serfs make it in secret, though we don't know who." She twisted her hands together. "We would never do it again, even if those men kept attacking us."

A strained silence fell. Ares nodded to Trinity again, suppressing his irritation.

"Where is this contraband now?" Trinity asked, her voice a little thin.

"It's gone," Erin said, lowering her head. "We drank it. It was a stupid thing to do.…"

"Yes," Trinity said, glancing at Ares to gauge his reaction. He indicated that she should continue.

She spoke to the other witnesses, who gave similar accounts of the event. In each case, they seemed too frightened to do more than speak as briefly as possible.

Without waiting for Trinity to rejoin him, Ares turned to the man on the bed.

"Are these accounts accurate?" he asked.

The man babbled incoherently about being forced to intimidate the young couple by his companions, and claimed not to understand the reason behind the assault. Even Trinity, who took Ares's place in questioning the serf, couldn't compel him to say more. By the end of the interview Ares was seething with anger.

"Hold him here," he told Jonathan, "and when he is well enough, confine him to the holding cell and do not release him until he is prepared to be more forthcoming. We will question Novak." He swept the other serfs with a severe gaze. "Return to your work. There will be no more of this." He turned back to the young couple. "If you repeat your infractions, you will be punished. Now, go."

They left as quickly as decorum would allow. Ares and Trinity went with Jonathan to the holding cell. Until now, there had never been a need for more than a single room.

But when Jonathan unlocked the cell door, they found only a body. Novak's body, sprawled in the corner as if he had indulged in too much of the alcohol Erin and Vijay had illegally procured.

"He is dead," Ares said, smelling the stagnation of blood that suggested the human had been gone for several hours.

Trinity quickly moved past him to crouch beside the body. She laid her fingertips against the serf's neck, as if she could not quite accept Ares's pronouncement.

"He's dead, all right," she said. "But there's no blood. No injuries, except a few bruises. Nothing to suggest…" She threw a quick glance at Ares. "He must have died of natural causes. A heart attack, a stroke—"

"At his age?" Jonathan asked. He glanced at Ares. "When I brought him here, my lord, there was absolutely no sign that he was ill."

"It's possible for younger men to die of heart attacks," Trinity said. "Sometimes they come on suddenly."

But she spoke too quickly, Ares thought. As if she desperately wished such an unlikely possibility to be true.

Yet the only reason she should have a personal interest in the death of a man she had defeated in a fight was because she felt she was to blame. She had been distressed by Leonard's death, and Ares had believed she felt genuine regret.

Or did she simply fear she had finally gone too far and committed an act that would compel Ares to punish her at last?

"Do you believe your fight with this man could have caused some internal damage that would not be immediately apparent?" he asked.

She bit her lip. "No. I didn't hit him hard enough anywhere to—" She broke off. "I don't know."

"Jonathan," Ares said, "bring Levi at once."

Ares and Trinity waited in silence until Levi arrived, carrying a bag and slightly out of breath. He knelt across from Trinity and Ares, his eyes scanning Novak's bloodless face.

"Can you determine the cause of death?" Ares asked.

Levi briefly met his gaze. "No signs of injury?"

"None, except the bruises that might be expected."

The physician studied the body more closely, examining the eyes, the tongue and the visible skin. "I think I'll have to take him back to the infirmary, my lord," he said.

"Of course." Ares rose. Trinity remained by the body, seemingly paralyzed. He pulled her to her feet. "Inform me of your progress," he said to Levi.

"Yes, my lord." Levi closed his bag. "Jonathan, will you find men to carry a stretcher?"

Once Jonathan was gone again, Ares led Trinity out of the room and back to his apartments. She said nothing until they were in the Great Room.

"Sit," he said, leading her to one of the couches. She obeyed, her limbs stiff and her face expressionless.

"What if I did it?" she whispered. "What if I—"

"Speculation is useless until Levi makes his report," Ares said.

"What else could it be?"

He sat beside her and grasped her by the shoulders. "Stop this. I have no use for a serf who wallows in self-pity."

Her gaze snapped to his. "Self-pity? Aren't you capable of understanding what it feels like to—" She laughed with a bitter edge. "Of course not. How could you?"

"You often seem to forget that I am not human."

"Yes," she said, meeting his gaze. "I do. Far too often."

"This is a tendency you must overcome," he said, "along with this useless guilt."

"Useless," she repeated dully. "I don't seem to be of much use to anyone. Including you."

Chapter 11

He pulled away from her, angered again by her assumption that she understood his motives. But when he searched her face, he saw in it something new—a deep sorrow that had nothing to do with her feeling responsible for the two serfs' deaths.

Rising quickly, he paced in front of the couch. "I told you what I wanted of you," he said.

"But you didn't take the one thing you seem to need most."

"I owe you no explanations," he said, his jaw aching as if he had been clenching it for hours.

"I know. But I also know you can die by not taking blood. You haven't been getting it from anyone else, have you?" She swallowed. "If I have something to do with this…refusal to take what you need, please let me make it right."

"Why should you think you have anything to do with my choices?"

"Instinct. Remember, we…humans have it, too."

Suddenly Ares didn't want to hear any more from her. He didn't want to be alone with her, didn't want to be tempted again to take her to bed and use her exactly as he wished.

It occurred to him that he had not seen Cassandra since their last conversation. She might have left the Household for a visit to the serf's gardens or simply to walk—she enjoyed showing herself off to Bloodlords and Bloodmasters who couldn't have her—but ordinarily he would know. He resolved to question Jonathan about it later.

For now, he needed to remind Trinity who and what she was—or was not—to him. "You continue to overestimate your effect on me," he said irritably. "You need a better understanding of life in Erebus. We will go out into the city, and I will have your impressions when we return."

Real interest brightened her lovely eyes. "I would welcome the chance to see more of the Citadel."

He stopped himself from telling her that the prospect of her enjoyment was not his reason for taking her. She was clearly unaware of what it would be like for her once they ventured beyond the walls of this Household.

Ares arranged for Abbie to help Trinity with the appropriate dress. He also summoned Daniel, who assisted him in donning the many layers of clothing demanded of Bloodlords and Bloodmasters when they left their Households—velvets, silks and brocades, many embroidered by his own skilled serfs. The coat came last, stiff with embroidery and embellishments of gold and silver.

Ares reflected with bleak amusement on how a simple excursion away from his own Household would be perceived by his fellow lords. He seldom visited the city proper, and by settled custom no Bloodlord or Bloodmaster would leave his Household without a company of at least two Freebloods, several vassals and senior serfs. He would be disregarding that custom today.

"You have already called for Gordianus and Thales, my lord?" Daniel asked cautiously, naming Ares's two client Freebloods as he finished lacing Ares's boots. "Which of the serfs—"

"Trinity and I will be going alone," Ares said, taking care to keep his voice level and unthreatening.

"Alone?" Daniel rocked back on his heels, clearly startled. "But Palemon…his allies…"

"I think I have a little time before they come after me. And if I hide here, they will be sure to think me weak."

Daniel had no argument for that. "Do you plan for a Procession later?"

The serf had always been perceptive. Ares had once again become an active participant in Opiri life simply by engaging in Challenge, and Daniel knew that Ares could not indefinitely put off the formal display of his wealth and status to his few allies and many rivals. Procession reaffirmed a Bloodlord or Bloodmaster's position at the top, and discouraged Challenge in the same way rutting stags flaunted their racks to ward off open battle.

"Yes," he said to Daniel. "Soon."

With a brief nod, Daniel rose and brought Ares his staff. Ares waved it away. In spite of his necessarily grandiose attire, he wanted to move as unobtrusively as possible.

When he was ready, he waited in the Great Room for Trinity to emerge. She glided through the harem archway like some ancient human queen, wearing a deceptively simple gown in Ares's house colors. Abbie had chosen a modest cut that set off Trinity's beauty without revealing too much, and had given her a pair of silver earrings and matching torc engraved with Ares's name in Opir script.

Trinity was obviously aware of the torc's purpose, and

she bowed deeply to Ares. He suspected irony, but refused to acknowledge it.

"You will follow three paces behind me," he said, "and say nothing unless I bid you to speak."

"Very clear, my lord," she said, gazing at the floor between them.

This time the mockery was obvious. He shrugged it off and strode to the door to the antechamber, aware that Trinity was not far behind him. He traversed the long, pillared hall and took the lift to the base of the tower.

The interior of the Citadel opened wide before him, a circular, domed space more than a mile in diameter and cast in perpetual twilight. In some ways, it resembled a human city, with residential blocks housing the large population of unattached Freebloods and lesser Bloodlords, open squares and plazas with gardens under special lights, warehouses and places of business.

Many of the buildings were painted with symbols significant to Opiri, like the corridors in the underground section. The architectural designs ranged from imitations of ancient Greek temples to Gothic castles straight out of the darkest Victorian fantasies. All were dominated by the nine towers and the cluster of imposing buildings where the Assembly and Council met to lay down laws, answer petitions, supervise formal Challenges and monitor human activities in the Zone and beyond.

And surrounding it all, built at a height with the roofs of the midlevel buildings, stood the elevated Causeway.

Trinity took a sharp breath.

"You may speak," he said, turning toward her.

"It's…not what I thought it would be when I saw it from the window," she said.

"Because you were told by your people that it was a hellish place, filled with fountains of blood and the bodies of drained serfs scattered on every street?"

"I don't know," she said. "It looks much more...human than I expected. You implied that many Opiri didn't share your admiration for our works."

"Most prefer to pretend that they have improved upon your species' creations," Ares said. Taking the moving ramp to ground level, he flagged down a public vehicle. He waited for Trinity to precede him inside, and soon they were skimming over the narrow roadways reserved for Opiri of high rank.

With no particular destination in mind, Ares instructed the driver to stop at the largest public garden. He climbed out of the vehicle and breathed in the scent of flowers, Opiri and air that held traces of the world outside. Public serfs diligently worked to cull and plant and groom under the lights, maintaining beauty where there was no true sunlight to nurture it.

Ares walked among the roses, constantly aware of his surroundings, of the low murmurings of the serfs, the distant, raised voices of a pair of Freebloods quarreling like tomcats, a Bloodlord and Bloodlady speaking of politics. He drifted closer to them, pretending to study some unusual hybrids created by a Bloodmaster particularly known for his horticultural interests.

One was a rich chestnut streaked with tones of red and gold, dubbed "Tigris" by its creator. It had no scent, but Ares paused to examine it more closely. He pricked his thumb on one of the large thorns. He examined the blood, aware of its dark color and the way the wound remained open far longer than usual.

When he returned to the Household, he must take blood. Cassandra was still his only real option, unless he broke his long-standing resolve and called on one of his other serfs.

Of course, public serfs could provide nourishment for Freebloods who had no humans of their own, and he could avail himself of one with no intimate contact involved. But that held no appeal for him, in spite of the sudden cramping in his stomach and racing of his heart.

Trinity came to join him, briefly touching his arm. "What's wrong?" she asked.

Ares stepped away before anyone could notice her lapse. "Merely a small prick," he said, displaying the puncture. "It is nothing."

Trinity stared at his thumb as if she would gladly have taken it into her mouth and licked the blood away. Ares hardened at the thought, though he could not have said why. She was human, not a drinker of blood.

Shaking off his surreal image of their positions reversed, he plucked one of the roses. "It suits you," he said. "Beautiful but dangerously barbed."

"Am I?" she asked, searching his eyes.

"You know you are beautiful. But you also continue to make mistakes when I have warned you of the consequences."

"I'm sorry, my lord." Her voice dropped to a whisper. "You looked dizzy, and I—"

"Be quiet," he said. He tucked the rose into the auburn hair Abbie had done up so skillfully. The flower seemed to glow above Trinity's downcast face.

He tipped her chin up. "Better," he said. "Now, pay attention to everything you see and hear."

Trinity nodded with all due respect. Ignoring his discomfort, Ares listened to the conversation of the two nearby Opiri. They were still speaking of politics, and he was reminded again of his ignorance of such matters. He had never taken his rightful place in the Assembly of Lords when it had first been convened at the founding of the Citadel, refusing to align himself with either major party.

Even when the Independents had risen as a viable force in the Assembly, he had avoided politics as yet one more disturbance of his highly valued peace. But he had begun to recognize that he could no longer maintain his neutrality. Trinity had compelled him to see just how important his active participation might become.

And as a major representative of the Expansionists, Palemon was highly influential in the Assembly. Ares intended to learn exactly what he and his party intended for the future.

"My lord," Trinity said behind him.

Ares turned. The Lady Roxana was striding toward him, her long, bright aqua tunic swirling around the tops of her gray boots, her pale hair so elaborately coifed and laced with jewels that it nearly overshadowed her piquant, almost elfin face. She wore a heavy neckpiece of silver made in the shape of a sea serpent coiling around and around upon itself. Her staff, carried by a Freeblood at her left hand, was headed with a trident, as if she were a goddess of the sea.

It was easy to observe that the serfs and vassals who accompanied her were at their ease. Their expressions were relaxed, and though they walked in a disciplined formation, they were clearly not afraid of occasionally stepping out of line. One tall serf followed very closely behind Roxana, and his dress suggested he was in high favor with his mistress.

"Ares!" the Bloodmistress said, holding her arms outstretched as if she would embrace him. She was the only one of their kind Ares would have permitted to touch him, but she stopped short and greeted him with a charming smile.

"I am truly shocked to see you here," Roxana said, her dark, lovely eyes searching her friend's face.

"One must occasionally keep up appearances, Roxana," Ares said, forgoing the usual formalities of greeting as she had done.

"Appearances," she scoffed. "This is what you call keeping up? When you've hardly shown your face in months and then Challenge Palemon and make yourself a potential target again?"

Ares smiled. "Your concern for me is gratifying, but I should think my victory would give other lords some pause in Challenging me again so quickly."

Roxana pulled a face. "If I didn't know it was you talking, I'd assume you were a new-made vassal. We both know perfectly well that Palemon can arrange for any number of his allies to Challenge you in rapid succession. All they need to do is force you to fight over and over again until they weaken you. Then, when Palemon comes after you…"

"I will deal with it when the time comes."

"The world—our world—is changing. You have to begin building new alliances *now,* Ares."

"I have you, do I not?"

"Of course. But you know I'm not enough." Her voice rose with urgency. "Take your place in the Assembly. Become involved, even if it is to help maintain a balance between Pax and the Expansionists." She leaned toward him, something like a plea in her voice. "More is at stake than you can imagine. There will soon be a dangerous imbalance that may result in worse than a return to war with the humans."

Ares shook his head, still resisting the decision he had nearly come to himself. "You truly hope to overcome the Expansionists?"

"Is it too much to expect that we should strive for something better than what we have in Erebus? We purport to be superior to humans. How can we be, when we consider achieving rank and power the pinnacle of existence?"

She knew him all too well. Her concern for him reminded Ares what it had been like when they'd been more than mere "friends" and allies. That time was long past, but he still respected and admired her immensely.

"I hope the serf you fought for is worth all this trouble," Roxana said, her expression a mingling of resignation and wry amusement. "She must be quite extraordinary for you to offer Challenge just because—" She broke off, and her gaze moved to Trinity. "And here she is, if I am not mistaken. Now that I see her, I am not surprised at your interest."

Ares had no intention of letting her sense his obsession with Trinity. Here, in Roxana's presence and among his own peers, he was keenly aware of his...

Weakness? Vulnerability? How could he have come to such a state without realizing the extent of his need for his serf? How could he have fallen so far?

"May I?" Roxanna asked, beckoning to Trinity.

With a quick glance at Ares, Trinity went to Roxana and bowed stiffly.

"What do you think of your new master, Trinity?" Roxana asked. "Has he given you as much pleasure in bed as he did me?"

Trinity didn't intend to blush. Yet she had learned that, in spite of their complex relationships, Opiri were fully capable of a bluntness that still surprised her.

And she was very much aware of the Bloodmistress's beauty, her confidence—and the fact that she had clearly been Ares's lover sometime in the past.

Swallowing her ridiculous jealousy, Trinity met Roxana's gaze. "He is very satisfactory, my lady," she said, lifting her chin.

The Bloodmistress broke into laughter. "I heard she was spirited, Ares," she said. "But this exceeds my wildest expectations."

Trinity could feel Ares's anger—or something very like

it. Humiliation, perhaps, at being spoken of as if *he* were the serf.

"Oh, don't look so sour, Ares," Lady Roxana chided. "It is very dull when one's serfs are overly respectful. And she must be as 'satisfactory' to you as you are to her, or you would not have brought her instead of Cassandra."

Ares moved up behind Trinity and gripped her shoulder. "Perhaps it was too soon to take her out in public."

"Not at all." Roxana gestured behind her, and the tall, well-dressed serf came to join her. His hair was red and his eyes green, and Trinity could tell that he had a special place in Roxana's Household. He wore a silver torc, also made to resemble twining sea serpents, and towered well above Roxana's modest height. He briefly met Trinity's gaze.

"My new Favorite," Roxana said, reaching up to tousle the serf's hair. "Isn't he pretty? Very few with this coloring, you know. Quite a lot of spirit and also excellent in bed."

If the serf resented being spoken of as an object, he didn't show it.

"Where did you get him?" Ares asked with polite interest.

"From Hannibal. He was ready to kill Garret, and I could not allow such a lovely creature to go to waste."

Ares's fingers tightened on Trinity's shoulder. She almost gasped.

"I think you're hurting her, Ares," Roxana said with a frown.

His grip eased, and he dropped his hand. "Hannibal is one of Palemon's allies."

"Precisely why you should take your place in the Assembly."

Trinity listened intently as Roxana chattered on about this and that, laughing as she spoke of the follies of her fellow Opiri. After perhaps half an hour, she signaled to her serfs and went on her way with a cheerful farewell.

"We should return," Ares said, his gaze detached, as if his mind had moved to some important thought that had nothing to do with meeting Roxana. He signaled to a garden serf, who summoned another car. Trinity noticed that a number of lords were watching them now, drawn by Ares's conversation with the Bloodmistress. She wondered what conclusion the observers might draw from the meeting, and whether it would benefit Ares or hurt him.

As she took her seat in the car, her mind returned to the men she'd fought near the mess, and Erin and Vijay's improbable story about smuggled alcohol. She'd had very little time to consider alternative theories, but one had inevitably come to mind.

What if the blackmail wasn't about smuggled goods, but an even more dangerous secret? What if the three men had discovered something that gave them power over those who would be considered traitors worthy only of painful interrogation and death?

She'd hardly had a chance to think about speaking to the Household serfs about the Underground, and she'd never expected that any members would simply reveal themselves to her until she gained their trust. But what if she'd stumbled right onto the very thing she was searching for?

She was going to have to speak to everyone involved very soon…and very carefully.

Lost in her thoughts, she hardly noticed when the car stopped near the ramp to the lifts. Ares dropped a handful of coins into the driver serf's hand, and the man rushed to hold the door open for him.

"We will go up to the Causeway," Ares said to Trinity. "I think you may find it of interest."

When they were at the lift level, Ares chose an unmarked elevator. It seemed built to carry its passengers to one destination, and when the doors opened again, Trinity saw that they were on the elevated road that ringed the interior of the Citadel.

"Come," he said. "We will continue along the Causeway."

But before Ares had gone more than a few paces, she felt the small hairs rise on the back of her neck. She stopped abruptly.

"Ares," she said. "It's Palemon."

Chapter 12

Ares snapped out of his detachment and grabbed Trinity roughly by the arm, nearly throwing her behind him.

"Having trouble, Ares?" Palemon asked, strolling to meet them. "I'm still prepared to take her off your hands."

Ares went utterly still. He had neither smelled nor heard Palemon's approach, and it appeared that the Bloodmaster had only just arrived on the Causeway himself, approaching from the second bank of lifts.

"Stay back," he warned Trinity over his shoulder.

Palemon was smiling in lazy amusement, his hand relaxed on his staff, which was topped by his emblem of a dagger-pierced heart. He was clearly not on an idle stroll; his retinue numbered at least twenty individuals. Vassals and serfs stood in precise columns behind him, and two Freebloods carried banners with the same heart and dagger. Directly behind Palemon, collared and on leashes like dogs, stood a woman and a boy.

The same boy who had been with Trinity during the

Claiming. His face was heavily bruised, his neck scraped and raw and his hollow eyes were nearly blank with terror.

Without thinking, Trinity moved forward. Ares pushed her back again.

"I see you still enjoy torturing helpless humans," he said, matching Palemon's casual tone. "So new and already so damaged."

"But so amusing," Palemon said, hatred a smoldering crimson haze behind his eyes.

"You'd best moderate your amusements from now on, Palemon," Ares said. "Fewer and fewer serfs are arriving every quarter, and you will not be able to waste the ones you have quite so freely."

The Bloodmaster chuckled. "How pessimistic you are, Ares. As long as there are humans, there will always be plenty of serfs."

"If I am pessimistic," Ares said, "you lean too far in the other direction."

"But you still hold yourself apart from our petty deliberations," Palemon said.

"I am considering taking my place in the Assembly."

Palemon lifted a brow. "Who would you join? Pax?"

"Would that distress you, Palemon?"

"Hardly, as I expect you to be gone before your presence alters the balance."

Gone, as in dead, Trinity thought. Her heart lurched, and Ares showed his teeth.

"You *are* an optimist, Palemon," he said.

"Perhaps if you stay out of politics, I may consider taking everything you have instead of killing you."

"I make no deals with you," Ares said with equal contempt.

Unable to remain silent a second longer, Trinity moved as close to Ares as she dared.

"Ares," she whispered, "there is one deal you *could* make. Save that boy."

Ares didn't look at her. "Why?"

"Because you're too good to leave him with Palemon."

"I am not—" Ares began.

"What is your little serf saying?" Palemon asked. "Does she think to get between the two of us, or is she hoping to protect you as she did before?"

Ares ignored the insult. "I'll buy one of your serfs," he said.

"Indeed? Which one?" Palemon glanced over his shoulder at the boy. "Of course. This rank sentimentality *will* destroy you, Ares."

"Will you sell him?"

Palemon tapped his teeth. "A trade for the girl, perhaps?"

"No," a familiar voice said. It was Daniel, who was suddenly beside Trinity and Ares. He faced Palemon squarely, though Trinity could see he was barely in control of his trembling.

"Take me," he said.

"Daniel!" Ares said sharply.

"He has wanted me back since you bought me from him," Daniel said, not a trace of the proper serf's humility in his voice. "I'll go."

"It seems your serfs do lead you around by the teeth," Palemon said. "But I'm prepared to take him in exchange for the boy. He's sired me promising human infants before, and I'm sure, with the proper persuasion, he'll do so again."

"You'll get none of my property," Ares said. "I offer one thousand for the boy. That is my *only* offer."

Palemon made a show of careful deliberation. "Very well," he said with a deep sigh. "The boy won't last much longer anyway. Weak and fragile, like most humans." He snapped his fingers, and one of his vassals, a painfully thin woman with pale hair, brought the boy forward, leading him by his leash. Palemon shoved the boy so hard that he fell at Ares's feet. Trinity moved at once to help the boy up. He winced in pain as she touched his arm.

"I will expect payment for the serf at my door by tonight," he said. "Send *him*," he said, pointing at Daniel. "I will take the rest of your possessions after the Challenge."

As if Ares had simply ceased to exist, Palemon strode past him, his Freebloods sneering at Ares as they followed, the vassals and serfs carefully avoiding him.

"Ares," Trinity said quietly, "this boy is very ill."

"Can he walk?"

The child only stared at Trinity, tears leaking out of his badly swollen eyes. Ares lifted the boy in his arms. Daniel glanced at Trinity and nodded, as if they had reached some kind of understanding.

His muscles taut with anger, Ares wasted no time leading them back to the Household. He delivered the boy to the infirmary, and then confronted Daniel and Trinity where they waited in the hall.

"I warned you, Trinity," he said. "And you." He stared at Daniel until the serf bowed his head. "You have done much to damage my status tonight. Daniel, go to your quarters and wait."

Daniel backed away, head down, and retreated quickly. Trinity stepped in front of Ares.

"I don't care what you do to me," she said, "but spare Daniel. He did what he did to protect *me*."

"Protect you?" Ares said, his voice growing hoarse as he spoke. "If Palemon didn't want him so badly, Daniel might have provoked him into killing him."

"Forcing you to Challenge him prematurely?"

"Palemon still isn't prepared to Challenge me. Not yet."

"Then the only thing hurt is your pride."

"My pride." He faced her with an expression she hadn't

seen since he had met Palemon in battle: the look of a savage. "You still do not understand, do you?"

"I *do* understand," Trinity said. "But you haven't lost status. You still got the better of him."

Ares turned on his heel, and Trinity followed him to his apartments. She accompanied him into his bedroom, where he nearly tore his fine overtunic in his haste to get it off. He tossed it on the bed as if it were no more than a simple house serf's shirt.

"Get out," he said, striding toward his bedroom.

"Let me stay, my lord. There are so many things I still don't understand…"

"Why should that matter to me?" He removed a half-empty bottle of wine from his sideboard. "You have learned nothing."

"But I want to. Truly."

He splashed wine into a clean glass. Trinity noticed that his hand was trembling and his skin was almost as white as that of an ordinary Opir.

She remembered how sick he had looked in the park. She knew the cause of his weakness, and she didn't understand why he was allowing it to continue.

"My lord," she said softly. "Wine is not enough. You *must* take blood."

She approached him cautiously. His back stiffened, and he returned to his office. She followed.

"I'm not trying to convince you to forgive me," she said, "and I'm not apologizing for what I did. I'm just asking you to stop torturing yourself."

With very controlled movements, he eased himself into the chair behind the desk.

"What did you think of Lady Roxana?" he asked, abruptly changing the subject.

"She is very beautiful."

"Even though she is a traditional Opir?"

"I'd say Garret finds her very attractive."

He lifted a brow. "How would you know that?"

"The way he looked at her, even when she spoke about him as if he weren't there. And I—" she glanced down "—I told you what I think of your appearance."

"As one who seems more 'human.'"

"Do you think that's the only thing that matters?" she hesitated, thinking long and hard about what she was going to say. "I think he loves her."

"Love," he muttered. "The pinnacle of human emotion. Lady Roxana would not return such feelings."

Trinity's throat tightened, and she berated herself for being an idiot.

"Because Opiri can't feel love, least of all for a serf. But I've heard there may have been…exceptions."

"You should never trust rumors, Trinity."

"You and Roxana were together once," she said.

"Yes," he said shortly.

"Does it happen often, male and female Opiri?"

"It is not common."

"Are you able to have children together, as humans do?"

"Surely you know we cannot. Our only offspring are those we Sire."

"But it's different with vampires and humans. Dhampires are the result."

"Because only human females can bear children in a mixed mating."

She pondered that for a moment, thinking of all the Opiri—including her own unknown father—who had taken unwilling human females during the War, up to the final days before the Armistice. Had they been driven by some primal instinct to reproduce in the conventional way?

"You can't take blood from Roxana, can you?" she asked.

Ares seemed to relax, as if such mundane subjects

were a balm to his frayed emotions. "Not of any nutritive value. But that hardly lessens the pleasure of the act itself, whether it is with serf or Opir."

"So who broke it off?"

"It was a mutual decision. Opiri never stay together as humans do."

"But I can see why someone like you would be drawn to her. She seems like a good person. Kind."

"Even though she spoke of you as if you weren't present?"

"That's part of your culture she can't throw off, no matter how enlightened she is." Trinity hesitated. "Were you offended when she asked me if you were—" she broke off again as her body flooded with heat and desire "—if you gave me as much pleasure as you did to her?"

"Why should I be offended?" He leaned forward, holding Trinity's gaze. "You said I was 'satisfactory.'"

She stifled a laugh. "I'm sorry. I didn't know what else to—"

"I think you have found me more than satisfactory."

For a moment she thought he was going to sweep her off to his very big bed and prove it again. She wouldn't object, and perhaps, at last…

She flushed. "Yes," she said. "Much more than satisfactory."

He leaned back again, in better control than she was. "Tell me more of your impressions."

"She talked about finding a better way of life for Opiri," Trinity said, eager to change the subject. "One that doesn't rely on Challenges and the constant struggle for rank and power. I thought that was a brave and wise thing for her to say." She hesitated again. "But maybe I'm being a little too frank."

"It is what I asked of you," he said, pushing his glass aside.

"She said you needed to build up alliances," Trinity went on. "That you had to take your place in the Assembly. She said you could provide some kind of balance between Pax and the Expansionists."

"You are familiar with them?"

"We've always known the Expansionists are the ones we have to fear most."

"And it is Pax you would look to for maintaining the peace."

She recognized that this part of the conversation could become much more than awkward very quickly. "If Aegis could meet with them directly…"

"And if they could? What would they ask?"

"That Pax work with us for our mutual survival."

"And what if your people had the advantage over *us?*"

"My people know as well as yours that they're running out of convicts to send here. There's either going to be another war that will destroy the world for all of us, or a compromise like the one you and your supporters once offered."

"My efforts were useless."

"Maybe. But now, if you could make a difference…" She inhaled deeply. If Ares did as Roxana suggested and joined the Assembly, she might finally gain some access to information that would be of use to Aegis.

If Ares continued to trust her.

"You've already made a difference," she said. "One human life may not mean much to you, but I want to thank you again for saving the boy."

His mouth twisted. "Because you continue to believe I am, like Roxana, a 'good person?'"

That predatory look flared in his eyes again, and she backed off. "What did Palemon mean when he said that Daniel had sired promising human infants for him?" she asked.

"Some Opiri breed their serfs," he said with obvious disgust. "It is illegal, according to our law and the treaty with the Enclave. But in the absence of an actual denunciation, the Council chooses to look the other way."

Trinity's stomach churned with horror. There had, of course, been rumors about such violations from time to time, but no one in Aegis had ever obtained proof that Opiri had so brazenly defied such a major provision of the Treaty.

"It had already begun before the War," Ares said, "even before the time of the Awakening, when the Bloodmasters walked the earth alone. It never entirely stopped, and lately it has been revived due to the decreasing number of serfs sent from the Enclave." His eyes sparked with anger and contempt. "Daniel's parents had no choice in their mating, and he was taken away from his mother when he was six."

And Daniel was about her age, perhaps a few years older. He had to have been conceived before the Citadel was built.

"Serfs are bred to be easily controlled. Evidently Daniel was forced to mate with Palemon's females before I obtained him. Nevertheless, he was not as easily dominated as they expected, and he suffered for it."

Trinity could only imagine what Palemon would have done to a rebellious serf. "How did you get him?" she asked.

"Eight years ago, he found a way to escape. He was found and brought back to Palemon's Household within hours. He was to be publicly executed to serve as a warning to other serfs, but I convinced Palemon to sell him to me."

"If he hates you so much, why would he do that?"

"Because I would have Challenged him." He shrugged with feigned indifference. "I saw some value in Daniel. He has been an excellent servant, even if he sometimes forgets his place."

It was so clear to Trinity now. Daniel's fierce loyalty, his willingness to stand between two angry Opiri and give himself up to Palemon was not only a mark of his courage, but also a testament to Ares's compassion. The "kindness" he denied he possessed.

But Daniel had never been free. Her heart ached for the man who had been so hostile to her.

"Perhaps I should have been more direct in my opposition to this practice," Ares said, his attention turning inward again.

If he'd involved himself more "directly" in other ways, Trinity thought, Erebus might be a very different place.

"You must know that if the Enclave even suspected such a breeding program exists," she said, "we'd cut off your supply of convicts completely. Those on both sides who favor a new war would find their excuse."

"That is a problem to be dealt with at another time," Ares said. "You and Daniel must face the consequence of your interference. I will have to confine both of you."

"In one cell?"

He frowned darkly. "You will both get your turn, two days apiece."

"I understand." She met his gaze. "But if I have to spend two days alone in a cell, would you consider…"

Rising from the chair, Ares circled around her. "Consider what?"

She turned to face him, knowing that she had this chance, this moment, to try again.

"I want you now," she whispered.

It seemed she was to get that chance. Ares closed his eyes and let her unbutton the high collar of his shirt. He didn't move as she opened his shirt. She kissed his chest just below the collarbone, running her tongue between his pectorals and across his nipples.

His breath came harsh, stirring her hair. She grabbed

the plackets of his shirt and kissed him, caressing every part of his chest, peeling his shirt back a little more to run her hands over his broad shoulders.

"Stop," he said hoarsely.

Trinity ignored him and tugged the shirt from the waistband of his pants. She didn't have to touch him to see how thoroughly he was ready to take her again.

But she had to make him lose control, forget whatever it was that had made him stop before. She unfastened his fly, removed his pants and released his cock. She knelt before him and closed her mouth over the silky head. Ares groaned. She took him in as far as she could, sucking and rolling her tongue over his hardness. He thrust his fingers in her hair, and Trinity knew she had him.

He swept her up in his arms and carried her to the bed. In seconds he had relieved her of her gown and was lying beside her, his body naked and glorious. He kissed her with a hunger that was anything but gentle, and she accepted and returned the kiss with equal ferocity. She arched her head back, all but begging him to take everything he wanted.

He ran his strong, elegant hands up and down her body, stroking her thighs and her belly and her breasts. But she could tell from the trembling of his fingers that he was in trouble, and she couldn't allow him to take his time with her as he had before.

"Please," she murmured as his lips grazed her jaw. "Please, don't make me wait any longer."

Chapter 13

This time he didn't stop, didn't hesitate. He rolled her over onto her belly and lifted her hips. She shifted to make it easy for him to enter her and nearly cried out as his cock probed between her thighs.

There was no foreplay. He thrust into her, grasping her hips to hold her still as he began an urgent rhythm as old as the earth itself. She gasped with every thrust, so painfully aroused that she had to fight to keep from coming every time he entered and withdrew. Again and again he moved inside her, harder and faster, and his mouth settled on the side of her neck, his tongue licking, sucking, paving the way for his bite.

She felt his teeth graze her neck, the slightest pressure before he broke the skin, and she shuddered in uncontrollable orgasm. But her body refused to let go, and she could feel it building again as his teeth slid across her skin, the promise of complete fulfillment only an instant away....

The instant never came. Suddenly he was gone again,

striding out of the room, and an icy weight settled over her where his body had been.

Cursing would do her no good at all. She rolled off the bed and went after him. He began to dress so hastily that he tore his shirt.

"Go back," he said without turning around.

"Ares," she said. "Please."

"I can't," he said. "For your sake."

"What are you afraid of?"

"Why are you so eager to be bitten?" He continued to dress. "I will summon Jonathan to escort you to the holding cell. You will be given meals and other necessities for the next two days." Without so much as a single glance in her direction, he strode out of the room.

Trinity collapsed into the nearest chair. How could she keep failing when he so obviously wanted her blood?

For your sake, Ares had said. What did that mean? He still didn't know what she was or recognize the possibility of addiction. Did he believe he couldn't control himself, that he'd become all predator as soon as he tasted her blood?

But it was rare that a Nightsider killed or seriously injured a human just by taking blood, unless that was his or her intention. Whatever it was that plagued him, she had to make him give way to an Opir's basic instinct for survival. Even if she had to take extraordinary measures.

Without bothering to dress, she looked around the bedroom and then in Ares's office for something she could use to cut with. She found the wineglasses in the sideboard, broke one against the desk and selected a shard of broken glass. She sawed off a piece of the bedsheet and then sliced the underside of her arm, careful not to sever any important blood vessels.

She bound the laceration lightly with the strip of sheeting. Given her half-vampire heritage, the wound would heal soon enough, but there was no point in letting the blood drip on everything in her path.

Ares was standing by the window when she entered the Great Room. His nostrils flared, and he turned to stare at her. In an instant he was at her side, grabbing her other wrist, dragging her into the serf's corridor and to the back stairs. A few startled humans watched him and Trinity pass, alarmed and bewildered.

A woman Trinity didn't recognize was tending the infirmary. The boy Ares had rescued lay in one of the beds hooked up to an IV, his head and arms bandaged.

The attendant stared at Ares, quickly dropped her gaze and waited for him to speak.

"Her wrist is cut," Ares said, pushing Trinity toward the woman. "See to it, and keep her here for observation for no less than six hours. Jonathan will come for her."

"Ares!" Trinity said as he swung around and charged back through the door.

But he was no longer there to hear her. She slumped, and the woman guided her to a chair.

"I'm Parvaneh," the woman said. "Let's look at the wound."

"I'm not badly hurt." Trinity unwrapped the cloth and, as expected, the laceration was already closing.

Parvaneh clucked in disapproval. "How did you do this?" she asked.

"An accident. But as I was trying to tell you—"

"Just keep pressure on it until I can treat it properly," the attendant said, hurrying toward one of the cabinets. "You may need stitches."

But Trinity knew that even when the wound was closed, she'd still be stuck in the infirmary. And then she'd be confined to a cell.

Out of Ares's hair—and his bed. And she still didn't know *why*.

She glanced at the boy in the cot next to hers. He was fast asleep.

"How is he doing?" she asked Parvaneh as the woman returned with a tray of medical instruments and bandages.

"He has been badly beaten and abused, but he'll pull through."

"What about Dwayne?"

"Levi took him to another Bloodmaster's physician for surgery. It must have cost Ares a pretty penny."

In spite of what Dwayne had done, Trinity thought. And she still had to question the man. Now there would be yet another delay.

"I never intended to do that to him," Trinity said.

"He deserved what he got. And so did the others."

"Did you know them?"

"Only that they were always bad news. Leonard and Novak were field serfs. I don't know why Ares brought them in."

"Where are they now?" Trinity asked.

"Leonard's body has been disposed of. Novak's is in the back. Levi's conducting an autopsy and tests as best he can without that kind of real training."

She set to work on Trinity's arm. When she was finished, she leaned back and met Trinity's gaze. "Now, why don't you tell me what you did to Ares?"

"What do you mean?" Trinity asked.

"He's been half crazy since you came here. Everyone has seen it. And then they way he looked when he brought you here—"

Levi suddenly emerged from the back room, his face pale. He pulled Parvaneh into the doorway and spoke softly to her, unaware that Trinity, with her keen dhampir ears, could hear him.

"Poison," Levi said. "Novak was killed deliberately, with drugs stolen from the infirmary." He glanced furtively toward Trinity. "Ares may kill *me* when he finds out."

"How did someone get to the drugs?" Parvaneh asked, clearly as frightened as he was.

"I don't know. I always keep those cabinets locked."

"It must have been a time when there was no one here," she said. "But the big question is…who did it? And why? Nothing like this has ever happened in this Household."

"It was bad enough when the other two—" Levi broke off and stared at Trinity. "All this happened since *she* arrived."

"How could she have anything to do with this? She's been with Ares nearly the whole time."

Trinity closed her eyes, pretending to be unaware of their private conference. Poison. Deliberate murder.

The first thought that came into her mind was that it *wasn't* a coincidence. In some way, Levi was right. This *had* begun when she'd arrived. The men she'd injured had been covering their tracks with the story about blackmail over stolen food. Vijay and Erin had confirmed the account, even though they risked bringing punishment on themselves.

Her mind reeling with all the possible motives for murder, Trinity sat up abruptly. Parvaneh looked toward her, her expression anxious.

Levi frowned at Trinity. "We'll discuss this later," he said, and left the infirmary.

"Is he afraid *I* poisoned Novak?" Trinity asked.

"You overheard us?" Parvaneh asked in alarm as she approached the cot.

"I heard enough," Trinity said. "I didn't kill Novak. But whatever happened with those men and the couple they were attacking must be connected to this murder."

Parvaneh sat down heavily in the chair beside the bed. "What are you saying?"

"Someone in this Household is a cold-blooded killer, and we have to find out who it is. And why he did it."

"I…can't believe this," Parvaneh said, shaking her head in denial.

"What if the killer was afraid that Novak might reveal something that could get him or her into trouble?"

"I have no idea what that could be. Leonard died of natural causes. Vijay and Erin already admitted what they'd done. I never heard of any other trouble like this, even if those three did have a tendency to throw their weight around." She shivered. "If this is even a possibility, we have to think of how to tell Ares."

"We can't."

Parvaneh stared at her. "Are you crazy? Do you have any idea the kind of uproar this will create in the Household?"

Trinity held the attendant's stare, trying to make her understand. "Yes, Ares was angry when he found out what I'd done to those men. He forgave me because he knew *why* I'd done it. But can you imagine how he's likely to react now? Even a good master has his limits."

"You want us to lie to him?"

"I want you to keep this under wraps until I can look into this myself."

"You're still an outsider here," Parvaneh said. "You don't know anyone, or who to ask. People know you can be dangerous."

"Then maybe they'll listen to me when I tell them what's going to happen unless we find the culprit."

"Why do you care what Ares does to us, as long as he trusts *you?*"

Trinity sighed. "I care what happens to everyone here, and I don't want to let a murderer escape."

"But when Ares learns we've been lying…"

"He never has to know. It's only the three of us right

now, and it can stay that way. I can take the blame for injuring Novak more badly than we suspected."

Parvaneh shuddered. "How can *we* trust you?"

"It's your choice. Risk dealing with Ares now, or let me see what I can do to mitigate the situation and keep it from getting worse." She slid off the bed. "I'm going to start right now."

"That's impossible," Parvaneh said. "He told us to keep you here."

"When Jonathan shows up, tell him I sneaked out while you were both examining Novak's body. I'll take the blame for that, too, since I'm already going to be punished. By the time Jonathan finds me, I hope I'll have learned something useful."

She could see that Parvaneh's resolve was weakening. The attendant removed Trinity's bandages carefully and raised a finely shaped brow.

"You heal quickly," she said. "Before you go, we should take a quick blood test to check for infection."

"There's no time," Trinity said, knowing what Parvaneh was likely to find. Disguising the smell and taste of her blood was one thing, but letting it be tested was quite another.

She started for the door. "Thanks again for patching me up." Without waiting for the other woman to answer, Trinity moved quickly and silently through the serf's corridors. Though the people she met were still wary of her, none showed signs of having heard the news of Novak's death.

Before she could confirm that what she'd guessed was correct—and she had to admit that it was only conjecture at this point—she had to proceed with caution. Because *if* those men had known about the Underground within Ares's Household, and if Leonard had been killed because he and the others were blackmailing its members, the Underground could be panicked enough to make dangerous mistakes that could expose them to everyone.

She had no idea how much Ares knew about the Underground in general, given his solitary life and disinterest in politics. He'd never mentioned it, even in passing. But she couldn't take the chance that he might begin to suspect.

Erin and Vijay got to her before she had a chance to find them. Vijay grabbed her arm and pulled her into a storage room near the mess hall. Erin was waiting inside.

"We know you're from Aegis," Erin said without preamble. "We know you're looking for the Underground."

Trinity faced them calmly. "How do you know these things?"

"Because we've been waiting for you." Erin pulled a face. "I mean, we all got word that someone would be coming to collect intelligence on the Council's plans."

Trinity didn't ask how they'd "gotten the word." The important thing was that they *had,* just as the Enclave had learned of the Underground via the messages of some unknown field serf.

"It was pretty obvious after you saved us from those men that you couldn't be an ordinary serf," Vijay said. "We just didn't know you'd end up in this Household."

"*We* didn't, either," Trinity said. "We had to trust in luck and in my ability to convince the right kind of master to claim me. We thought a less rigid Household might be more likely to shelter covert members of the Underground."

"Yes," Vijay said, "And you were very lucky to end up with Ares."

"I'm aware of that," Trinity said, shifting uncomfortably. Erin's keen eyes noticed her slight movement.

"Rumor says he hasn't taken your blood," she said.

Thank God, Trinity thought, that that was the only kind of rumor circulating in the Household. Erin and Vijay didn't know she was a dhampir, but a lot of people could be talking about how she'd overcome three strong men with such relative ease.

"It's only a matter of time," she said with more confidence than she felt. "He already treats me very well, and once he *has* taken my blood, I should be able to obtain more information we might find useful. Right now I need to know how those men realized you were in the Underground, and when they started blackmailing you."

Erin and her partner exchanged knowing looks. "You realized all along that we were lying about the smuggling?" she asked.

"I only had a gut feeling. Until now."

Vijay cast a nervous glance at the closed door. "After you interfered to protect us, we thought those men would talk. But Novak disappeared, and then Leonard died. Dwayne must have thought he'd be tied in with the Underground if he said anything."

"How did they find out about you in the first place?"

"We don't know. But they were becoming a real problem for us."

"And now two of them are dead," Trinity said.

"Two?" Erin asked, clearly startled.

"Novak was poisoned."

"Poisoned," Vijay echoed. "You don't think *we* did it?"

"It would be stupid for us to try something like that," Erin snapped.

"Even if it wasn't just stupid," Vijay said, "we don't kill people. We help badly treated serfs escape when we can and try to get food to the public serfs, who are practically starved since they belong to the Citadel and don't provide any status." He swallowed. "Do you think Ares suspects—"

"As far as I can tell," Trinity said, "Ares doesn't know much, if anything, about the Underground, let alone that there might be members in his Household. How many of you are there?"

"Five," Erin said. "Three besides me and Vijay."

"Then unless someone else has another motive for wanting Novak dead—and maybe Leonard as well, if he didn't die of his injuries—there's a very real possibility that one of you *did* murder him. I need to make contact with whoever runs the Underground in Erebus and pick up any intelligence I can. I also expect to get more information from Ares, even if he doesn't have any idea of what I'm looking for."

"And what intelligence do you hope to get from him?" Erin asked. "Even if you've become his new Favorite—"

"I'm not his Favorite. At least not that he's told *me*. I know he hasn't called for Cassandra since soon after I arrived, but that's not the problem we're facing right now. We have to find this killer and make sure he or she doesn't strike again."

"Even if we find the murderer," Erin said, "getting rid of him or her won't be easy. Especially if the killer really is a member of the Underground."

"Whoever did this is a potential danger to all of you and to my mission," Trinity said. "I need the names of the other members of the Underground in this Household."

"Let us talk to them first." Erin said.

Trinity released a breath. "All right. But don't let anyone know you heard that Novak was murdered. And I'll need you to put me in touch with the Underground leaders in Erebus as soon as possible."

Erin opened her mouth as if to protest, and quickly shut it again. "We'll try to arrange for you to speak with someone who's likely to know more than we do."

"Good. You'll have a couple of days to arrange it. Ares is sending me to the holding cell as punishment for defying him, but I expect him to call me back when I've served

Send For
2 FREE BOOKS
Today!

I accept your offer!

Please send me two
free Paranormal Romance
novels and two mystery
gifts (gifts worth about $10).
I understand that these books
are completely free—even the
shipping and handling will be
paid—and I am under no obligation
to purchase anything, ever, as explained
on the back of this card.

237/337 HDL F455

Please Print

FIRST NAME

LAST NAME

ADDRESS

APT.#   CITY

STATE/PROV.   ZIP/POSTAL CODE

Visit us online at
www.ReaderService.com

HARLEQUIN® READER SERVICE—Here's how it works:

Accepting your 2 free books and 2 free gifts (gifts valued at approximately $10.00) places you under no obligation to buy anything. You may keep the books and gifts and return the shipping statement marked "cancel." If you do not cancel, about a month later we'll send you 4 additional books and bill you just $5.69 each in the U.S. or $5.99 each in Canada. That is a savings of at least 17% off the cover price. It's quite a bargain! Shipping and handling is just 50¢ per book in the U.S. and 75¢ per book in Canada.* You may cancel at any time, but if you choose to continue, every month we'll send you 4 more books, which you may either purchase at the discount price or return to us and cancel your subscription.

*Terms and prices subject to change without notice. Prices do not include applicable taxes. Sales tax applicable in N.Y. Canadian residents will be charged applicable taxes. Offer not valid in Quebec. Credit or debit balances in a customer's account(s) may be offset by any other outstanding balance owed by or to the customer. Please allow 4 to 6 weeks for delivery. Offer available while quantities last. All orders subject to credit approval. Books received may not be as shown.

▼ If offer card is missing write to: The Harlequin Reader Service, P.O. Box 1867, Buffalo, NY 14240-1867 or visit www.ReaderService.com ▼

NO POSTAGE
NECESSARY
IF MAILED
IN THE
UNITED STATES

BUSINESS REPLY MAIL
FIRST-CLASS MAIL   PERMIT NO. 717   BUFFALO, NY

POSTAGE WILL BE PAID BY ADDRESSEE

HARLEQUIN READER SERVICE
PO BOX 1867
BUFFALO NY 14240-9952

my…sentence." She glanced toward the door. "I have to go. Carry out your end of this, and I'll take care of mine. We have to do everything possible to keep whoever did this from exposing all of us."

Trinity was on her way back to the infirmary, grateful that she could now spare Levi and Parvaneh any blame for her "escape," when she was accosted again. Cassandra, dressed in simple serf's clothing, stood just outside the door to the infirmary. She smiled as Trinity came to a sudden stop.

"And how is Ares's little plaything today?" she asked. "I hear he finally took you to bed, but didn't finish it. Why is that, do you suppose?"

Trinity started to walk past her. "I'm not in the mood for sparring, Cassandra. I never meant to take your place, but it's not as if I had any—"

"Choice?" Cassandra blocked Trinity's path, tossing her golden hair around her shoulders. "It seems that Ares has regretted his choice about *you*."

Trinity shrugged. "I guess we'll find out soon enough."

"After you embarrassed him in front of Palemon?"

"How did you hear about that?"

"Didn't you know that serfs have their own ways of communicating between Households? Plenty of Palemon's serfs witnessed what happened." She clucked in disapproval. "You really haven't learned anything about Opiri, have you?"

"I'm learning more all the time," Trinity said, holding Cassandra's hostile gaze.

"Maybe you just need to learn a few tricks from an old hand," Cassandra said. "I can tell you some of the secrets I used to please Ares, particular things he likes. Maybe that will help you win back his favor."

"Why would you *want* me to take your place?"

"Because I know if Ares lets me go, he'll give me the

choice of any Household and Master I choose. And I'm sure I can find a better one."

"I'm glad for you. Now, if you'll excuse me—"

"You're going to make a mistake," Cassandra said as Trinity moved around her. "It's only a matter of time."

Chapter 14

More angry than she had any reason to be, Trinity struggled to regain control of her emotions. Cassandra was just a little too smug for her own good. What was she after? And how could Trinity use Cassandra's "ways of communicating" with serfs of other Households?

She had no time to explore the possibilities. Four hours after she returned to the infirmary, Jonathan came to escort her to the holding cell. He locked her in with a cot, a small table with a chair and several books, promising to bring her food and let her out for breaks at regular intervals.

"A light punishment," he remarked from the other side of the door, "in view of your stupidity on the Causeway."

"Did you get that information from the inter-Household rumor mill, too?" Trinity asked, watching his face carefully. "Or did Daniel confide in you?"

Jonathan hurried away without answering. Trinity sighed, sat down at the table and tried to distract herself with one of the books, a volume on Greek philosophy by a mid-twentieth-century author.

It was dry reading, but she stuck with it, and soon enough she received her meal. A few hours later Daniel paid her a visit.

Everything Ares had told her about Daniel's origins flashed through Trinity's mind, and she felt a fresh wave of pity. But there was nothing pitiful about Ares's valet. As deeply respectful as he was of his master, he was not without his pride. He'd proved his courage and loyalty. And he'd lived through a hell found only in this Citadel, the kind most people outside could never understand.

"How is Ares?" she asked as he entered the cell.

"Getting weaker," Daniel said. "He's trying to hide it, but he's losing more and more strength every hour, and if he doesn't do something about it soon…"

"I tried more than once to get him to take my blood," Trinity said, rising to meet him. "But he keeps rejecting me."

"Do you have any idea why?" Daniel asked, leaning against the cold cement wall. "Have you discouraged him without realizing it?"

"After all his kindness, I'd never push him away, even if I could."

Daniel watched her with a brooding expression. "I would have understood if he'd refused because of the way we defied him. But—"

"The way *I* defied him," she interrupted. "You were trying to save me."

"Only because I knew what would happen if Palemon pushed too hard. Ares wasn't ready."

"Then I'm grateful to you for distracting both of them."

"Your gratitude doesn't interest me. Getting him to take nourishment does." He hesitated, clearly considering how best to continue. "He's not like other Opiri, and there are…

reasons he doesn't like being reminded how different he is. He doesn't want to believe he needs anything from you. Or any serf."

"But that still doesn't explain why he wouldn't call Cassandra or someone else," she said.

"That I don't understand," Daniel admitted, shaking his head. "He doesn't have any emotional attachment to her."

Trinity shivered. "But you think he does to me?"

"I've never seen him like this before. You're the only thing that's different."

"Then believe that I don't want to see him suffer any more than you do," she said. "I'll keep trying to get him to take my blood, or someone else's."

"I believe you," he said slowly. "But whatever you do, don't make him feel weak."

"No matter what he may feel about me, I don't have that power."

"Don't you?" Daniel's voice turned cold. "I'm not supposed to be out of my quarters, but I risked coming here to make sure we were in agreement about Ares."

"We are. And I want to thank you for what you did out there. You're a good man, Daniel."

"If I am, it's because Ares gave me the chance."

Trinity offered her hand, but Daniel ignored it and left the cell.

That man, Trinity thought, was probably the single most important ally she could have in Ares's Household. But she couldn't believe Daniel was one of the Underground. His loyalty to his master was too great for that. And he didn't seem to know that Novak had been murdered.

He was still not above suspicion. But she couldn't think of a reason he'd poison Novak.

Frustrated by her inability to pursue the matter, she returned to her book. There was nothing more she could do until she got out of the cell and received the information she needed from Vijay and Erin.

And found a way to make Ares take her blood.

She had no sense of time while she served out her sentence. After what seemed far longer than two days, Jonathan came to release her. He took her to her room in the harem, where he left her with the warning that she should be grateful Ares had taken her back. He told her the master was out, and that she should prepare to humble herself when he returned.

Trinity sat on the edge of the bed after Jonathan left, considering what more she could do to push Ares over the limits of his control. She was certain that Ares's inexplicable will to resist was beginning to break down.

But she had to come up with an argument he could accept. Another way of making him give in without making him feel weak.

Moving very quietly, she crossed the Great Room and entered Ares's private suite. Two doors led off the bedroom: one, she knew, led to Cassandra's chambers, and the other opened onto a grandiose bathhouse, adorned with marble tile and pillars and life-size sculptures of ancient warriors standing in niches set into the walls.

Leaving the door cracked slightly open, Trinity pulled off her clothes and left them in a heap beside the bathing pool, as if she had entered on a whim and intended to leave soon. She slipped naked into the water. It was warm but not hot; it slid over her skin like a caress, and she sank to let her back rest on the sloping side, just her head above the surface.

She didn't have to wait long for Ares's return. Less than fifteen minutes after she'd entered the pool, she heard the sound of voices from the Great Room. One of them was Ares's. And the other...

Lady Roxana's.

"I'm only concerned for you," the Opir woman was saying as their footsteps crossed the Great Room. "Whatever the reason you are going without blood, it isn't good enough."

"Must we cover this subject again, Roxana?"

"After a decade together, I would have thought you'd accept that I will never stop worrying about you."

"And I must remind you that your worry is a burden you need not carry," Ares said, his voice brusque with irritation.

"You and your discipline," she said, a laugh in her words. "Forever denying yourself what you need just to test your ability to endure privation."

"There was a time when such privation was not a choice," he said.

"Yet that was so long ago."

"Such circumstances may come again. Fewer serfs come from the Enclave every year."

"That only worries monsters such as Palemon, who never have enough," she said.

"It should worry all of us. Would you like wine, since you insist on staying?"

"Don't try to distract me, my friend. I won't leave this Household until I'm sure you've taken at least enough blood to feed a bat." She chuckled at her own joke. "Isn't your pretty new serf around here somewhere?

"She's being punished."

"Oh? For what?"

"For rank stupidity when we met Palemon on the Causeway, after we left you."

"You met Palemon?" Roxana said with real concern in her voice. "What did Trinity do?"

Ares told her. "Would you take her," he asked, "if I decided to let her go?"

Trinity gasped.

"A little too spirited for you?" Roxana asked. "That isn't like you, Ares. Perhaps you felt obliged to punish her, but I know you admire her courage."

"She has become too much trouble."

"You went to a great deal of trouble to get her. If you can't tolerate such minor challenges from humans, what will you do when you finally face Palemon?" She sighed. "Give it up, Ares. You can't pretend with me. I think you must feel about your new serf as I feel about my Garret, and that bothers you excessively."

"Are you alluding to something other than physical needs?"

"We Opiri like to believe we aren't subject to the weakness of human emotions."

"We are not human."

"There are theories that the earliest of our kind *were* human, even before the first *Homo sapiens* were converted. Mutations of some kind."

"No Opir accepts such theories." He exhaled sharply. "Go back to your Favorite and tell *him* of your feelings."

After a long silence, Roxana spoke again. "I also asked to speak with you for another reason. I will be attending a party given by Phoibos in ten nights. Have you received an invitation?"

"From Phoibos?" Ares said, his voice rising in surprise. "I have had no dealings with him in years, and even then we were never allies."

"He really isn't such a bad sort, in spite of his odd style of living. And he *is* a member of the Council. Attending the party would be an excellent way to reintroduce yourself to society in a less dangerous environment." She paused. "Bring Trinity. The other lords and ladies will wish to view the female that inspired the reclusive Ares to Challenge a dangerous Bloodmaster."

"I will not. She isn't prepared—"

"She'll never be able to function safely in our world if you don't take her out in it. Of course, there is the matter of sharing, and I know you wouldn't force any of your serfs to attend any more than would I. But some should be willing, for additional privileges." Another pause. "Will you come?"

"I doubt it."

"Well, if you change your mind—" She broke off. "Why, you deceiver. You have had her here all along."

Ares strode a little unevenly into the bathhouse, followed by Roxana. Both stopped dead when they saw Trinity. The Bloodmistress lifted her pale brows in amusement.

Ares's eyes were cold, though he couldn't hide the hunger in them. Trinity forced herself to look down.

"I came only when I was released from my punishment, my lady," she said.

"And you knew your lord would find you here." Roxana sauntered over to the side of the pool. "Get rid of her, indeed. She feigns humility very poorly, but for that you should be grateful, Ares. You have been alone far too long."

"Get out, Trinity," Ares growled, though it could not be more evident that his body's desires were very much at odds with his mind. Trinity remained where she was.

"I think she plans to defy you, Ares," Roxana said with a touch of humor. She smiled at Trinity. "But somehow I don't think you've had anything to do with his refusal to take your blood."

"I have not, my lady," Trinity said quietly. "I have offered it freely."

"Of course you have."

"Roxana," Ares warned.

"Ah." Roxana turned back to Ares. "You *do* have feelings for this human, but you cannot accept them. So you turn her away, hoping to dismiss what you cannot acknowledge."

"You go too far, Roxana," Ares said through his teeth.

"Where is my disciplined, unshakable friend now?" she asked. "You're angry, Ares. And I know why. You haven't taken any blood at all because you want only hers, and *that* is a weakness you cannot abide. I advise you to overcome your irrational behavior at once."

Ares was so tense that Trinity was afraid he might shatter, mentally if not physically. "If you were not an ally," he said to Roxana, "I might Challenge you for your insults."

"Insults?" She chuckled. "You'd best get a handle on that pride of yours if you don't want to become like Palemon." She strolled to the doorway. "Don't go without blood too much longer, my friend. You know you will need all your strength."

"Farewell, Roxana," Ares snapped.

"Until the party. And do be sure to bring Trinity."

"I told you—"

"We shall see." She smiled at Trinity once more and left the room. Ares stared after her as if he wished he might call her back simply to put off the inevitable.

"Ares," Trinity said.

His back was rigid, every part of his body clenched in resistance. "You had no right to enter this room without my permission."

"I…needed to see you. To apologize for what I did, for trying to manipulate you. I should have known it would never work."

"Yes. You should have."

"Would you really give me to Roxana?"

"Perhaps I will."

"Then you've found the worst punishment of all," she said.

He turned his head halfway toward her, and she could see the strength and stubbornness in his profile, the rigid set of his jaw. "You will be treated well there."

"But I won't be *here*." She hugged herself. "I never thought you were weak because you treated me with respect. I only wanted to be with you."

At first she thought he had stopped breathing. He stood absolutely still, like one of the statues in its niche.

"Do not think that the Bloodlady Roxana's speculation about my 'feelings' means that I am capable of such emotions," he said.

"I understand." Suddenly there were tears in her eyes, though she knew they meant nothing. Nothing at all.

She scraped them away with a swipe of her arm, leaving a trail of water across her face. "You wanted me to be more than a source of blood and sex to you," she said. "You wanted me to share my opinions and experiences, and I…wrongly began to interpret your treatment of me as one of my kind would. That was stupid. But it's also very human." She paused, lowering her head. "Obviously I've failed in almost every way. But I still don't want you to die because you refuse to take blood. I'll beg, if that's what you want. And when you're finished, I'll go wherever you want to send me."

"You would have no choice in the matter."

"You'll always have the power, my lord, whatever Lady Roxana may imply. I can't take anything from you that you aren't willing to give."

He swung around, his expression so furious that she expected him to reach into the pool, drag her out and force her back to her quarters. But after he'd looked her over again, he had quite a different expression on his face.

Trinity knew she'd finally won.

Chapter 15

Ares tried to look away from her. He tried not to see the beauty of her glistening hair; her breasts lying just above the surface, nipples drawn into stiff peaks; the wavering image of her belly and hips and slightly parted thighs.

Lust was driving his heart with such fury that it shook his entire body. His mouth was dry, his breath short, his sex so taut and hard that he thought it might be visible from halfway across the Citadel if anyone were to see him at this moment.

Opiri could suffer from something akin to fever, but only when they were very near death. Ares wasn't that close, yet his blood burned as if his body would turn to ash in the way of the old human legends.

He hated to admit it, but Roxana was right. It *was* highly irrational to let his concern over losing control with Trinity prevent him from taking her blood.

Trinity belonged to him. If she misinterpreted what she saw as his "kindness," it was none of his concern. If his muscles tensed and his heart raced whenever he was in Trinity's presence, it was only because of his physical need.

If he had been more vulnerable to emotion since he'd claimed Trinity, he had no one to blame but himself. He *would* master his desire to make Trinity his vassal. And when he had sated himself with her, he would never face these fears again.

He would take Trinity's blood. Take it, and finally be free of her.

She watched him from beneath her thick lashes as he stripped out of his clothes and dropped them next to hers. He eased himself into the water beside her, feeling the heat of her body swirl around him, vividly remembering the way she'd taken him in her mouth, teasing him with her tongue and grazing him with her teeth. He seized her lips with his and gently pushed her back down onto the sloped surface of the pool.

Trinity bent her head back, slipping easily into the position for which this portion of the pool had been designed. He smelled the scent of her readiness mingling with the water.

Her body made very clear that he didn't have to take his time. He didn't want to. But he wanted to see her at the pinnacle of her pleasure before he bit her, taste the sweetness of completion in her blood.

The pulse in her neck beat rapidly as he kissed her again, more gently this time, and cupped her breast in his hand as he eased himself between her thighs. She gasped a little as his sex touched hers, but he didn't enter her. He bent his head to take her nipple into his mouth. She shuddered and moaned softly. He explored the puckered, slightly rough texture with the tip of his tongue, probing the indentation, covering it with his lips.

Trinity shifted underneath him, drawing her knees up, rubbing herself against him. He held to his resolve and turned his attention to her other breast, kissing and tasting every part of it as he cupped her bottom in his hands. Her breath came in urgent puffs as he let his other hand slide down over her stomach, moving against the water's resistance, and dipped into the soft indentation hidden beneath her curls. She began to buck, arching her back, crying out as she had done the last time he'd taken her.

Again she tried to work herself into a position that would compel him to enter her. Instead, he eased away, lifted her hips above the water and tasted her, running his tongue between the soft folds of flesh, stroking over the nub, circling her entrance without breaching it. She reached down and grabbed at his hair, pulling at it without regard to the discomfort she might cause him.

But he welcomed her grip, the way her fingers opened and closed in time to his caresses, knowing it was a futile effort to take some control again. He wouldn't let her. He pushed his tongue inside her, and she cried out once more.

If he didn't stop, she would finish, and he wanted to be inside her, moving hard and fast, when she did. He let her slide back into position and parted her thighs, pushing her knees to either side of his body so that he would have complete access. He stroked himself against her moist heat, letting her feel it, anticipate what he was about to do.

When he could bear it no longer, he thrust into her. She had been tight before, and he'd known she hadn't had a man inside her for many years. But now she stretched to fit him like a glove, warm wetness enveloping him, pulling him deeper. She wrapped her legs around his hips and gripped his shoulders, gasping each time he withdrew and thrust again.

He put his lips to her neck, just where it joined the shoulder. Her blood throbbed with such force that Ares barely had to break the surface of her skin. The rich, warm blood flowed into his mouth and over his tongue, as unique in its vintage as that of any human he had ever tasted, and yet a thousand times more potent. She released her breath in a long sigh, and then gasped again as he began to move inside her with greater urgency. Her blood heightened his pleasure to a degree he could never have imagined, a drug so intoxicating that he lost his sense of himself, of every part of his body but his mouth and his sex.

When he came, it was as if every nerve in his body was exploding at once. Trinity cried out again, and he felt her come with him, tightening, pulsing, closing around him as if she would keep him inside forever. She trembled, stubbornly holding on to the moment, trying one last time to make her own rules.

It worked. He stayed firm inside her, so much so that he knew he could start all over again.

But whatever her enthusiasm, her body would not be as ready to repeat the exercise so soon. He eased out of her, slowly realizing that he had not done what he had feared.

He had controlled the act of will that would have changed the chemicals in his body, altering hers, as well. He had not made her his vassal. She was still only a serf, belonging to him in body but not by bond of blood.

Sealing her wound, he drew back. She continued to clutch at his shoulders, her eyes closed, her lips parted.

"Is that…" she whispered. "Is that what it's always like?"

Always? Ares laughed under his breath. It had *never* been like that. Not in all his long life.

But he could let her go now, knowing that she had chosen this willingly and he had not taken something vital from her because of his own uncontrolled instinct.

He rolled onto his back, letting his mind drift. Trinity's blood had made him drowsy and content and not inclined to move. Nor did he feel the need to send her away immediately, especially because she, too, would be feeling the lingering effects of his bite and her loss of blood.

After she was recovered, he would decide whether or not to give her to Roxana. Now it would truly be *his* choice. He could go back to Cassandra.

He closed his eyes, aware of Trinity's warm body pressing close to him, her wet hair brushing his face, her cheek coming to rest on his chest. Without thinking, he moved his arm and put it around her shoulder, his palm resting on her hip.

For a while, all he did was savor her intimate presence, knowing it would be the last time he would avail himself of it.

"Maybe now," Trinity said, breaking into his peaceful reverie, "you can tell me why you sent me away before instead of taking my blood."

He was inclined to leave her then, reluctant to delay the inevitable parting with unnecessary conversation. He owed her no explanation, and to confess the truth would be pointless.

But it would be a kind of weakness to conceal his reasons, as if he feared what *she* might think and feel.

"You did nothing wrong," he said, turning his head so that his lips brushed the top of her hair. "I believed that as soon as I tasted your blood, you would become my vassal."

She inhaled sharply, though if it was in fear or surprise he couldn't tell. "It takes an act of will for a Sire to create a vassal," she said.

"Yes."

"And you thought you might not be able to stop?"

"Yes."

"But you...didn't want it to happen."

He shrugged, sending ripples across the water. "It was an irrational impulse. There is in all of us the instinct to make vassals. It is another mark of power and is, as we discussed, the only way we reproduce."

"But when you had the impulse, you couldn't do it?"

"I would not convert any of my serfs against their will."

"What if a serf wanted it? Would you do it?"

"Perhaps," he said.

He half expected her to ask him to make her his vassal right then and there, but she was silent. Clearly it was not her wish.

For reasons beyond his comprehension, anger swept through him. He had not wished to make her his vassal, and she had no wish to be one. It was all perfectly reasonable. Trinity had said she wanted him, craved his lovemaking and his bite. She had hinted at feelings for him. But why should she desire to be bonded to him forever, when she knew he could never return those feelings?

"May I speak to you frankly, my lord?" she asked, shifting to look into his eyes.

Aware that he was risking the possibility of losing his temper with her, he was slow to answer. "You may," he said, "within reason."

"How did the first Opiri come to be?"

Ares well remembered Roxana's mention of the highly unpopular theory that Opiri had somehow descended from the first intelligent humans—a kind of mutation, stronger and faster and keener of senses, perfect predators of mankind.

"Our origins lie in a distant past no human ever recorded," he said, relieved that they had returned to a largely intellectual subject. "Our own ancient writings tell us that we evolved long before humans became capable of reason."

The water rippled again as Trinity shifted position, her breasts brushing his side.

"Did Opiri…mate with humans then, the way they did during the War?" she asked.

"It is likely the males did. Our writings do not record such relationships."

"Of course. They weren't important." Her body tensed. "Have *you* ever fathered children with a female human?"

"No," he said, startled by the question. "I never touched a human female in that way before the War or afterward."

"And during the War?"

"I will not justify myself to you. I never left a child and its mother abandoned to fend for themselves."

"But you *could* father a child on a human woman. What if you…one of you made a serf pregnant here in Erebus?"

"The Opiri who attacked your female soldiers and civilians during the war were almost certainly Freeblood troops," he said. "They do not yet have the full control over their bodies that Bloodmasters and Bloodlords have attained, which is why they cannot reliably convert humans. They could not prevent a pregnancy from occurring."

"But you can?"

He narrowed his eyes. "Are you concerned that you might bear a half Opir child?"

"A dhampir," she murmured. "The best agents the Enclave has ever produced, thanks to your Freeblood soldiers."

"In Erebus, such a child would be claimed by the Council and raised as a serf," he said, regaining his composure.

"Because dhampir blood is a special treat to Opiri, isn't it?"

"How would you know this? Have you lost some of your agents to Erebus?"

"We have no knowledge of dhampires entering the Citadel. But we learned things before the Treaty was signed."

"You captured Opiri and experimented on them," he said coldly.

"How is that worse than what you did to us before the War ended, and are still doing now? Your people would let that dhampir child grow up and then sell her to some Bloodmaster for his pleasure."

"That will not happen," he said. "You will bear no child of my fathering."

Trinity pulled away as if he had struck her, though it was clear that the idea of bearing his child was repulsive to her. "You've taken my blood," she said. "Shall I go now?"

He found it difficult to believe he had thought he could send her away less than an hour ago. Already he was hungry for her blood again. Starving for it.

"I have changed my mind," he said, pushing himself up to the edge of the pool. "You will stay with me, as my Favorite."

She blinked rapidly several times. "You want me instead of Cassandra?"

He reached down to touch her hair, the wet strands spreading over her shoulders like those of a mermaid emerging from the sea. "Yes," he said, "if you have no objection."

"I have no objection," she said softly.

"And you must forget what Roxana said of 'feelings,' and dispense with her foolish notions."

"I understand. What will you do about Cassandra?"

"I will deal with her."

Trinity was silent for a long while. "I was wondering…"

"Again?" he asked, twisting a strand of her hair gently between his fingers.

"Lady Roxana mentioned a party—"

"What did I say about Roxana and her foolish maunderings?"

"I know." Trinity laid her hand on his thigh, provoking a nearly instantaneous erection. "But I've barely been outside this Household since you brought me here."

"You saw the Citadel."

"I saw a garden and some buildings through a car window."

He looked down at her, wondering why he should be surprised that she chafed at her confinement. "The party to which Roxana referred is being given by an Opir known to be eccentric," he said, "and his gatherings are not to my taste. But we will find some other way to get you out of the Household in a manner that is safe for you and doesn't tempt you to cause more trouble."

With a sudden, unexpected burst of motion, Trinity jumped out of the pool and bore him onto his back, straddling him as she kissed him hard on the mouth. He overcame his surprise quickly enough, and in a few seconds he was inside her again. She rode him with her head thrown back and her face rapt with ecstasy. She sprawled across his chest at the last moment, presenting her neck, and he bit her again, coming almost as soon as he tasted her blood.

After it was over, he lifted Trinity in his arms and carried her to his bed.

"Stay with me awhile," she said, grasping his hand. "Even Opiri need rest."

He sat on the bed beside her. "Only vassals truly sleep."

"Please. Just for a little while, until I—" She yawned.

"You must remember," he said, "that giving blood is tiring for humans."

She stretched her arms above her head. "It's a wonderful feeling. I hope you never stop."

"Sleep," he said. "You will need it."

"How long?" she said with a sly smile. "An hour? Two?"

"If I were to take your blood too often, you could become seriously ill."

"I don't think so." She looked into his eyes, her face losing its playfulness. "I think it's going to make me stronger."

Ares shook his head. "Rest now. That is a command."

Closing her eyes, she rolled onto her side. Ares covered her with the silk sheets and waited until her breathing grew steady and gentle with sleep. Then he strode into the Great Room and opened the shutters on the window overlooking the city.

His heart would not be still. He knew it was only because he'd never experienced such physical pleasure as he had when he'd taken Trinity's blood. It had almost been unreal, as if it were part of a dream.

But he had maintained his control. And he would be certain to regulate his taking of Trinity's blood so that he would not become too dependent on it.

Or her.

Before noon the next day, after Ares had gone out on business, Trinity went down to the serf's common room and carefully listened to various conversations, observing every man or woman who entered to play chess, read or engage in other amusements provided to them.

It wasn't easy to concentrate on her job when she was also trying to process her last conversation with Ares.

The part she couldn't get out of her mind was his confession that he had feared he might be driven to make her his vassal. She had taken the proper precautions to prevent Conversion, but they were far from foolproof. The possibility that she could truly become his in every way, blood bound to him until such time as he wished to convert her to a Freeblood, was a real concern.

If Ares maintained his much-valued "discipline," that possibility, and all its inherent dangers, might never arise. Still, she was very much aware that she and Ares had become closer since he had taken her blood. Just as she had intended.

But would he fall prey to addiction? Would it be possible for her to manipulate him into becoming more active in Opiri government, and provide her with the intelligence she sorely needed?

She had no way of knowing. That had always been the difficulty of the whole mission—the fact that so much of it could not be planned in advance. She had to be ready to jump in any direction circumstances required.

And all that was made far more complicated by her realization that she wanted Ares more than ever. Wanted his body, his respect, even his companionship.

She was close, so very close to forgetting her whole purpose for being in Erebus. So close to…

"Trinity," Erin said quietly, sitting down beside her at the otherwise empty table. The rebel looked around them quickly and released her breath. "I've spoken to the person you're supposed to meet. You're not going to see this person's face. You'll hear the voice, but you can honestly say you aren't sure who it is if someone questions you."

Trinity nodded. "When and where am I to meet this person?"

"At 2:30 a.m. in the cold-storage room by the kitchen. Most of the staff are off duty by then."

Which meant, Trinity thought, that she'd have to make sure Ares didn't see her sneak out at an hour when the Household's humans, except for the scanty night shift, were asleep.

"I'll be there unless it's impossible for me to get away," she said. "Have you or the others learned anything about who might have killed Novak?"

"Nothing so far. But we're watching and listening, just like you." She took Trinity's hand, squeezed it hard and let go. "Good luck."

When Trinity returned to Ares's apartments, he had finished whatever business had taken him away from the Household. She hardly had a chance to greet him before he swept her off to bed.

It had been slightly less than twenty-four hours since he'd last taken her blood. Ordinarily, she would have expected him to hold back out of fear of weakening her too much. But he seemed to recognize that she was not reacting as most humans would and gave way to a drive he could not control.

That was the first time Trinity suspected that he might be in the early stages of addiction, though the speed with which it had happened surprised her.

At two-thirty the next morning, after she and Ares had discussed the human perspective on the origins of the Opir language and she'd retired to rest, she left her quarters for the kitchen. She waited in the appointed place until a very young kitchen serf took her by a service corridor to the cold-storage room. Once they reached the door, the young serf vanished.

The time for answers had finally come.

Chapter 16

It was freezing inside the room, and very dark. That presented no problem for Trinity, though of course no one in the Household knew she didn't need light to see. She wove a path among the hanging carcasses and shelves of frozen food toward the back of the room.

Someone was waiting for her, his or her head and body covered with black fabric. The person's scent, which ordinarily Trinity would have been able to identify, was masked by the smell of meat and the icy cold.

"I'm sorry it has to be this way," the figure said. "But I have to stay hidden."

It was definitely a woman's voice, though she'd lowered the pitch to the point where Trinity didn't recognize it.

"I'm glad you agreed to see me," Trinity said, taking a seat on a crate a half-dozen feet away. "You know why I'm here."

"Yes," the woman said. "All of us have been hoping that someone from outside would get in after you began picking up the messages our field serf left outside the Citadel."

"They stopped not long before I was sent here."

"Our agent was killed for straying too far outside the boundaries of the fields. The bloodsuckers never suspected anything, but we couldn't risk more messages."

Trinity knew how painful it was to lose a comrade in a dangerous fight. "I'm sorry," she said.

"We all know what we're getting into when we join the Underground. We risk our lives whenever we communicate. We do it for ourselves and for the Enclave, even though they sent us here." She laughed bitterly. "Even though most of us have done things that would have gotten us little more than a slap on the wrist five years ago."

"I know," Trinity said softly. "Don't think the Enclave isn't grateful for your loyalty under these extraordinary circumstances."

"We don't want gratitude. We want freedom, and we have no chance of that—ever—if the Nightsiders win the next war."

"And you believe that war is coming."

"We've heard bits and pieces of information that indicate it, but we have no details. That's why we needed someone trained by Aegis to help us."

"Understood," Trinity said. "It was my intention to make contact with members of the Underground—presuming they existed within whatever Household I joined—and then find a way to use my assets as a means of gaining additional information from my new master. But as you must know, Ares doesn't have much to do with his peers or the government. Yet."

"We know that Lady Roxana's been urging him to join the Assembly," the woman said. "You may already be having some influence on Ares's decisions, which means you're doing something right."

Ares seems to think so, Trinity thought, distracted by the flood of warmth rushing through her body.

"It's not enough yet," she said. "Fortunately, he's interested in my opinion of the Citadel and Opir society. Of course, I have to be careful about what I tell him. Gaining some measure of his trust is one thing, but I'll need access to what he learns if he becomes more active in the government."

"Yet you feel you're making progress?"

"As much as I can in such a short time, yes. And I have additional…resources I hope to make use of if it becomes necessary."

"What was your plan for escaping the Citadel?"

"We'd hoped the Underground could help arrange it."

The woman sighed. "We'd anticipated that. But we can't promise we'll succeed. If it were easy, we'd have helped many more serfs escape." She was silent for a few moments. "You said you wanted to meet the man who's more or less the leader of the Underground in Erebus. You should be able to learn more from him, and he wants to speak to you, as well. He's set things up so that you can meet him soon, if you do your part."

Trinity leaned forward. "What's my part?"

"You know about the party being held by the Bloodmaster Phoibos?"

"Yes. Roxana invited Ares to attend, but he declined."

"You'll need to convince him to go and take you with him. Our leader will find you there."

"I'll manage it somehow," Trinity said.

"Good. And there is one other thing you should consider. If Ares takes his place in the Assembly, you may actually be able to gain direct access yourself."

"How is that possible?" Trinity asked, her heart beating faster.

"By becoming his vassal. They're often allowed to observe the proceedings from the upper galleries, and occasionally they're permitted to act as secretaries to their Sires."

That was something Aegis hadn't known, Trinity realized. All the thoughts she'd had about the subject earlier that day flooded back into her mind. It could change her mission in a way she had never anticipated.

"Of course, you understand that this is only permitted because vassals are blood bound to their lords," the woman said. "They literally can't betray the Opir who Sired them."

"That's a pretty big complication," Trinity muttered. "I was given an injection to prevent Conversion, but it's experimental, and—"

"*If* you were to become a vassal," the woman said, "it would be virtually impossible for you to escape Erebus, regardless of how much useful intelligence you collected. Even if you got out of the Citadel, you wouldn't get more than half a mile away before you'd feel the pull of the bond."

The woman was right. If Trinity's injections failed, she would be forced to remain here and live on blood for the rest of her life. Forced to stay with Ares.

Would that be so terrible after all?

The treacherous thought stunned her. She'd known all along she'd be betraying him, using him in any way she required in order to complete her mission. The very notion of remaining here under any circumstances, especially as a blood drinker, should have sickened and horrified her. No matter how much she valued Ares's companionship, it should have been utterly unthinkable to any operative of the Enclave, especially a dhampir.

The fact that she felt even the slightest sense of longing made her doubt everything she had ever believed about the world…and herself.

She banished the unconscionable notion from her mind. "I couldn't be sure I could get that information to someone who *could* leave Erebus," she said, her voice unsteady. "I think we'd better forget about that strategy. But I'll do what I can to make sure Ares attends the party and takes me with him."

The woman rose, black fabric rustling around her. "I've told you all I can for now. I'm sorry I couldn't give you more information."

"You've given me more than I expected," Trinity said. "Thank you."

The woman nodded beneath her veil. "If you figure out how to make this work," she said, "we'll do everything we can to help you."

Trinity rose and stood aside to let the woman precede her out of the room. A moment later she followed, waiting until she was certain no one would see her.

She was nearly to the doors of the mess hall when she realized that Ares was very close. She kept walking, concocting a ready excuse to explain her presence in the serf's area at three in the morning.

He rounded the corner as she was headed for the serf's stairs.

"Trinity," he said, striding to meet her as she came to a stop. "Where have you been?"

Swallowing, she stared at the floor. "I'm sorry you had to come looking," she said. "If I'd known…"

His fingertips brushed her cheek, urging her to look up. "I didn't need you. I am merely surprised to find you here."

Likewise, Trinity thought. Her heart was still drumming because of the close call. If he'd shown up a few minutes earlier…

"I was looking for a snack," she mumbled.

"You can call for a meal at any time without leaving your quarters," he said. "There is always one serf on duty in the kitchen."

"Yes," Trinity said, meeting his gaze, "but I decided not to bother him."

"Are you still hungry?"

"No," she said hastily. She studied him more closely, struck by the pallor of his normally golden skin, the haggard look of his face, the shadows under his eyes. He appeared about as unhealthy as any Opir could without being seriously ill…exactly as he'd looked before he'd broken down and taken her blood.

She'd wondered if it was possible for an Opir to become dependent on dhampir blood so quickly. Now she was certain Ares *was* already addicted, even though he couldn't possibly realize it.

At least not yet.

Guilt locked a fist around her heart. He would continue to weaken each time he went without her blood for any length of time, and she hated the sight of him so physically vulnerable. If things went as she expected, he'd be unable to let her leave his side for long, and he would continue to take her blood more than he ordinarily would deem safe for a human.

Eventually he'd figure it out and try to separate himself from her. His pride would demand it, and his fury could be deadly. As much as she regretted—loathed—what the addiction was doing to him, she simply had to delay that moment of reckoning for as long as possible.

"If you were human," she said, trying to take a lighter tone, "I'd say you had insomnia."

He focused on her again. "I had not walked in the serf's area of the Household for years before the incident with you and the extortionists."

"Why now?" she asked, careful not to make her question seem like a challenge.

Running his hand from her neck to her shoulder, he

smiled. "If I came here by day, I might frighten the serfs again. I have no wish to do so."

"You wouldn't frighten them if they saw you more often. If they get used to you, they'll behave in a more natural way, and you might learn a little more about humans."

"A wise observation, and one I should have grasped long ago," he said, stroking her arm. She shivered violently, and his brows lowered in concern. "Are you cold?"

"No. Thank you."

His gaze fell to her neck and lifted again quickly. "Let us walk," he said.

So they did, through the silent corridors, encountering no one except a serf on night duty. The young man pressed himself to the wall and lowered his head. Ares paused to question him about his work, and the serf, clearly startled to be addressed by his master in such a conversational way, responded with a shy glance at Ares's face.

Once the Bloodmaster had dismissed the young man, Trinity touched Ares's arm. "You set him at ease," she said. "You see, I was right. It won't take much to convince them that they have nothing to fear from you, no matter what happened a few days ago."

"Perhaps," he said. He listed to one side, nearly hitting the wall, and Trinity grabbed for him. He shook off her hold, clearly disturbed. She didn't dare suggest they return to his apartments.

"I haven't spent much time around here, either," she said, watching him out of the corner of her eye as they turned toward the common room. "I still don't know what half the serfs do. How many are there?"

"Forty, I believe," he said absently.

"But you don't really need all of them to run your Household," she said.

He glanced aside at her. "No. The serfs primarily run the Household for themselves."

"I imagine that's true of most Households."

"Indeed." He seemed lost in his own thoughts again, but Trinity saw no reason to delay working up to the subject of the party.

Slowly.

"You told me that all your serfs would go to the winner of any Challenge called against you," she said.

His teeth glittered in the dim light along the corridor. "And I believe I told you that would never happen."

"Even if Lady Roxana was right, and Palemon sends his allies to Challenge you one after the other, until you aren't fit to face him?" She searched his eyes. "You need your own allies, and quickly."

"It is not your—"

"Concern. I know. But what if you're wrong? Can you really allow every serf here to suffer under a monster like Palemon?"

Ares was silent, but Trinity could see she was getting to him. She pressed her advantage.

"This party Roxana mentioned," she said, touching his face. "She said you might find some allies there."

He jerked back, his eyes fierce and hot with hunger and fevered rage. "Roxana knows nothing."

Ares turned and began to walk away. Suddenly he stopped, his back rigid.

"You are right," he said. "I cannot disregard the possible fate of my serfs."

Breathing a silent prayer, Trinity went after him. "Then you will find your own allies?" she asked.

"Yes." He sighed and turned to face her. "I will attend this party. But you must understand that it is likely I will also meet some of Palemon's allies. Phoibos has never made his guest list dependent on political affiliation."

"You mean they might actually Challenge you there?"

"It is possible. Only to injury or debilitation, of course.

Almost certainly only to first blood. They would dare no more, since duels to the death are infinitely more complex, and affect the entire Citadel."

"But they still have to meet you one by one, right? How much would these allies do for Palemon? What do they get in return?"

"Protection from stronger Bloodlords. Serfs. Other favors."

"Then when they actually come face to face with you, they may decide what they're getting isn't enough."

He smiled. "Sometimes you think almost like an Opir, Trinity."

At that moment she was once again torn between her duty and her desire to keep Ares safe, something she knew she could never do. He would face those Challenges, either at the party or in a place where his enemies might try something much worse.

"When you beat them," she said, "it'll get more Opiri on your side, won't it?"

"Perhaps." His smile faded. "I will take Roxana's advice. I will attend."

"And I'll go with you."

Chapter 17

Suddenly he had her against the wall, teeth bared. "You will not."

She pressed her hand against his chest. "Please listen to me, Ares," she said, softening her voice. "Lady Roxana was right about something else, too. My life is at stake here as much as yours. You wanted me to observe, to look at Opiri society as an outsider who might be able to remain at least a little objective. As a former soldier, I can watch and evaluate the behavior of Opiri at the party while you're otherwise engaged."

He released an exasperated breath. "Do you have any idea what dangers you will be exposed to?"

"Once everyone's had a good look at me, I'll become invisible like every other serf."

"You, invisible?" he said wryly.

"I'll also be a living reminder of how you won your last Challenge. A psychological advantage."

"Trinity," he said, shaking his head. "This is no game. It will not be a pleasant experience for you."

"It couldn't be worse than the—" She broke off with a grin. "You said 'will.' Does that mean—?"

"I'll permit you to accompany me. But you will do nothing to draw attention to yourself beyond what your beauty and circumstance attract. And you will *not* behave as you did on the Causeway, no matter how strongly provoked. You will remain silent throughout the party."

"Of course," she said in a small, humble voice.

"You take too much on yourself."

"I know what I'd like to take now," she whispered, pushing against him.

It was an extremely reckless thing to do, considering the possibility that someone might walk past them, but Ares clearly felt no concern for the risk. He worked her pants off, shed his own and lifted her against the wall. She wrapped her legs around his waist, gasping when he entered her in one long, smooth thrust. He held her up easily with one arm and locked his arm around her waist to steady her as he settled into a vigorous and lusty rhythm.

When she came, she came hard. His teeth grazed her neck, and he bit her. A moment later he finished with several powerful thrusts and shuddered against her. He rested his forehead on the wall, his cheek touching hers, and slowly eased her to the floor.

Nothing more was said. He swept her up in his arms, carried her back to his apartments, and took her to her room in the harem quarters. He stripped her and laid her down on her bed. Then he tucked the sheets and blankets around her as tenderly as a human parent might his child. Or a man his lover.

Trinity stared at the ceiling for a long while after he had gone, waiting for her heartbeat and breathing to return to their normal pace. She tried to sleep, without success. She ran through her discussion with the Underground representative, remembering what the woman had said about Trinity's becoming a vassal, truly bound to Ares for all time.

Once again she felt herself torn in two by conflicting feelings that should never have existed at all. She could tell herself that she simply admired his treatment of his serfs, his interest in a human's opinions, his willingness to save the boy and protect her and Daniel at all costs. Or simply that he was a superb and generous lover. All the things about him that made him "good," in spite of her former prejudice against his kind and his own denial.

But now there was something more. Something that had unexpectedly found its way into her heart.

Do not think that the Bloodlady Roxana's speculation about my 'feelings' means that I am capable of such emotions, he'd said.

But she *was* capable of such emotions. And she was still afraid to admit just how far they extended.

She tossed and turned the rest of the morning and woke up late. She found a breakfast tray waiting for her on the small table near the wall opposite the bed, complete with eggs and sausage under a warmer, pastries and a selection of fruit. Trinity didn't question who'd sent them. She sat at the table and began to eat ravenously, replenishing her strength.

When she had finished her meal, bathed and dressed, she started for the Great Room.

As she approached Ares's office, she heard voices coming from within, one of them Cassandra's. Although Trinity couldn't make out all the words, it was clear to her that Ares was calmly explaining that Cassandra would no longer be serving him as his Favorite.

Trinity remained just inside the doorway of the harem quarters until the voices fell silent. Cassandra moved with her usual grace as she entered the Great Room, her gown sweeping behind her, her chin high. She caught sight of Trinity, and for a moment an expression of terrible anger marred her lovely features.

The anger didn't last. Cassandra's face went blank, and she swept out the door into the antechamber of Ares's apartments.

Knowing full well that she'd made a lasting enemy, Trinity hesitated to go to Ares. But he emerged from his private rooms a moment later and saw Trinity in the doorway. He was dressed informally, in the simplest tunic and pants, barefoot and free of all ornamentation.

"Trinity," he said. "Come."

She went to him and saw immediately that he was neither troubled nor angry. And yet, after less than twelve hours, he was developing those shadows under his eyes and cheekbones, the paleness that came with his increasing need for her blood.

Nevertheless, his gaze, when it met hers, was warmer than she had ever seen it—not only filled with the usual physical hunger for her, but also something she would have identified as affection in any human being.

Hadn't she wanted this even from the beginning, knowing how it would ease her mission? Didn't she crave it now, for completely unacceptable and very personal reasons?

Or was what she saw in his eyes simply some side effect of the addiction, reminding her how far she was from completing her duty?

"I saw Cassandra," she said.

"Yes." He gestured for her to sit in the chair near the front of the desk. "She has been informed of her change in status. I have, however, offered her compensation for her loss of rank and privilege. I believe she will be satisfied."

Trinity didn't ask what that "compensation" entailed, though she remembered Cassandra boasting that she'd be given her choice of new Households. She hoped Cassandra's severance package would make the former Favorite content enough that she wouldn't try to cause trouble for Trinity.

"I'm sorry for her," she said softly.

"There is no need." Ares smiled at her, a genuine smile, without any showing of his teeth and with that same unexpected warmth. "She will be accompanying us to the party, where she will receive her reward for exceptional service."

That was a pretty cold way of putting it, Trinity thought. But she couldn't feel too upset about Ares's dismissive words.

"What do I need to know before we go?" she asked.

"I will see that the nature of this gathering is explained to you well beforehand. You may still change your mind if it seems too demanding."

"I won't." She dared to lean forward and kiss him. "Thank you."

He responded eloquently to her boldness. "You may have cause to feel differently later," he said when they were disentangled again.

"I don't think so."

This time she took the lead, and they made love on one of the couches in the Great Room under the broad fronds of the potted plants Ares kept in one corner. Ares hesitated to bite her when they were at the height of their passion.

"Go ahead," she said hoarsely, gripping his arms. "You can't hurt me."

Still deep inside her, he lifted himself on his arms and searched her eyes. "I have taken too much already," he said. "I...have not been thinking clearly. Surely you should have become ill by now."

You're the one who's become ill, Trinity thought with the shame and guilt that had been haunting her with increasing frequency.

"I'd tell you if I felt weak or sick," she said, arching her neck and wrapping her legs around him. "I want it, Ares."

She could see his will struggling with his need, but the need won. She came to glorious completion as he bit her, and he followed quickly. Soon afterward, as they lay in each other's arms, she could see the color returning to his face, the hollows filling out again.

All because of her.

The next week passed by in a blur. She was able to learn nothing more about Novak's death, and had few chances to observe or speak with the other serfs. She spent nearly every moment with Ares, discussing human history and languages and evolution but almost never touching on Opir matters. When they weren't talking, they were making love or she was sleeping in his arms or, on rare occasions, in her own bed.

Ares was more tender than he had ever been, gentle even in his hunger for her, and more than once she was certain she heard real affection in his voice and felt it in the way he touched her. He began to relax more, to smile, even to laugh when she least expected it.

Still, she couldn't be sure that he was entirely himself. He continued to take her blood at least once a day, usually much more often, but he never seemed to recognize that something might be wrong or wonder why such frequent feedings didn't weaken her as it would an ordinary human. She was torn between a strange, fragile happiness and disgust at the way she was deceiving him so.

Near the end of that wonderful, terrible week, Trinity was forced to face a problem she had let slip by too long. Now that she was where she'd intended to be and had won Ares's trust, she was completely dependent on *him*—on his ability and willingness to talk about his own people and their Citadel.

Though she spoke to him frequently about his becoming more active in Opir politics for the reasons Roxana had urged, he showed no inclination to take the Bloodlady's advice. Twice he took her on a tour of the city in one of the public transports, but he didn't allow her to leave the vehicle. His obvious fear for her safety was stronger than ever—and so was his possessiveness.

Trinity knew that even after she spoke to the Underground's leader at the party, she could only succeed if she was able to push Ares into certain actions, and convince him to tell her things he ordinarily wouldn't share with a human. Not even with her.

But that was something she couldn't rush, not without arousing his suspicion, and the addiction gambit didn't seem to be helping at all. If anything, it was making things harder for her.

There was only one other path she could take. And it would rob her of her humanity forever.

"What would you do if I became your vassal?" she asked the day before the party, lying curled against him with her head tucked in the crook of his shoulder.

His hand stilled on her hair. "Why ask this now, Trinity?"

"I know we talked about what it meant before. But what would change? Would you still keep me here, with you?"

He rolled over until he was half on top of her and leaned on his elbow. "Vassals always remain with their Sires."

"Do Sires keep vassals as Favorites?"

His gaze was intense, his expression guarded, as if he was suspicious of her sudden interest. "There is no rule against it," he said, "though perhaps it is less common."

"But the blood is different?"

"Somewhat." He ran his fingertip along her nose, smiling faintly. "It would make no difference to *me*."

"Would I be in less danger?"

Again he stiffened, his dark brows drawing down over his eyes. "In what way?"

"Would you worry less about me?"

He rolled over onto his back, withdrawing his arm from around her. "Do you know what becomes of vassals when their lord is defeated in a Death Challenge?"

"Do they go to the new lord with the defeated Opir's serfs?"

"No." He stared at the ceiling, his mouth set. "It is difficult for an Opir to override the bond of the former lord. It can be done, but it requires effort, and not many Opir are willing to do so."

"So the new lord kills them."

"Yes." He sighed and pulled her close again.

"And I thought you only hesitated because you didn't want to do anything against my will."

"I might have changed my mind," he murmured into her hair. "But it would not be necessary. You would never leave me, even if you had the choice."

Concentrating on her operative's discipline, Trinity managed to keep her heartbeat steady. Ares had once told her very clearly that she was his property, body and soul. But this was different. Was it merely the addiction speaking? Or had he become convinced that she had truly developed such powerful feelings for him that she would refuse freedom to remain by his side?

What in God's name did he expect her to say?

Test him with the truth, she thought. It was the only way to know.

She propped herself up on her elbow and met his gaze. "You wanted me to be honest," she said. "I haven't heard of many humans escaping Erebus. But if I had a chance, I might try. Because it's no one's natural state to be slave, no matter how well treated."

He was still for a long while. When he spoke again, his voice was calm and measured.

"I believe you would choose to stay," he said.

And Trinity knew they wouldn't speak of it again. She had told him the truth, and she had no reason to feel guilty about it.

That evening she returned to her room in the harem quarters. She spent most of the night trying to quiet her thoughts by reading one of the old novels on the bookshelves. Someone knocked on the door just after dawn.

It was Daniel. Trinity pulled her robe closed around her neck.

"What are you doing here?" she asked. "It's barely—"

"Ares sent me to explain about the party and the Procession," he said as she climbed out of bed.

"Procession?"

"No one ever mentioned it to you?" he asked, entering the room.

Something in his voice put her on her guard. "No," she said, tightening her sash. "But why did you come now?"

"You need time to consider what will happen tonight." He leaned against the wall, folding his arms across his chest. "I know you convinced him to attend this party."

"Lady Roxana brought it up. She urged him to go, and I thought her reasons were good ones."

"You're both right," he said, frowning at the floor. "It can't be helped."

"But you'd rather he didn't go?"

"A human can't stop an Opir from whatever he decides to do," Daniel said, sidestepping her question. He looked up and began to speak quickly. "Let me explain about the Procession. You already understand that Opir society is based on competition and the constant struggle for status and property."

"I have good reason to know," she said.

"A Procession is the way high-ranked Opiri show off their wealth and power to their peers and inferiors. The custom developed as a way to help keep the peace, to prevent unnecessary Challenges and stabilize Nightsider society and government."

In spite of herself, Trinity shivered. "A way to keep the peace," she said with a touch of irony. "Like what happened between Ares and Palemon on the Causeway."

"Ares was at a disadvantage then. He hasn't made Procession in years. His life may be riding on the impression he makes now."

"I understand."

"Yes," Daniel said with a grim twist of his lips. "I think you do."

"What is my part in this Procession?" she asked.

"Purely ornamental. A reminder of Ares's recent victory, as you will be at the party. Abbie will be coming up to make you as beautiful as possible. Stand wherever Ares's Freebloods indicate."

"I'll finally meet them?" she asked.

"Don't expect them to pay any attention to you. Until Ares chooses to reward them with one of his serfs, they'll pretend we're invisible."

"He'd give one of us away?"

"He won't risk it until he finds his clients to be mature enough. And even then he wouldn't force any of us to go." Daniel shrugged. "There isn't much more to tell. But be warned…don't chance what you and I did with Palemon. Ares can't be made to look as if he can't control his serfs a second time."

"If it hadn't been for that boy—"

"I know."

They stared at each other again, silently appraising. Daniel broke away to examine the books on the shelf, obviously weighing something he wanted to tell her. "Ares is...more content than I've ever seen him," he said. "Now that he's finally taken your blood, he can't stay away from you. That means he could be distracted when he can least afford to be."

"You have to believe what I said before, Daniel. I want him to live. Not only to secure my own survival, but because of what he is."

"But he doesn't know about *you,* does he?"

Trinity froze. "I don't know what you mean."

Without a second's warning, Daniel spun around and rushed her. She dodged him instinctively, but he caught at her arm and twisted it behind her with surprising strength. Almost immediately she freed herself and counterattacked. He slid out of her path, but she hit him hard on the shoulder and kicked at his knee. He began to fall, caught himself and backed away, holding his numb arm against his side.

"What in hell are you doing?" she gasped, remaining in a fighting crouch. "If Ares found out—"

"Yes," Daniel said, his breath coming fast. "If Ares found out what you *truly* are..."

Chapter 18

"I don't know what you're talking about," she said, swallowing her alarm. "I think you should leave."

"Not yet." He winced as he rotated his shoulder. "You're good. You're also stronger than any normal human should be. It was obvious to me when you defeated Novak and the others, even if no one else recognized it."

Trinity remembered how he'd all but accused her then, before they'd been interrupted by Ares's arrival at the scene. She should have remembered, realized that Daniel was bound to bring it up again, even if he hadn't indicated that he still held suspicions about her.

"I was well trained by good teachers," she said. "So, apparently, were you."

"You were more than just trained, Trinity. You're a dhampir."

"And you're crazy."

"No. I suspected it very soon after you arrived."

"And just how many dhampires have you seen, Daniel?" she asked.

"Enough to recognize one, even without the eyes." He touched his temple. "Contacts? Capped teeth? Genetic alteration?"

"I don't see any reason why I should—"

"I *know*," he said, shaking his head with obvious weariness. "The question is what I should do about it."

Trinity saw no point in trying to deny it again. Daniel was certain, and he wasn't going to back down.

But she had one thing in her favor. Daniel hadn't mentioned the addiction. He'd said Ares couldn't stay away from her, but he didn't seem to have connected that with any kind of dependence on her blood.

Maybe the serf was unfamiliar with the condition. She might still salvage the situation.

"What do you *think* you should do?" she asked.

"Were you sent here as a spy for the Enclave?"

She snorted. "I was a soldier, as I imagine you know by now. I was convicted of treason and escaped execution by secretly joining the Deportees."

"A dhampir wasted as a common soldier?"

"I've always hidden what I was. My mother didn't want me becoming an unwilling operative for Aegis, forced to risk my life in the Zone until some Citadel agent killed me. She got me special contacts for my eyes and caps to cover my teeth. I kept my secret when I joined up."

It was clear from Daniel's expression that he wasn't convinced. "I want to believe you, for Ares's sake," he said. "But I can't trust you. As long as you do nothing to betray him, however, I'll leave you alone. *If* you do as I ask."

"What do you want?"

"I know you're in contact with the Underground."

The second revelation hit Trinity with the force of a bullet to the heart. "You should talk to Levi," she said coldly. "He may be able to give you something for your delusions."

Daniel gave a short bark of laughter. "I've felt for months that something strange was going on in this House-hold," he said, matching her icy tone. "But as I've been watching you, I've also been watching others. They hide themselves well, but one of them made a mistake."

Trinity worked to regain her composure before she spoke again. "What kind of mistake? Who?"

"It doesn't matter. I know they exist, and you've joined them."

"Why would I?" she asked. "I've only been here a little over two weeks. The Enclave isn't even sure this Under-ground exists."

"But you found them. And having any communication with them is enough to condemn you to a painful death, even though the Assembly and Council refuse to admit that serfs are clever enough to organize any kind of Re-sistance."

"How *can* it be a Resistance?" Trinity asked. "You your-self said there's nothing any human can do to—"

"Not directly," he said. "I know they help abused serfs escape. But they also gather information they hope to send to the Enclave."

"And you're too well trained a slave to think that's a worthwhile effort," she said, "even if it might stop another useless war."

The muscles in his jaw flexed. "Do you believe I'm in-capable of compassion because I was bred like an animal?"

Trinity flushed, remembering what Ares had once told her. *He was not as not as easily dominated as they ex-pected, and he suffered for it. He was to be publicly ex-ecuted to serve as a warning to other serfs.*

Before Ares had saved him.

"Don't pity me," he said harshly, as if he'd read her

mind. "Think carefully about what I'm about to tell you. If you and your allies were to be discovered, you'd all be killed. But you wouldn't be the only ones to suffer. Ares could be brought up before the Council as an Opir unfit for his rank because he failed to expose the traitors in his own Household. He could be stripped of all his property and his serfs would be put up for Claiming by any Blood-lord or Bloodmaster strong enough to take them."

Shaken to the core, Trinity wondered why no one in the Underground had bothered to explain the other consequences of exposure.

But what Daniel said made perfect sense. She should have realized it from the beginning, knowing what she did of the Opir attitude toward weakness of any kind.

"We've done everything possible to avoid exposure," she said. "There's no sign that anyone else knows what's going on here."

"Don't think you're safe," he said. "If I found you, so can someone else who'd be willing to tell Ares immediately. And our lord would be compelled to give them up, or watch every one of his serfs go to other masters. There are far more like Palemon than like Ares."

"I'll warn the others," Trinity said, heading for the closet.

"That's not good enough," Daniel said. "You have to get them all out."

She turned to stare at him. "Excuse me?"

"You said it yourself. The Underground can do it. I want you to arrange to get the members here out of the Citadel before one of them betrays himself—and Ares."

She paused with her robe hanging loose from her shoulders. "Do you have any idea what you're asking?"

"Perfectly. I know someone high up in the Underground will be at the party tonight."

"How did you—?"

"I *know,*" he interrupted. "You get the message to that person and arrange it. Otherwise, I'll have to tell Ares what I've discovered. He'll know you've betrayed him, and that might kill him."

Did *Daniel know about the addiction after all?* Trinity asked herself. Did he believe Ares might die if she and Ares were separated?

Or did he mean something else entirely?

"Will you do as I ask?" Daniel said.

"You aren't leaving me much of a choice, are you?" She ran her fingers through her tangled hair. "And what about me? Should I leave the Citadel, too?"

"Don't you want to?" he asked, observing her carefully.

"I don't know," she said, realizing she was speaking the unvarnished, unacceptable truth.

"You know what you have to do," Daniel said. Without another word, he strode out of the room. He nearly collided with Abbie, who drew aside with a startled look and stood in the doorway staring after the valet.

"What was that all about?" she asked, her elegant brows high over inquiring eyes.

Trinity remembered to breathe. "Daniel came to explain the Procession to me," she said.

"Oh. I suppose that's why he looked so upset," Abbie said wryly. "Jealousy, I suppose."

"Why?" Trinity asked.

"Because Ares used to talk more with him, almost as if he were a son. Now you've taken that place."

"But not as a son," Trinity said, still unable to think clearly.

Abbie laughed. "I stand corrected." She strolled into the room. "I know it's early, but we have a lot of things to do. I already have someone working on your gown, so I can spend a little time with you." She gestured toward Trinity's dressing table. "Take a seat. I need to look at your hair."

Trinity hesitated. The other woman grabbed her hand and pulled her to the chair. Once Trinity had perched nervously on the edge of the seat, Abbie scooped up a handful of her loose hair and frowned at their joint reflections in the mirror.

"At least I have something good to work with," she said. She set down a small case of various grooming implements and began to comb out Trinity's hair, twisting it into experimental ropes and coils. After much clucking and frowning, she swept Trinity's hair on top of her head and pushed in a long silver hairpin.

"There," Abbie said, stepping back. "What do you think?"

Trinity had to admit that the woman had done an extraordinary job, using a few pins to hold Trinity's hair in place while making it seem as if the entire concoction might come loose at any moment.

Breakfast—very generous, as before—arrived a few moments later. Abbie let Trinity's hair down again.

"I'll be back later to do it up properly and help you with your gown," Abbie said.

"You can stay for breakfast," Trinity said as the kitchen serf laid the meal out on the small table.

"No, thanks. You have no idea how much I have to do today." Abbie grabbed a pastry from a plate and gripped Trinity's shoulder. "Courage, my friend."

Then she was gone. Trinity forced herself to eat. The last thing she needed was to be physically weak during this Procession, or the party afterward. And Ares was likely to take her blood before they left.

And then what? she asked herself. *Do what Daniel says? Is there any other choice?*

His final words to her had convinced her that she'd been right the first time. He didn't know about the addiction. But she couldn't trust him not to expose her as a dhampir, no matter what he'd promised. The mission was compromised, and maybe the best thing she could do was cut her losses.

And leave Ares to fight the inevitable withdrawal alone, without knowing what it might do to him? If she became his vassal, she could break the addiction.

Even though it meant betraying the Enclave once and for all.

She had no answer. And she had a feeling she wouldn't have one until the events of the coming night played out.

All eyes fixed on Ares when he entered the assembly hall. The casual, comfortable clothing he wore in his apartments had been replaced with a dazzling, jewel-spangled sapphire tunic, calf length and slit nearly to the waist, with loose-fitting, intricately embroidered pants tucked into boots of hand-worked leather dyed the same blue as his tunic. He wore a plain silver circlet around his head, but it only added magnificence to his appearance and emphasized the sculpted masculinity of his face.

Trinity was nearly overwhelmed by his powerful appearance. Even though she was far from his bed, her body responded to the strength he wore like a mantle, the sheer exotic force of his nature, the heat of his stare as his gaze swept the room and found her.

Then he looked away as his senior client—a Freeblood who had adopted the name Gordianus—brought him the staff Trinity had first seen during the Claiming. A moment later Cassandra strode into the room, dressed in a gown of vivid red. She wore gold hoop earrings, a gold torc set with rubies and matching bracelets. Tiny, reflective disks glittered on her cheeks.

She smiled at Trinity with full, scarlet lips, and then dismissed her former rival with a toss of her head. Trinity picked Vijay, Elizabeth and Levi out of the crowd. She had no way to warn Vijay and Erin about what Daniel had told her, even if she knew it was safe to do so.

Ten serfs, in addition to Jonathan, Diego, Daniel and Ares's two Freebloods, were gathering to accompany Ares. It was evident to Trinity that nearly every human in the room was nervous and uncertain.

Did any of them suspect how much danger was bubbling under the Household's once serene facade?

Before Trinity had a chance to observe more closely, Jonathan indicated that she was to take her place at the fore of the Procession, just behind Ares. The Freebloods, carrying banners with Ares's device, had fallen in to either side of their sponsor.

Given the gravity of the situation, Trinity didn't expect Ares to notice her. He'd been preoccupied most of the day and had taken her blood much more perfunctorily than usual only a few hours before. But when she fell in step behind him, he gave her a brief, intimate smile, and his eyes told her she was beautiful and desirable and worthy of every privilege he could bestow on her.

Privileges that would mean nothing if Daniel ever told him the truth about her. She couldn't forget that, no matter how many times Ares smiled at her or held her in his arms.

The remaining serfs, all in the equivalent of their "Sunday best," had formed a two-column formation behind the seniors. Altogether, they looked to Trinity like a troop going off to war.

And that, she thought, wasn't far from the truth.

With Ares striding ahead of them, the entire assemblage walked through the wide, "public" halls of the Household and to the main lobby with its single elevator. Large as the lift was, it couldn't accommodate the entire Procession. Ares, Trinity and the Freebloods with the banners went first, followed by the senior serfs and Cassandra, and finally the remaining serfs. When everyone had reached the proper floor, they took their places again.

The interior of the Citadel, darkened by the night sky outside the dome, glittered with a thousand points of light, meant to be decorative and yet practical for serfs traveling through the city. Once again Trinity was amazed by the complexity of it—and by the degree Opiri borrowed so many aspects of design from their supposed "inferiors."

"What do you think of the city?" Cassandra asked, slipping out of her place to join Trinity at the head of the ranks.

Oddly enough, there was no hostility in the woman's voice. She spoke in an almost friendly way, which Trinity trusted about as far as the Freebloods could toss their banners.

"I've already seen it several times," Trinity said. "But it always seems different."

Cassandra laughed softly and moved away. Trinity looked along the Causeway. The elevated walk paralleled the curve of the dome, and she could make out other large groups moving at a measured pace in the distance. Opiri of the more common sort, primarily Freebloods, watched from benches on either side of the walk, or from balconies on the taller buildings in the vicinity. Trinity wondered if rumors of Ares's Procession had spread throughout the Citadel, and if the sheer rarity of such an event had captured the interest of its inhabitants.

A sudden tension in the air called Trinity back from her appraisal. She looked up at Ares, who was standing very straight and holding the staff slightly tilted forward. He began to move, graceful as a leopard prowling its territory in complete confidence of its ability to defend it against all comers. As the retinue passed the first observers, Trinity felt their stares move from her to Ares and back again with something much more intense than mere curiosity.

Ares appeared not to see them at all. When another Procession approached, led by what Trinity assumed was a Bloodlord, the two Nightsiders stopped and stared at each other over an empty space of a dozen yards as if they had reached invisible barriers neither dared cross.

That, Trinity surmised, wouldn't last long. And she was right.

"Ares," the Bloodlord said, dipping his own staff ever so slightly. His hair was the bleached white of the typical Opiri, done up in an elaborate style, and his eyes were a deep purple.

"Eucleides," Ares acknowledged, holding his staff upright.

"I heard of a Challenge," Eucleides said in a formal voice.

"A Challenge was offered and accepted." Without looking away from the Bloodmaster's dark eyes, Ares gestured to Trinity. She stepped forward and bowed her head.

"A fine prize," Eucleides said. "May you take her blood with pleasure."

Ares nodded acknowledgment of the other Nightsider's respectful words. Trinity returned to her place behind him, walking with shoulders back and head held high.

Eucleides signaled to one of his own Freebloods, who in turn spoke to his vassals. The entire retinue moved to the side, making room for Ares and his followers to pass.

It had been so quick, Trinity thought, so simple. Yet there was no mistaking the change in scent, the vibration in the air, the new tension in Ares's body. The sensations swept back in a wave to engulf her, and her knees almost buckled.

Moving more quickly than even she could detect, Ares caught her arm with his free hand and held her up until she had her feet underneath her again. His skin, normally cooler than hers, seemed to burn. His eyes were hardly recognizable, nearly all pupil. Trinity almost believed he could see through her lenses and recognize exactly what she was.

"Are you ill?" he asked.

"No, my lord," she said, pulling herself erect.

He released her and indicated that the Procession should move on. Trinity continued to tremble, shaken by Ares's firm, gentle touch and her own utter hypocrisy.

The next two Bloodlords didn't so much as exchange words with Ares; they simply bowed and pulled their retinues out of Ares's path. The Procession had gone about a quarter mile farther along the Causeway when Ares suddenly turned onto a ramp ascending to another tower. He signaled a stop.

"Remember what I told you," Daniel said, coming up beside Trinity.

"Aren't you coming?" she asked.

"Not this time," he said, and vanished among the other serfs. All at once the formation reversed position, and the common serfs and their guardian Opiri marched back the way they had come, leaving only Cassandra, a female serf named Xiu Li and the two Freebloods carrying Ares's banners. Xiu Li, adorned with a cascade of ebony hair, wore a sleek green gown slit almost to the waist on both sides.

They all followed Ares up a ramp through an arched entrance between two Grecian columns and across an elegant lobby with three elevators. Trinity assumed that this tower, like Ares's, contained the Households of high-ranked Bloodlords or Bloodmasters. The devices on the elevator doors comprised a wolf, a lyre and a joker's mask.

The small party entered the elevator marked with the mask and rode it to the top. That floor's private lobby was decorated with a mural that was obviously Opir art, strangely alien to a human eyes. Several life-size and very realistic nude marble figures, human and Opir, flanked the very wide doors, which were carved with erotic imagery. Only the long hair of some of the figures, weaving among the other bodies like tentacles, identified the Opiri from the humans.

A little shocked, Trinity looked away. It wasn't as if she hadn't seen erotic art before, but this was so brazen that it sent shivers through her body.

Ares glanced at her as if to reassure her and advanced to the doors. He tapped the head of his staff against a figurine of a writhing Opir body, and the doors swung open.

Chapter 19

The three humans, or vassals, who greeted him were as startling as the carvings on the door. One of the males, extraordinarily tall, wore nothing but a very brief loincloth, and his entire body was covered with tattoos of Opir pictographs. The two females were equally exotic, one dark-skinned, completely bald and dressed in a body suit of spotless white that fit her like a second skin. The second had golden hair that literally brushed the floor, woven with a thousand glittering strands of ribbon that also seemed to wrap around every part of her otherwise naked body. Her brilliant blue eyes were framed in wide bands of glittering copper paint.

All three bowed to Ares and then straightened with welcoming smiles that seemed quite genuine. The woman in the body suit offered Ares the blood cup. He took a very small sip, nodded, and allowed the three humans to precede him through another set of doors. Trinity didn't look at the reliefs carved into their surfaces, but the glimpses she caught as she passed suggested images that bordered on the truly obscene.

The tall man led them through one more set of gleaming gold doors and into a large dining hall that held more than a dozen Opiri, lying on couches in the ancient Roman style and surrounded by serfs who wore a wide variety of costumes or nothing at all. They served the Opir with smiles and even laughter, dropping playfully into Nightsider laps, kneeling to present all sorts of delicacies favored by their masters and offering their necks to any Opir who might want a taste of their blood.

Everyone stopped to look at Ares as he entered. One of the Freebloods stationed himself at the door with the banners, and the other, who took Ares's staff, indicated that Trinity, Cassandra and Xiu Li should follow Ares into the room.

"Ares!" one of the Opiri said, rising from his couch. He was plump and wore flowing robes sewn with gold thread and jewels to such excess that Trinity could hardly believe he was able to move at all. She was astonished to see him open his arms and embrace Ares, who bore the gesture without complaint.

"So glad you could come," said the Opir, stepping back. "Roxana has talked ceaselessly of your new Favorite."

"Phoibos," Ares acknowledged calmly, as if the other Opir hadn't just broken a major unwritten rule of Nightsider protocol. "I am honored to be present in your Household."

Phoibos rolled his eyes. "Elders," he said in mock disgust. "Always so *formal*." He stepped around Ares and stood in front of Trinity, who met his curious stare before dropping her gaze. "Ah. Now I understand." He tipped up Trinity's chin. "There *is* something special about her."

Ares pinned Phoibos with a hard stare. "She is not for

sharing," he said in the dangerous voice Trinity knew all too well.

Raising his hands in a placating gesture, Phoibos backed away. "I never presumed otherwise," he said. He examined Ares's former Favorite with an open leer. "The legendary Cassandra. She has not faded in the past several years."

"My gift to you," Ares said, inclining his head slightly.

Trinity stifled a gasp. She stared at Cassandra, who seemed neither surprised nor upset. If anything, she looked like the cat who'd gotten into the cream. She caught Trinity's gaze and winked.

"What a very fine present," Phoibos said, gently taking Cassandra's arm. "I hope you won't think it rude if I sample her soon. But not right now, of course." His bright gaze swept over Xiu Li. "This one is for sharing?"

With a sweep of her gown and a very unsubtle display of creamy thigh, Xiu Li bowed to Phoibos.

"A dancer," Ares said. "Very talented, but I have little occasion to make use of her skill."

"Of course you haven't, you dull dog," Phoibos said, rubbing his hands. "Well, we shan't make her experience here too miserable, I think."

Suddenly Trinity put it all together. *Sharing.* Roxana had mentioned it, stating that Ares would never force any of his serfs to attend the party. Did this mean that the young woman would be passed around like a bottle of wine, to be sampled by every Nightsider in the room?

Trinity's first impulse was to ask, even beg, Ares not to give Xiu Li to these Opiri for their pleasure. Considering the circumstances, she knew she'd be incredibly stupid to interfere.

But she did so, nevertheless. "Ares," she whispered as Xiu Li flowed gracefully across the room to join another cluster of serfs who were, to judge by their very colorful dress, the "entertainment." "Do you have to give her to all these Opiri?"

His gaze was distant and strange when he looked at her. "You are not to speak unless you are asked," he said, all the warmth gone from his voice and his eyes. "It is for your own protection."

Then he was taking her arm and following Phoibos to a couch set aside for him, supplied with a small ottoman where Trinity was to sit. Occupying the couch beside Ares's was Roxana, with her Favorite, Garret, standing behind her. Trinity scanned the room, wondering who among these serfs was the leader of Erebus's human Underground.

And wondering what in hell she would say to him.

"I think you know everyone here," Phoibos said to Ares, stroking Cassandra's neck as she took her place at his side, "but perhaps you require a small reminder."

He proceeded to name the Bloodlords and Bloodmasters on their various couches, each with a Favorite standing or sitting close by. A pair of lords and one lady were preoccupied with taking blood from serfs who wore torcs with the mask device embossed on their golden surfaces. Another lord was intimately caressing a female serf sprawled across his lap.

Ares reacted to none of this. He nodded to several of the Opiri. Most of them seemed interested in Trinity and respectful of Ares.

Two were not. "Hannibal and Medon," a male voice murmured in her ear. She started, turning to find Roxana's Favorite beside her. "Allies of Palemon. Lady Roxana has informed me of the situation." He gazed at her gravely with his striking green eyes. "You know there's a chance one or both of them might offer Challenge while they're here."

"I've been told," Trinity said. "Hannibal and Medon had better watch themselves."

He chuckled. "My name is Garret." He offered his hand.

His grip was firm, and Trinity matched its strength. He showed no surprise.

"Welcome to the party, Trinity," he said. "Or perhaps I should say orgy."

"I saw the carvings," she said. "Is that what I can expect here?"

"Oh, I doubt Ares will join in," Garret said. "Roxana certainly won't. But whatever you see, don't react. Just do whatever Ares tells you to do, and you'll be fine." He glanced at Ares, who was speaking with Roxana, and bent closer. "It's important that we speak later, in private. In a few hours none of the Opiri will even notice we're gone."

Trinity had no chance to ask why. He was already with Roxana, smiling, kissing her hand. She stroked the side of his face.

As Trinity's surprise faded, she realized what Garret had meant. *He* was the Underground's leader. And it was abundantly clear that Trinity had been right when she'd first seen him and Roxana together. He was very much in love.

Ares had denied Roxana could return his feelings. And if Ares had known what Garret was, he would no doubt claim the serf's obvious devotion was all a ploy to camouflage his membership in the Underground.

It wasn't a ploy, of that Trinity was certain. But if he loved a woman he might be forced to betray, how could he be trusted?

The party was, as Garret had intimated, just short of an orgy, with apparently willing serfs continuously moving among the guests offering delicacies, wine and themselves.

Trinity understood now why Ares had been so reluctant to attend. He hadn't wanted to be part of this, or allow *her* to be. She was, as he had warned, subjected to a great deal of attention, much of it openly lascivious. Ares ran interference between her and the worst of his peers, but she knew he was aware that too much protectiveness would expose a point of vulnerability his enemies could use against him.

But he wouldn't permit anyone to touch her, and his stare warned off any Opir whose behavior became overly bold or insolent. When he glanced in her direction, his gaze expressed the concern his dispassionate expression hid so well.

And his face revealed something else…a weariness, a look of gauntness about his face, the paleness of his skin and shadows under his eyes. It had only been six hours since he had last taken her blood, and already he needed it again.

She leaned close to him, bracing herself for a public display she would have given almost anything to avoid.

"My lord," she said softly. "Would you have blood?"

But Ares no longer seemed to hear her. She was forced to withdraw again as he engaged in conversation with another Bloodlord.

Knowing she didn't dare press him, she bided her time and continued to observe as she had promised, assessing to the best of her ability which Opiri would make good allies. The ones who seemed most restrained and gentle with the serfs? Or were there other qualities an Opir would recognize that she could not?

She turned her attention to Medon and Hannibal. Many of the Opiri appeared to be drunk, but Palemon's allies seemed unaffected. They remained alert, and their stares were focused on Ares. He gave them no more notice than he did the debauchery going on around him.

Nor did he pay any attention to the "entertainment." The human jugglers using sharp or dangerous objects as props were by far the least disturbing part of it. Other serfs, many naked or barely dressed, performed astonishing acrobatics, some blatantly reminiscent of the erotic door carvings.

Xiu Li, who appeared last, was indeed a very talented dancer, her skirts swirling, her thighs flashing through the slits as she leaped and twisted in midair. By then, many of the Opiri had lapsed into a contented stupor or were engaged in desultory conversation with their neighbors.

All but Hannibal and Medon, who surely recognized on Ares's face the signs of weakness any predator looks for in likely prey.

Trinity began watching for another chance to speak to him without attracting too much attention. His withdrawal had gotten out of hand. It was no longer a matter of pitting one set of consequences against another.

Either she would have to make him drink, or tell him the truth, before—

"Ares!" a male voice shouted, and Trinity realized it was already too late. Medon was on his feet, weaving as if he were intoxicated, though his eyes were hard with purpose.

"You haven't taken blood at all tonight!" he said loudly. He looked around at the other Nightsiders, drawing their attention. "The mighty Ares is above his company!"

With a sigh, as if he were dealing with a boastful child, Ares rose from his couch. "Medon," he said. "I confess that there is some truth to your assertion, at least where you are concerned."

Trinity tensed. Every Opir face focused on the unfolding drama, and even the half-unconscious Nightsiders began to stir. Hannibal rose with a lazy smile.

"It's all in jest, Medon," he said. "Can't you see that Lord Ares was only attempting to amuse the guests with his quip?"

Ares walked slowly to the front and center of the room, where the serfs had recently been performing. "Perhaps you require lessons in understanding the difference between jests and derision, Hannibal," he said.

"I hear you are receiving lessons in submission from

your new Favorite," Hannibal said. "Your submission to *her,* of course."

The room virtually throbbed with barely veiled hostility. Hannibal was using Ares's own apparent "weakness"— compassion for his humans—against him. As all of Erebus would use it against him if his peers discovered that he had allowed the Underground to operate in his Household.

"Your own habit of submission has made you find it everywhere you look," Ares said. "Because Palemon clearly uses you as a serf, you should be grateful when he lets you off the leash."

The two Opiri glowered at each other, and a wash of sound swept the room as the other Nightsiders murmured excitedly amongst themselves. Suddenly Garret was beside Trinity again.

"Hannibal will have to offer Challenge now," he said, "or face humiliation he'll never be able to live down."

"Ares did it on purpose," Trinity said, matching his low tone. "I didn't expect—"

"This way he comes off strong," Garret said. "Palemon has at least four allies here, and Ares has only Roxana. He's showing the guests that he's willing to face all of his enemies in successive Challenges."

"You have no idea what he's risking."

Garret glanced at Ares. "I can see there's something wrong with him. What is it?"

"He needs to take my blood," she said. "Even if I have to get between two Opiri who'd like to kill each other."

Garret peered into her eyes. "Why?"

"Because he grows progressively weaker the longer he goes without it."

His gaze narrowed, but before she could speak again, Roxana called for him. The Bloodmistress was leaning forward with as much a show of anxiety as Trinity had ever seen in a Nightsider.

As she and the other guests watched, Hannibal snapped his fingers, and a lovely female vassal with haunted eyes brought him his staff.

With a theatrical gesture, Hannibal banged the head of the staff, a charging boar, on the floor with a cracking thud. "I Challenge—" he began, and then paused dramatically. "I Challenge Ares to first blood for ten of his best serfs, and five thousand bloodmarks."

A hiss of approval echoed around the room. Trinity had to clench her fists and press her lips together to keep from shouting out her disdain for all of them.

"Ten thousand bloodmarks only," Ares said.

Hannibal made a show of weighing the offer. Trinity felt such irrational hatred for Palemon's ally that she began to shake.

As if he sensed her thoughts, Ares turned to look at her. His eyes seemed to be the only source of warmth in the room. The corners of his lips curved upward.

"I accept," Hannibal said.

Ares glanced at the Freeblood who held his staff. The man hurried onto the floor and gave it to Ares with a deep bow. Ares cracked the head of his staff against the floor as Hannibal had done.

"I accept," he said.

A vassal approached the challengers with a large, two-handled blood cup. Eyes downcast, he offered it first to Hannibal.

The Bloodlord drank a full measure, his mouth painted with blood as he lifted his head. When the cup was brought to Ares, he scarcely touched his lips to the rim. There was another murmur among the Nightsiders, so Trinity guessed his lack of enthusiasm must be a breach of protocol. Or another sign of contempt.

Ares's and Hannibal's retainers moved to retrieve the staffs, and the two Nightsiders faced each other across the room, Hannibal smiling slightly, Ares wrapped in unassailable dignity. But Trinity saw the almost imperceptible twitches in his fingers, the muscle jumping in his jaw, the slight tilt in his stance. No matter how powerful he was, Ares was going to fail before the Challenge was over.

Taking a desperate chance, she walked out onto the floor and knelt between the two Opiri, facing Ares.

"My lord," she said, bowing her head. "I beg you to accept my blood before the Challenge begins."

Absolute silence filled the room. Trinity knew her fate, and perhaps Ares's as well, hung by a thread. The other Opiri might consider her out of control. They might demand that she be severely punished in a way Ares would never permit under ordinary circumstances. She couldn't even be sure that Hannibal wouldn't demand her death.

"What have we here?" Hannibal asked with a curl of his lip. He reached down to grab Trinity's loosened hair, twisting a large portion of it in his fist. "The rumors were right. You have no control over the human bitch. She—"

Ares had Hannibal's wrist in an iron grip before the other Opir could finish his sentence. He forced Hannibal to release Trinity and shoved him away.

Hannibal nursed his wrist. "I call all Opiri to witness this disgraceful breach of conduct," he snapped. "I demand the surrender of this serf to me for punishment, and penalties against my opponent."

Openly snarling, Ares advanced on Hannibal, his steps slightly unsteady. "I will accept penalties," he said, "but you will not touch her."

Trinity, her heart in her throat, heard a shuffle as several Nightsiders rose and approached. One was Roxana, one Medon and the third Phoibos.

"This human has earned punishment," Phoibos said with uncharacteristic gravity. "No serf is permitted to interfere in a Challenge, on pain of death."

"There will be no killing of serfs today," Ares said, turning to stare at the three Nightsiders, and beyond to the silent observers. "I will deal with her later."

"You will do nothing, Ares," Medon said. "We all know you too well. You'll never touch a hair on her pretty head."

As if to prove his enemy wrong, Ares pulled Trinity to her feet. He looked more bestial than human, his eyes sunken and glittering, deep shadows under his high cheekbones. He jerked her off to the side of the room.

"Go to Roxana," he said hoarsely.

"No." She looked into his burning eyes, her throat choked with tears. "You're not yourself, Ares. If you meet him like this, you'll lose." She closed her eyes. "You have to bite me, Ares. Make me your vassal."

Chapter 20

Ares stared at her as if she'd lost her senses. "Why?" he asked. "Why now?"

"Don't argue with me!" She lowered her voice still more when she remembered how well the other Opiri could hear. "You're addicted, Ares. Addicted to my blood. You have to take as much as you can right now, and convert me so that you can break the addiction."

The little color still left in his face drained away, and soon there was nothing left of the Ares she knew, only a dangerous and hungry predator.

"You betrayed me," he growled.

"I want to stay with you. Ares…"

Without a word, he yanked her against his chest and bit her. She had never felt so much discomfort from one of his bites, and it lasted a very long time.

"Another infraction!" Hannibal cried.

Wiping his mouth with the back of his hand, Ares pushed Trinity away and returned to the floor. "Take your own blood, Hannibal," he said. "Then we will be on equal footing."

Hannibal turned on his heel, marched back to his couch and grabbed his Favorite, a frail-looking young woman who seemed as though she might fade away a little more each time her blood was taken. Trinity staggered toward Ares's couch, dizzy and sick with self-disgust and the changes that were surely beginning to take place within her. Hannibal finished with his Favorite and returned to face Ares, not bothering to wipe the fresh blood from his lips.

"Now we are back where we began," he said with open contempt.

"Are we?" Ares asked. His voice was rough with anger, but Trinity could already see the difference in his stance, feel the energy radiating from his body in almost tangible waves, the solid readiness of a soldier who had trained for war all his life.

Hannibal must have felt it, too. "The serf must still be punished," he said.

"Not at your hand," Ares said.

"Then I, too, Challenge Ares," Medon announced. "To disabling injury. And if he falls, the serf goes to the victor."

Half-blind with pain and nausea, Trinity fell onto her ottoman. Immediately Garret was at her side.

"If he refuses," Garret whispered, "they can take you by default. But he'll have to fight them both in succession. If he beats Hannibal to first blood, he'll still have to fight Medon to disability. If he loses either one…"

"How is that…fair?" Trinity gasped.

"Fair, among Opiri?" The serf helped her up and squeezed her shoulder. "If he'd given you up for punishment right away, maybe this wouldn't have happened. But he wants to protect you. At any cost."

And I begged him to let me come, Trinity thought. *I put him in this position. I'm responsible.*

"Where is Roxana?" she asked, realizing that the Opir woman had disappeared.

Garret shook his head, and a deeper fear sank its teeth into Trinity's heart.

"You have to come with me now," he said. "It's the only way we can be sure you'll be safe."

"Safe?" A harsh laugh caught in her throat. "Ares has just made me his vassal."

Garret's eyes widened. "Why? If Ares loses and they find out you're his vassal, you'll die."

"Everything's changed," she said. Of course Garret didn't know that she'd admitted to betraying Ares, even if the Bloodmaster didn't yet understand just how thoroughly she'd deceived him. Garret didn't know that Ares would almost certainly never trust her again, and that she would never get the information she needed to complete her mission.

"I'm no good to you now," she said, nearly weeping with exhaustion and fear for Ares. "I can't just walk away."

Anything Garret might have said was lost as Ares's voice rose in barely restrained hatred, answering Medon's Challenge. A pair of strong vassals took up positions on either side of Trinity, clearly intending to keep her from leaving. Garret cast Trinity an almost despairing look and disappeared.

Numb both mentally and physically, Trinity watched as Hannibal and Ares shed their tunics and silk shirts, passing them to waiting serfs. Hannibal was far less imposing than Ares, but Trinity didn't underestimate his strength and she knew Ares wouldn't, either. The two faced each other across the floor, preparing for battle, muscles tensing, teeth bared.

Within seconds they were at each other, their shallow

veneer of civilization shed like a snake's old skin. They grappled violently, neither one landing a strike that drew blood. Hannibal sprang back, and Ares circled him, half-crouched and hands raised. He flung himself at Hannibal again, punching the other Nightsider's kidney with his fist as he lunged for his enemy's neck.

He failed to make contact. Hannibal spun out of his reach. They stared at each other, gauging strength and possible angles of attack. Ares's muscles bunched and relaxed under his golden skin, every move powerful and predatory.

But something went wrong. Between one moment and the next, in a motion too fast for Trinity to follow even with her superior dhampir vision, Hannibal darted in and raked his long nails across Ares's chest.

Trinity struggled to her feet. One of the vassals pushed her back down. Ares leaped away from his opponent. Hannibal, breathing heavily, looked toward Phoibos.

"Hannibal is victor," the Opir announced with no sign of pleasure. Hannibal grinned and licked Ares's blood from his nails. Ares hardly seemed to notice his injury.

Trembling with alarm, Trinity felt her pulse throbbing under the healing wounds on her neck. If not for the guards, she'd have gone to Ares now, fought by his side even if it meant her death.

But that wasn't an option. She could only watch, her nails digging into her palms, as Medon swaggered up to face Ares.

Trinity could tell immediately that this fight would be different. Ares attacked like a tiger, bearing Medon to the ground with his first charge. He didn't keep his opponent down long, but she understood his simple strategy. He had deliberately let Hannibal win the first duel. He'd saved all his strength and anger for his second opponent.

The battle was almost as savage as Ares's Challenge with Palemon had been when he'd claimed Trinity. Medon fought with his long nails as well as his hands, feet and teeth, but Ares had an edge in speed and agility, punching and kicking in moves Trinity recognized as similar to the ones she had been taught at Aegis.

But Medon found the opportunity he so desperately needed. He managed to clamp his teeth around Ares's arm, more brutal than any animal, and Trinity heard pointed incisors grate on bone.

She hardly had time to cry out. Ares swung his free hand at Medon's head, pounding his opponent's skull with a fist like a sledgehammer.

It took nearly a dozen blows, but Medon finally released his arm with a grunt of pain. Bleeding profusely from his injury, Ares kicked a staggering Medon in the genitals. With a shriek of agony, Medon collapsed. Ares put his booted foot on Medon's outstretched arm and bore down. Bone snapped.

The only sound Trinity heard then was the roaring of her pulse in her ears. Ares had disabled Medon, but he showed no satisfaction in his victory. His gaze seemed focused on something only he could see.

Realizing the danger was finally over, she became aware of the loud applause and of Roxana's fingers digging into her right shoulder while Garret's hand pressed down on her left. The men who had held her down were gone.

"Elders," Roxana breathed, releasing Trinity. Garret also withdrew his hand, but not before Trinity noticed that it was shaking. She blinked tears from her eyes and focused on the voices around her, hearing words of praise and admiration, with notable silence from a handful of Nightsiders Trinity assumed to be aligned with Palemon.

The enemies were outnumbered, however, and soon several Opiri had risen to congratulate the victor. Ares came back to himself and responded quietly to the guests gathered around him. He ignored Medon, who moaned as two vassals ran to help him.

"Ares should walk out of here with no less than four new allies," Roxana said, satisfaction in her voice. She eyed Trinity. "You played a very dangerous game."

"He had to have my blood, or he would have lost," Trinity said, never taking her eyes off Ares.

Roxana and Garret exchanged glances. "Ares wants you to come with me," the Bloodmistress said. "He has business to take care of."

"You expect me to leave now?"

Roxana pulled Trinity up with her full Opir strength, and Trinity was still too weak to resist. The Bloodmistress led her out of the dining hall, through a broad corridor and into a small waiting room, furnished with ridiculously gaudy chairs and couches, some of which seemed designed for blood taking in the act of sex. More erotic frescoes covered the walls.

"Sit," Roxana said. "Garret?"

A knowing look passed between the Bloodmistress and her serf before she left. "It's as safe as it's ever going to be," Garret said to Trinity, closing the door and moving to stand beside her.

"Ares didn't ask Roxana to bring me back here," Trinity said, meeting his gaze. "She knows, doesn't she?"

"Yes," he said. "She knows about the Underground. She's one of us. And considering what's just happened, we've had to change our plans." He cleared his throat. "We have to try to convince Ares to join us."

Trinity dropped onto the couch. "Ares?" she repeated, feeling lightheaded.

"It wouldn't be without precedent," Garret said. "Roxana isn't the only Nightsider who knows about us, though there are only a handful of direct supporters."

"How... Why did she become involved?"

"I didn't plan it this way," Garret said with a crooked smile. "Believe me, I hated them as much as anyone when I was sent here. As soon as I realized that Roxana was a liberal Mistress and I had some freedom to move around, I joined the Underground. I rose in the ranks to where I am now. But it became harder and harder to betray her, and…"

"You trusted her enough to tell her," she said. "Because you're in love with her."

"Yes." He met her eyes. "The same way you're in love with Ares."

Trinity began to rise. "But I'm not—"

"It was hard for me to admit it, too. But after a while there wasn't any point in denying it. And pretty soon it was obvious that—"

"She loved you, too," Trinity said, swallowing the lump in her throat.

He looked down at the carpet. "We were wrong to believe they aren't capable of it."

Aware of how little time they might have and more than eager to change the subject, Trinity caught his gaze. "I was given a message to meet with the leader of the Underground at this party, but I was also made to understand that there's not much you can do to help me with my mission. That you'd called for the Enclave to send an operative because you hoped one of us would do what you couldn't."

"Roxana and a few other Opir allies have been attending every Assembly, trying to find out what's going on behind the scenes," Garret said, knotting his hands behind his back. "They know how precarious the balance is between the Expansionists, the Independents and Pax, and now we have reason to believe that secret plans are being made in the Council…plans for war of which no one else in the Assembly is aware. But we've used up most of our resources."

"And now you need Ares."

"We know he has a powerful sense of justice, and he realizes what will happen to his relatively peaceful existence if a new war breaks out. Roxana has had him pegged as a possible ally for some time. But the Expansionists—and plenty of Independents—won't consider the possibility that their way of life may destroy them as surely as humanity might." He hesitated. "There's something else you should know. We asked Erebus to send a well-educated operative because Roxana knew that Ares had developed a strong curiosity about the human viewpoint and would value such a serf. Roxana convinced Ares to attend the Claiming, hoping that he'd choose whoever Aegis sent."

"You *planned* it?" she asked, truly astonished.

"As much as we could, given that we couldn't guarantee anything, or even know exactly how Aegis's operative and Ares would interact."

"I was told nothing about this."

"Our communication was tenuous at the best of times. If Aegis didn't tell you, they must have thought you'd be more effective not knowing." He grimaced. "We should have asked them to send someone less beautiful. Ares wouldn't have been strongly influenced by appearance, but we weren't prepared for Palemon's interest."

"Or for what could happen if they sent a dhampir."

His eyes widened in shock. "You're a—"

"Yes. I guess they didn't manage to get *that* information to you." She leaned forward. "Listen. I've met two of the Underground members in Ares's Household, but I don't know the name of the person who told me to meet you. I need to know who she is."

Visibly reluctant, Garret unclasped his hands. "Cassandra," he said.

Trinity jumped to her feet. "Cassandra? You're kidding, right?"

"She isn't what she may have seemed to you," he said. "She was playing a part, as many of us are. She was working toward a time when she could tell Ares at least part of the truth, and she felt she was on the verge of that when you arrived."

Trinity shook her head. "I don't believe it. Not Cassandra."

"Listen to me, Trinity. If she ever resented you, it was because she'd lost her chance to complete her own mission. She was afraid you wouldn't trust her once you found out who she was."

"I still don't."

"Whatever you may think of her personally, Cassandra's part in this has been vital."

"Why did she come to Phoibos?"

"He's one of those Nightsiders we might be able to influence. In spite of his strange habits, he treats his serfs very well and gives them a fair amount of freedom."

Trinity wondered if that was really all there was to it, but there was nothing she could do about the situation at the moment.

"I have a message for you," she said. "And you're not going to like it any more than I do."

"What is it?" Garret asked, a note of alarm in his voice.

"Someone in Ares's Household has discovered the Underground presence there."

"Who?" Garret asked, taking a step toward her.

"I can't tell you that. If I do, he could go to Ares and inform him…which he *won't* do if we remove the members from the Household and get them out of the Citadel."

"One of Ares's serfs would expose his fellow humans to an Opir?"

"A loyal serf who's worried about what will happen to Ares if someone discovers the Underground operating under his authority. What would happen to Roxana if anyone found out she was involved?"

Garret sank into a chair and gripped the arms with clenched fingers. "All throughout history," he said, "the rulers of societies run on the labor of slaves have feared uprising, and Opiri are no different. An Opir working against her fellow Opiri on behalf of serfs would be an abomination to them. But we thought the members in Ares's Household were—"

"Safe?" she asked. "What about the serfs who have been covering up what's going on, even if they weren't members themselves?"

"We've had to take many risks," he said, his voice hardening. "Exposure would be bad for Ares. But it will be much worse for Roxana."

"Why worse?" Trinity asked with an unsettling premonition that what he was about to tell her would change everything.

Garret closed his eyes. "She's pregnant," he said.

Trinity pressed her hand to her mouth, remembering her long conversation with Ares about interbreeding and his promise that he would never make her pregnant.

"You're the father?" she whispered. "But I thought only male Opiri could—"

"Obviously it's not true. We never intended it to happen. We've been together far longer than I've officially been her Favorite. I don't know why her precautions failed, but now she's carrying our son. And the children of female Opiri and male humans are killed at birth."

"But if they're…if they're dhampires—"

"They aren't. There's something different about them that Opiri hate, and they're taken away from their mothers as soon as they're discovered."

"My God," Trinity said. "Why hasn't Roxana fled the

Citadel? They might think she was crazy, but any Blood-mistress can do what she pleases. No one could stop her."

"The Council doesn't trust any Nightsider to leave since the new colonies were formed in the Zone."

"Humans and Opiri living as equals," Trinity murmured.

"If she had taken me with her," Garret said, "the Council would know where we'd be headed. I tried to make her leave alone, but she refused." He paused, panic hovering behind his eyes. "This serf who threatens us… Do you have any idea why he chose this time to do it? Does he know you're from Aegis? That you're a dhampir?"

"He guessed that I wasn't human, yes. He asked me if I was a spy, but I think he believed me when I told him I wasn't."

"Just knowing you're a dhampir is bad enough." Garret released his breath. "Does he have any idea how difficult it is for us to get someone out of Erebus? We only manage it a few times a year, at best, and we're lucky if one or more of us doesn't 'disappear' afterward."

"He obviously knows it's possible."

"And what does he expect Ares to do if several of his serfs go missing?"

"He didn't tell me *what* he expected. I haven't even had a chance to warn the two members I've met face-to-face. But if we don't comply—"

Garret rose abruptly and paced across the room, muttering under his breath. When he came to a stop, his expression was as rigid as one of the Nightsiders' sculptures.

"It's Daniel, isn't it?" he asked.

"What difference does it make?" Trinity said, her chest beginning to tighten with foreboding.

"Because he'd do anything to protect Ares. Anything." Garret stared at Trinity. "There's only one thing we can do. You'll have to kill him."

* * *

Garret's ruthlessness stunned her. Aegis operatives were prepared to take stringent measures in the Enclave's service, but this—

He's the leader of the Underground, she reminded herself. *He has to protect dozens, maybe hundreds, of people. Not to mention the woman he loves and their unborn child.*

"What you're asking is impossible," she said, torn with a deep and bitter pain. "I couldn't get away with it. He may have some way of getting the information about the Underground to Ares if something happens to him. And I'm willing to try just about anything else before I'll even consider it."

"There is only one other way," Garret said. "The one I suggested before. Recruit Ares to our side."

"Did it ever occur to you that he might refuse and turn us all over to the Council?"

"Is that what you really believe?"

"Have you forgotten that I'm his vassal now?"

"I still don't understand why you did it," Garret said. "How could that possibly have aided you in your mission?"

"Cassandra told me I could gain access to the Assembly. But that wasn't the reason I asked Ares to convert me. It was necessary to save his life. He'd become addicted to my dhampir blood." She looked away. "It was a weapon I could use if I needed to. Aegis gave me the means of stopping it from happening, but I had to make sure Ares kept me close, bind him to me somehow, and at the time…" She met Garret's gaze. "I didn't realize how bad it would be. How much it could hurt him."

"Hell," Garret swore, running his hands through his red hair. "This couldn't be—" He stopped. "You can use this, Trinity. Use it to convince him to come over to us."

She laughed. "Even if I thought it would work, he won't be addicted anymore. Not since he converted me."

The door swung open. "That is fortunate," Ares said as he walked into the room, Roxana at his heels. "Otherwise, it might have been necessary for me to kill you."

Chapter 21

"Ares," Roxana said softly, touching his arm.

He shook her off. "Take your serf away," he said, "before I kill him, too."

"No!" Roxana said, stepping between him and the humans. "You won't harm Trinity. It's not in your—"

"Get out of my way," he said, staring at Trinity through a red haze of rage.

"Not until you've calmed yourself," Roxana said.

"You're a traitor," he said, baring his teeth at her. "I should call Challenge on you."

"You mean you won't turn me and Garret and your own serfs over to the Council right away?" she asked. "You'd slake your bloodlust first?"

He shouldered past her, nearly knocking her over. Garret stepped up in a hopeless bid to protect her. Ares lifted his hand to strike the serf down.

But suddenly Trinity was there, inches away, her gaze meeting his with sorrow and defiance.

"I know you'd never do that to Roxana," she said. "She's not the one who betrayed you. *I* did."

His instinct was to grab her by the throat and squeeze until she begged for mercy. He remembered the crucial moment when he had decided to look for Trinity, who had mysteriously disappeared along with Roxana's Favorite. The moment when his victory over Medon had turned to ashes.

What he had overheard had been a jolt to the gut and a blow to the mind. It had gripped his body and nearly doubled him over with shock. If he surrendered to his basest instincts now, he would lose what little sanity remained to him.

He dropped his hands to his sides, clenching them so hard that the bones threatened to snap.

"She didn't betray me?" he asked with a bitter laugh. "She merely arranged for me to attend the Claiming in the hope that I would choose you. She always knew my Household harbored members of this Underground."

"I was waiting for the right time to—" Roxana began.

"Recruit me? It appears you have always found me weak."

"Not weak," Roxana said. "Wise enough to see the only solution to an untenable situation."

"I know what you find untenable about it," he snarled. "Get out."

Keeping just out of Ares's reach—as if that would protect him—Garret took Roxana's arm. "Please," he said.

Her gaze met Trinity's. "I'm sorry," she said. Backing away, she and her lover left the room. Trinity remained very still. "How long were you listening?" she asked.

"Long enough," he said, curling his lip up over his teeth. "Where to begin? Which betrayal should be given the most attention? That you have been in contact with the Underground? That you are a dhampir and addicted me to your blood in order to 'bind' me to you? Or perhaps that you are an operative of Aegis, and never said or did anything that was not in the service of your Enclave?"

"They're all the same," she said, as unflinching as she had ever been. "All part of my mission. Get into Erebus and find out if your Council was planning another war and, if so, determine how close they might be to provoking one. Use any means at my disposal, at my own discretion."

"Including this addiction."

"I couldn't be sure what would happen when you took my blood. I hoped you would eventually trust me enough to share information about the current situation in Erebus, give me a chance to observe the state of affairs with my own eyes. We were never sure it would work, but we couldn't leave any possibility unexplored when the fate of humanity was at stake."

"It must have disappointed you greatly to learn that I had little to do with political matters in Erebus."

"You also said you had no interest in acting against the Enclave. The disruption of a new conflict would only disturb your life as you wished it to be."

Ares remembered speaking such words to her and meaning them. He remembered how earnestly Roxana had urged him to take his place among his peers in the Assembly. She had spoken of the body becoming polarized, unbalanced, driving inevitably toward disaster for humans and Opiri alike.

He had chosen to ignore her warnings, and the wisdom of words that had been true, even as she deceived him: *Is it too much to expect that we should fight for something better than what we have in Erebus?*

But she had been nursing other, far more personal reasons for wanting something "better." And his life had already been utterly changed. It might never again be set right.

He wiped his lips with the back of his hand and turned away, his mouth remembering the taste of Trinity's blood as if he had just bitten her.

"How did you hide what you are?" he asked.

"Look at me," she said.

Resisting the instinct to berate her for daring to speak to him in such a manner—a ludicrous impulse under the circumstances—Ares turned and met Trinity's gaze. She touched her eyes one by one, blinked several times, and showed him the almost invisible lenses in the palm of her hand.

There was no loss in the beauty of her eyes and only a slight change in the color. But he detected a reflective layer behind her irises, like those of a cat or an Opir, and her pupils were more oval than round. Ares knew that if he were to shine a bright light into her face, those pupils would constrict into slits.

And when she reached into her mouth to remove the caps that covered her teeth, he already knew what he would see.

"Why?" he asked. "Why hide it?"

"It was a trump card I could play if it became necessary," she said in a dull voice, as if giving up the secret had finally drained her of her unquenchable spirit. "I could use it if I thought it would get me the kind of master I believed I needed."

"One you could manipulate."

"If I ended up with a bad one, being a valuable dhampir might protect me. The possibility of addiction was another factor that might work in my favor. But now I've learned that Roxana…"

"Encouraged me to attend the Claiming and arranged with Aegis to present you as the perfect bait."

"But the Underground didn't know I was a dhampir," she said.

Ares wondered if Palemon had felt the truth of her nature when he had attempted to claim her. Had *he* felt it, ignorant of the source of his own desires?

"If Palemon had claimed you," he said, "you would have had no time for betrayals. You would have been kept chained to his bed until he used you up or killed you."

"I told you more than once how grateful I was that you claimed me instead," she said, her eyes glimmering with unshed tears. "That has never changed, no matter what else I had to do."

He ignored the sadness in her gaze. "You knew that if you were caught, you would die."

"Yes," she said. "I'm still prepared to pay that price. But if you have any mercy in you, Ares, don't take what I've done out on your serfs or on Roxana and Garret. Take *me,* and be content with that."

"*You* make demands of me?" he asked with a brief laugh.

"Requests," she said. "Perhaps hopeless ones. But you know that Roxana isn't helpless, either. She'll fight to protect what she cares about, and you'd have to kill her to stop her. If you could give her a chance to get the others out of Erebus—"

Ares raised his hand, and Trinity braced herself. The resigned look on her face stopped him cold.

She was finally giving up.

He grabbed her arm, pulled her over to the couch and forced her to sit. "You're my vassal now," he said. "I can make you do whatever I choose. I can force you to disclose the names of the other traitors in my Household and tell me everything you had planned."

"You heard what we've had planned. And I don't think it would be difficult for you to figure out who two of the other members are."

"Erin and Vijay," he said. "The extortion—"

"Exactly, though at the time I didn't know why those three men were attacking them." She hesitated, as if she were considering telling him something more about it, but kept silent.

"Whatever you've held back from me," he growled, "I can still compel you to tell me."

"I always knew the consequences of becoming your vassal."

"And you only urged me to make you one because you wished to save me from this addiction to your blood, not because you might gain access to the Assembly?"

Trinity visibly winced at his sarcasm. "You were becoming too dependent," she said, her voice thick with regret. "When you took my blood, it would temporarily strengthen you, but the effects wouldn't last." She closed her eyes. "I couldn't stand what it was doing to you."

Ares almost believed her. Worse still was that he *wanted* to.

"Why do you believe the change would save me from this dependence?" he asked, feeling his righteous anger beginning to desert him.

"My blood changes, too, doesn't it? The addictive quality will be neutralized." She swallowed. "You'll probably have to go through some kind of withdrawal, but it's been such a short time—"

Short, Ares thought wearily. It seemed a lifetime. "Apparently Garret believes you are 'in love' with me," he said, lacing the words with an almost gentle irony. "Have any of these feelings you've claimed to have for me been genuine, or were they merely part of your game?"

"The feelings weren't all lies," she said, dropping her gaze. "I wish they had been."

So did he. His life could have continued along its peaceful course, and she would have remained no more than his serf, easily discarded when he tired of her. Considering it wise to put more space between himself and Trinity, Ares paced to the opposite wall.

"Where is Cassandra?" he asked.

"I don't know," Trinity said. "I only became aware she was part of the Underground when Garret told me."

"So she, too, was attempting to corrupt me. She was simply not as clever about it as you were." He turned to face Trinity again. "I shall have to tell Phoibos about her... if *he* isn't involved, as well."

"Roxana hoped that he would eventually—"

"And what of Daniel?" he said, cutting her off.

"Daniel kept it from you, yes," Trinity said. "He didn't want me and the others to suffer the likely punishment we'd face if we were discovered, but he would have exposed us if it was the only way to protect you."

"Protect me? As you have tried to do?"

"He also knew what you'd be forced to do if *you* discovered them. Could you have killed them yourself?"

Ares refused to let her see how well she had read him. Even on those rare occasions when he had felt the urge to punish his serfs with more than mere imprisonment, he had never laid a hand on any of them.

Except Trinity.

"Daniel knew what that would do to you," she said. "You know he'd die for you. If you were to condemn him, he wouldn't make excuses. And neither will I."

"Would you have killed him to silence him, as Roxana's Favorite urged you to do?"

A tear escaped her eyes, and she wiped it away with a fingertip. "Once I wouldn't have hesitated. I would have done whatever it took to protect myself and complete my assignment. But now—" she caught her breath, as if the words she spoke were as new to her as they were to him "—now the price is too high. I said I knew the consequences of becoming your vassal. I wouldn't be able to get away from you even if I got what I needed. But I…" She lifted her chin. "I made my choice."

"And thereby destroyed any hope of fulfilling your mission." Ares clenched his fists behind his back. "Unless you convince me to do as Roxana wishes."

She remained silent, but Ares's thoughts were racing. He knew what Trinity was capable of, her fierce courage and ability to adapt. She'd deceived him again and again, but this "choice" she had made was real. Perhaps it was the only true thing in this disastrous, almost farcical situation.

"Whatever your noble intentions," he said, hardening his voice again, "you have placed me in a position that would rightly earn my own execution. Yet you wish me to support the rebel organization that has endangered me and all my property."

"Do you even know what the Underground is, Ares?" she asked. "Its entire purpose is to provide support for those humans who are suffering, and occasionally get the most endangered out of the Enclave. Every member constantly risks death or capture." She leaned forward earnestly. "*You* save abused serfs, too. The only difference is that you won't be killed for it."

"And I am to fight for a place on the Council only to turn against my own people and allow yours to revolt against us?"

"No," she said urgently, rising to join him. "The Underground isn't out to overthrow the Erebusian government. That would be impossible. As for Aegis and the Enclave, all we wanted to know was whether or not the rumors were true, if the Citadel was planning to attack us again. *We* would never have moved against you."

"And you are part of your own ruling council, your Senate? You can guarantee this?"

"You must know I can't. But you told me that most Opiri were prepared to make a deal with humanity before the

War, to offer the chance for my people to give blood willingly rather than have it be taken from them."

"And the Enclave clearly meant to make it appear that no such offer was ever made. Do you now blame your own people for the War?"

"No." She reached out as if to touch him, froze and then dropped her hand. "Ares, if we can admit we were wrong—*both* sides—there has to be a way to reach a better agreement." She flexed her fingers as if she were still fighting against the desire to touch him. "I believe in your strength, Ares. In your ability to see beyond yourself. In your sense of what's truly right, no matter how different we are."

"Your admiration moves me deeply."

"It's more than that, Ares. Garret was right. I love you."

Ares went still. It wasn't as if she hadn't implied it before, and Roxana certainly believed it. But he had no reason to believe Trinity had ever been sincere. The words were meaningless coming from her.

"Even if Garret is correct in his claim that Lady Roxana *loves* him," Ares said, "I have told you many times that I am not capable of such—"

"Whatever you stated then has nothing to do with what I'm telling you now," she said, her eyes brimming with emotion. "I think I must have loved you from the moment you claimed me, though until then I hated all your people. I saw that a Nightsider could be kind and generous and honorable. And then I found out that you tried to help make peace between humans and Opiri. You rescued Daniel and that boy, even though you wanted to keep your life as it had always been. You—"

"Stop," he ordered, raising his hand to silence her. "I have no interest in these claims of devotion, which you so easily set aside when it suited you. They change nothing."

"Maybe not," she said quietly, "but perhaps you'll appreciate the irony. I used to be considered the cold one among our operatives, the one who never let anything as trivial as human feelings get in the way of my missions. And I never did. Until now."

"And would you continue to assert this 'love' were I to refuse to help your Underground?"

"Yes." She stood erect and defiant, like a soldier facing the rifle she knew would kill her. "It's all up to you. It's all in your hands—whether to choose the side that would destroy us or the one that believes there has to be another way." She bowed her head. "As I said before…whatever you decide for me, I'll accept. But Roxana and Garret and their child…the others…"

He moved away from her again, afraid even to be near her. "I can only admire your selflessness, foolish as it is."

She met his gaze. "I don't think you're that different from the rest of us, Ares."

"Again and again you make the same mistake," he said, overwhelmed by sudden despair. "Because you stand between two worlds, *you must make yourself believe that peace is possible.* But even if you were free—even if your world and mine reached a final, lasting truce—could *you* find peace?"

"I had it once," she said. "And I know how to find it again."

Suddenly Ares wanted to be rid of her, as he was now apparently rid of his need for her blood. Or soon would be.

But to be rid of her meant only one thing: help her to escape, along with the other traitors in his Household.

He laughed under his breath. Even that wouldn't save him. Once she was outside the Citadel, she wouldn't get very far from Erebus before the pull of their bond, Bloodmaster and vassal, forced her to stop.

"Peace is an illusion," he said at last. "Disguise yourself."

As soon as Trinity had replaced the contact lenses and

the caps, Ares grabbed her arm and stalked into the corridor. There was no sign of Roxana, Garret or Cassandra.

As he and Trinity entered the dining hall, all conversation stopped. Medon and Hannibal had already left with their retainers.

Ares paused to exchange a few words with Phoibos. The Bloodlord hadn't seen Cassandra since he'd first availed himself of her blood, though he was clearly disturbed by her absence. Ares's Freebloods and Xiu Li joined him and Trinity, and they set off for home, Ares moving at such a fast pace that the others could hardly keep up. Once they had entered the Household, Ares ordered the others back to their living quarters and all but dragged Trinity to his rooms.

He closed the door to his private chamber, pulled Trinity into his arms and kissed her, thinking only of the moment, of the end of something he had never expected to have. She responded with the same sense of desperation, tangling her fingers in his hair and exposing her throat.

His mouth moved from her lips to her neck, and he bit her, grinding his hips into hers. At the same time, he unfastened the back of her gown and pushed it away from her shoulders and down her back. The silky fabric slid down her legs. He cupped his hand around her bottom, caressing her naked skin as he continued to take sustenance. He was so aroused, torn between anger and grief, that he was truly afraid he would finally lose control and hurt her.

He lifted his head and looked into her eyes. She took his hand and led him to his bed. Ares flipped back the covers and she climbed up.

In seconds he had torn off his bloodstained shirt and removed his pants and boots. He turned Trinity onto her belly, lifted her hips and entered her with one hard thrust.

Trinity groaned, but it was a sound of pleasure and desire, and she gasped again and again as he moved inside her. He wasn't overly gentle, but he knew she had no need or desire for gentleness. This truly might be the last time, and she knew it.

She came an instant before he did, and they shuddered together, her body clenching around him as he finished in a series of urgent thrusts and finally let go.

He withdrew slowly, swung his legs over the bed and walked away, leaving her sprawled and silent among the sheets. He found a fresh shirt and pants in his armoire and pulled on the clothing with no thought to the dried blood on his chest and shoulders, or the sense of betrayal that still lingered like rancid perfume.

"What will you do now?" she asked, rolling over onto her back. She made no move to cover herself. She was utterly vulnerable, ready to accept whatever sentence he imposed upon her.

He strode into the Great Room and opened the window shutters. He heard Trinity move up behind him on bare, almost silent feet. Dhampir feet.

He gestured at the view of the city below. "This is my home," he said. "This is what I am. I can never be what you ask. But Roxana has been my…friend, as you would call it, for a very long time. I would not see her killed because of a lapse in judgment. If there is a way to get her and her Favorite out of Erebus, I will attempt to arrange it."

"And the others?"

"Those who betrayed me in my own Household must be punished." He closed the panels and buzzed for Jonathan. The serf came quickly, his skin ashen. Ares had no doubt that he and the other serfs suspected what had happened. They almost certainly knew that their lives hung in the balance.

"Where is Daniel?" he asked.

"I…I don't know, my lord," Jonathan stammered. "He hasn't been seen since the Procession."

"Continue to look for him," Ares said, cold to the depths of his being. "No serf is to leave this Household for any reason. Trinity, return to your room."

Jonathan hurried out, but she lingered in spite of his orders.

"You're going to interrogate them, aren't you?" she asked. "Especially Erin and Vijay."

He gazed into her eyes, always lovely no matter how she displayed them. "Do you know the names of the other members and their supporters?" he asked.

"Only the ones I've told you about."

"Then go to your room," he commanded, "and remain there."

Her jaw set, and he could feel her fighting him, resisting the absolute hold he had over her as her Sire.

"Please, my lord," she said, "consider this. Go to the assembly hall. Ask the members of the Underground to give themselves up in exchange for the safety of the others."

"Ask," he snarled. "Ask traitors to betray themselves."

"You said you can admire humans for their capacity for selflessness. I can't guarantee anything, but you can still interrogate them if they don't respond."

The portrait of Van Gogh seemed to mock Ares from its place on the wall, and he was tempted to break it in two. "And when I have the traitors," he asked Trinity, "what do you advise I do with them?"

"Meet with the serfs," she said softly. "Speak to them first."

He stared at her for a long time, sickened yet again by his own weakness and the hold she still had on him, even after all she had done.

"Is this your last request of me?" he asked.

"Yes, my lord," she said, her breath catching as she spoke.

"Then dress yourself, and wait." He buzzed Jonathan again and gave the order.

Chapter 22

When Ares and Trinity reached the assembly hall, the serfs, most of them roused from sleep, looked up with expressions that suggested they expected to be devoured on the spot. Jonathan, Diego, Levi and Elizabeth stood near the front, eyes wide and faces taut with fear.

Ah, yes, Ares thought. *They knew.*

Striding to the dais at the front of the room, Ares struck the floor with the butt of his staff and took the single, ornate seat resting on the platform. Trinity stood slightly behind him, a vital presence he could neither repudiate or ignore.

"I know many of you are aware of the presence of insurgents in this Household," he said, his voice ringing in the wide space.

No one moved. Trinity's hand came to rest on the back of his chair, and from the corner of his eye he could see her fingers tighten.

"I have come to give you members of the so-called Underground a chance to save those who have hidden and protected you," Ares said. "If you surrender yourselves now, there will be no further inquiry. If not, it will be necessary to question every member of this Household, and I cannot answer for the consequences."

There was still no answer. Ares clenched his teeth. It was clear that whatever Trinity had expected, the guilty serfs would not surrender themselves to save their fellow humans.

"May I speak to them?" Trinity asked, her lips close to his ear.

He nodded brusquely, and she moved to the side of his chair.

"Very early this morning," she said, "I was sent by a member of this Household to contact the leader of the Underground in the Household of Lord Phoibos. Lord Ares discovered my purpose, but has shown mercy and chose to speak to all of you before he passes judgment. He knows the actions of the Underground within this Household could lead to its downfall."

A slow murmur began in the back of the hall, loud to Ares's ears even though it was hardly more than a whisper. He waited, counting the moments until he could end this farce.

Then the first man stepped forward, trembling all the way down to his shoes. It was Vijay.

"I am…" He swallowed loudly. "I'm a member of the Underground."

The room echoed with a collective moan. A moment later Erin walked toward the dais and bowed.

"So am I," she said quietly.

After that, a dozen serfs came forward to admit to their knowledge of the Underground, including Levi and Elizabeth. Finally, Abbie came to stand before the dais.

Ares was aware of Trinity's underlying tension, the

change of her scent as she heard the woman's confession of membership in the Underground. "You can see they're willing to die so that the entire Household doesn't suffer," she murmured.

"*They* brought danger upon it," Ares said without looking at her. "They took advantage of my leniency."

"They did what they believed they had to do," she said.

"As I must," he said. "Abbie."

The woman bowed. "My lord," she said.

"What was your intention in becoming a member of this Underground? Were you not treated well here?"

"I…" She straightened, meeting his gaze. "I didn't intend to cause you trouble, my lord. I would never have turned against you."

"Yet you have acted directly against the Citadel. You took serfs from their masters and harbored an agent of the Enclave. You know what will happen if other Opiri discover that I have permitted this behavior, even unknowingly."

"We know we have to pay the price," Abbie said. Vijay and Erin moved up beside her, lending their tacit agreement. "We're ready."

Ares rose abruptly. Everyone bowed. And awaited their sentence.

"Jonathan," Ares said. "Confine those serfs who came forward to the holding cell."

The Master of Serfs bowed. "Another must see to it," he said, his voice unsteady. "I knew about the Underground, as well."

Staring into Jonathan's eyes, Ares summoned the Freebloods waiting near the wall. Gordianus signaled to several serfs who hadn't come forward and moved quickly to obey Ares's orders.

"The rest of you remain here until you are dismissed,"

he said, feeling a sudden wave of nausea. "Jonathan, return to your quarters and wait for my orders."

When the prisoners and the two Freebloods had retired, Ares rose and quickly left the room. Once he was in the corridor, he leaned against the wall and tried to catch his breath as his vision darkened. Trinity moved as if to support him, but Ares's savage glance held her back.

"I had hoped this wouldn't happen," she said, holding out her open hands in a pleading gesture. "Your addiction *will* be broken, but I told you I thought you might experience symptoms of withdrawal."

"And so I'll continue to need your blood until it ends," he said with a short laugh. "How, then, can it end at all?"

"If you quit cold turkey, without tapering off—"

"I will not take it."

"You still don't know what's going to happen. Palemon will still be after you. Even if you turn the Underground members over to the Council, there will be inquiries, right? You have to be able to defend yourself physically and mentally."

"You no longer fear for your fellow humans?" he asked, straightening again.

"I wanted you to see that these people you call traitors stood by the courage of their convictions," she said, looking up into his eyes. "We remind each other that we aren't only things to be used, but intelligent beings with pride and dignity that can't be stolen. Yet, in spite of all that…" She leaned her cheek against the wall, as if she, too, had lost her strength to the burden of her actions. "No matter what you decide to do with me, I will love and respect you until the moment of my—"

"Stop," he rasped, his throat constricting.

But as she gazed at him, he saw the truth that had always been there—the remarkable woman who had never left him, even when duty had bound her to work against him.

And all at once his anger was gone. He felt a peculiar resignation, as if the very worst had already happened and all that remained was to live out the fate that had been determined long ago.

"I will not order you to the cell with the others," he said. "You will return to the assembly hall while I send a message to Lady Roxana."

Hope flashed across her face. "Ares—"

"Much of what happens will depend on her cleverness," he said. "I will advise her to use any means necessary to arrange the escape of my rebel serfs as well as herself and her Favorite, and I will help as much as I can. She will need to determine what to do with her remaining serfs to keep them safe, and with decent masters. It will be necessary for her to find Cassandra and convince her to leave, as well."

Trinity curled her fingers into fists at her sides as if she feared her feelings would overwhelm her. "Do you mean it?" she asked.

"You have succeeded in your goal. I have finally grasped the human point of view through your stubborn refusal to surrender, even when the situation seems most hopeless."

"Surrender...to you?"

"To fear. To despair. And because you—" He shook his head, inadvertently increasing his dizziness. "I will Challenge for a place on the Council. Such a rare and unexpected event will attract the attention of the entire Citadel and give Roxana and my serfs a better chance of escape. If I succeed, I may be able to do as Roxana hoped and influence the decisions of the Assembly with regard to future relations with the Enclave." He gulped in air as his chest seemed to tighten around his lungs. "But first I must win. That means I must make that Challenge before Palemon offers his, because the first takes precedence. I cannot risk being weakened beforehand."

Her bright eyes gleamed with moisture, and for a moment he thought she would fall on her knees before him. He caught her shoulders and held her up. She bent her head against his chest.

"Thank you," she said, her voice muffled in his shirt.

"Perhaps you should withhold your gratitude for the time being," he said. "You know what will happen if I lose. That is why I am sending you back to speak to the serfs, to make them understand what will happen if I fail."

She stood on her toes and kissed him, barely brushing his lips. "They would all stand behind you and fight with you if they could."

"Oddly enough, I believe you."

"Then believe this. None of it will matter if you don't survive to carry out our plans." She bared her neck to him. "Take it, Ares. Please."

Even if his will could resist her, his body could not. He drank, sealed the wound and took a deep, fortifying breath.

"Go back to the assembly hall and do as I have asked," he said, touching her cheek. "Then report to me in my apartments."

She frowned. "Are you sure—"

"Enough. For once, do as I've bid you."

She grinned at him fiercely, turned and entered the assembly hall.

Ares made his preparations carefully. He sent his message to Roxana, opened one of his books on human philosophy and read a little Marcus Aurelius and Charles Darwin. Then he dressed in his finest clothes, wondering again where Daniel had gone. In spite of his valet's behavior, he was genuinely concerned. He had no idea if the young human was safe, or if he had—

"Ares," Trinity said, striding into his bedroom. She slowed when she saw him. "You look magnificent."

He glanced down at all his finery. "Not practical for fighting," he said wryly, "but the Assembly will expect no less." He fastened the clasp of his high collar. "You have a report to give me?"

"Yes." She perched on the edge of the bed. "Every serf in the room supports what you're about to do, whatever the risks."

"They are prepared to lose what little freedom they have if I should fail?"

"I think most of them would sacrifice their lives for you."

"Then they are very—"

"Human."

He looked gravely into her eyes as he took his heavy gold gorget, a mark of Bloodmaster rank, and raised it to his neck. Trinity jumped down from the bed to help him fasten it, lifting his hair to fix the clasp.

"Have you sent someone to look for Daniel?" she asked, echoing his thoughts.

"He would not have run away," Ares said heavily, "even had there been a place for him to go."

"I think he loves you as a father," Trinity said, biting her lip. "There's no telling what else he might do to protect you."

Ares reflected grimly on how easily he had taken Daniel for granted, even though he had spoken to him more freely than to any other serf, before Trinity had come into the Household. He wondered how it must have felt to Daniel to lose that closeness, and to be berated for his rightful suspicion of Ares's new acquisition.

Trinity had made him see so many things more clearly.

"I am concerned for his well-being," he admitted. "It is not impossible that Palemon—"

"Don't say it," she said, lifting a slender finger to his

lips. "There are people here who'd be willing to look for him, if you asked."

"No," he said. "I'll put no one else in danger."

"Yes, you will," she said, in that particular tone of voice that meant trouble. "I want to stand beside you in the Assembly."

He laughed. "There has been enough foolishness today."

"I mean it, Ares. I'm not afraid."

Taking her by the shoulders, Ares gave her his most quelling glare. "You have no idea—"

"I know vassals are permitted to attend with their lords," she said.

"You'll be helpless if I lose."

"It doesn't matter where I am if that happens," she said, "and I'd rather die by your side."

"No. I have arranged for Roxana to get you out of Erebus along with the others."

"I won't go."

He pulled her against him. "Trinity, your courage does you credit. But it is useless now. You can do nothing to help me."

"I have to be with you if you have more symptoms of withdrawal. They're not over yet. And it's not just because of the Challenge," She drew away to look into his face. "What you're about to do is likely to cause chaos in the Assembly. If it does, if it comes to a bigger fight, I need to be there."

"You would die in a matter of moments, no matter how skilled a fighter you are among your own kind."

"I told you my life won't mean much of anything if you're gone."

He gazed into her eyes for a long time, wondering how he could even consider granting her request. But she was correct: if he *did* suffer additional symptoms and could not reach her, he might very well lose any chance of victory.

Defeat would mean utter disaster for far more than one
woman. The woman he...

"Very well," he said harshly, turning away. "But you
will not be permitted on the floor of the Assembly. I will
take your blood just before I enter the chamber. After that,
you must remain in the gallery above, with the Freebloods
and other vassals. Do not interact with the observers more
than is necessary. And do not interfere unless I call for
you."

"Yes," she said, her eyes growing bright again. "I'll do
exactly what you say."

Less than half an hour later, Trinity and Ares left the
Household, she wearing her best serf's tunic and pants, he
in his princely robes, carrying his staff and moving with
the grace of a leopard.

Though she still wore the contacts and the caps on her
teeth, Trinity kept her head down, remaining close beside Ares as they caught a ground car and passed the gardens and squares where Freebloods loitered, looking for
fights, and serfs rushed about their morning duties in the
semidarkness.

The car let them off at the Assembly precincts with its
wide, columned courtyard, grand arcades and series of
porticos resembling a reasonably attractive blending of
Greek and Babylonian architecture. The courtyard was
deserted except for a few serfs trimming hedges under
growing lights, but a large number of humans was waiting outside the imposing entrance.

Ares took her arm. "Nearly the entire Assembly must
be present today," he said. "You must take great care. A
side entrance is available to Freebloods and vassals. Follow
the arcade between the columns and climb the stairway
within. If anyone attempts to detain you, speak my name."

He waited until she had passed behind the columns and then strode toward the front doors. Trinity watched him climb the broad steps and disappear into the building, and then started in the direction he had indicated.

She'd gone no more than a few paces when someone stopped her. Daniel seemed to run directly into her path, his eyes wild, hair streaked with blood, cuts and bruises marking his face and several half-healed bites on his neck.

"For God's sake!" Trinity said, catching him as he began to fall. "What's happened to you?"

"What are you doing here?" he gasped, looking over his shoulder. "Where's Ares?"

"He's gone to the Assembly."

Daniel cursed. "That's…the last thing he should do."

"Ares is trying to save all of us," she said. "Where have you been?"

"I…tried to make a bargain with him," Daniel said, panting with pain and exhaustion.

"With whom?" she asked, sickened by Daniel's physical state and what she feared was coming.

"Palemon," he said, looking over his shoulder again.

"What bargain?" she demanded. "Did you tell him about the Underground?"

"No!" He scraped blood-matted hair away from his face. "It isn't what you think. I would never…" He coughed as if he had swallowed broken glass. "I was willing…to give myself to him for…breeding stock. He said he wouldn't… send anyone else to fight Ares before *he* was ready to Challenge him." Daniel leaned on her heavily for a moment and then straightened, visibly struggling to take hold of himself. "Once Palemon had me, he…laughed and told me he had information about Ares helping the Underground. He expected me to confirm it." Daniel grinned with a strange, almost triumphant ferocity. "I didn't."

So he'd been tortured, Trinity thought. The brave, loyal idiot.

"I was supposed to help set a trap for you," Daniel said, closing his eyes. "He wanted you, too, before the Challenge. He knows Ares is coming to the Assembly today, and he will…accuse Ares of harboring members of the Underground."

"With what proof? What does he know, Daniel?"

"He didn't…see the need to tell me. But I know who told *him*." Daniel's eyes, filled with pain as they were, darkened with hate. "Cassandra. I think she's been Palemon's spy since Ares first claimed her, and she's been deceiving the Underground, as well. She…told me she poisoned Novak because he was about to expose her as a double agent." He gripped Trinity's arm with desperate strength. "Hannibal and one of Palemon's other allies are following me. You have to go back to the Household. Hide yourself." He shoved at her weakly. "I'll lead them away."

"I'm not going anywhere. I'm here to help Ares."

"You can't. Even as his vassal…"

"How did you know? You weren't at the party when he—"

"You forget how long I've been in Erebus," he said. "There are many ways—"

He broke off, and Trinity barely kept him from falling again. "When will Palemon be here?"

"He's been spreading the word…that something big will happen in the Assembly this morning, but he's making Procession." He choked on a laugh. "You know how arrogant he is."

"Then we have a little time. Ares is going to Challenge for a place on the Council."

Daniel pulled a hand across his haggard face. "We have to delay Palemon. Distract him somehow."

"Listen to me," she said, gripping his shoulder. "Ares

has become addicted to my blood. He's in withdrawal now. I have to stay with him."

"Then I was…right," he said, stumbling away. "You were betraying him all along, like Cassandra."

"But I'm not now."

"How can I trust you?"

"Daniel, I care about Ares as much as you do. You have to believe that." She searched the man's accusing eyes. "I can't ask you to put yourself in Palemon's hands again. But if you can figure out anything, anything at all that will keep him away a little longer…"

"Where is Lady Roxana?" he asked urgently.

"She's supposed to be helping the Underground members in Ares's Household get out of Erebus."

"If she's still at Ares's Household, we may have a chance. But only if she's willing to put herself in danger for Ares's sake."

Trinity closed her eyes. She didn't want any harm to come to Roxana or Garret, and the other serfs might never get out of Erebus. But it seemed there was no choice.

"If you have a plan," she said, "you have to try." She looked over Daniel's shoulder. "Someone's coming. You have to leave. Now."

He took her hand, his grip surprisingly firm in spite of what he'd been through. "Do what you can for him. He'll…take strength from your presence. From his feelings for you."

His feelings. Trinity still didn't know exactly what they were, and yet…

"I hope you're right," she said. "Can you make it?"

"I got away once." He grinned bravely and dropped her hand. "They…always underestimate us."

"Go, Daniel. And for God's sake, be careful."

He held her gaze for a long moment, nodded and backed away, dragging one leg a little as he began to run.

Trinity turned and sprinted along the arcade, aware that she and Daniel were both racing against time. And they, like Ares, had to win.

Chapter 23

It wasn't easy getting to the side door. Trinity paused twice to hide behind a thick column when Opiri in their brilliant tunics passed by on their way to the main entrance.

But once she'd reached her destination, she knew she was safe. For the time being. The door opened onto a hallway with a narrow set of stairs rising to the right. As she climbed them she began to hear quiet voices, the rustle of many bodies above and louder voices somewhere below.

At the top of the stairs was a wide landing where an arched entrance led to a gallery overlooking a cavernous chamber. She saw immediately that most of the observers were Freebloods with the typical Opir coloring, though there were also a handful of still-human vassals. She walked boldly through the open doorway, and almost at once several dozen sets of eyes turned toward her. Nostrils flared and pale faces tightened in hostility. The vassals hastily crowded against the rear wall of the balcony.

One of the male Freebloods left his place by the railing

and stalked toward Trinity, his long tunic swirling around his boots. He sniffed the air.

"New," he said, narrowing his eyes. "Who are you?"

"Keep your distance," Trinity warned. "I'm here with Bloodmaster Ares."

The Freeblood hesitated and began to speak again. But there was a swell of raised voices from the chamber below, and the Freebloods returned their attention to the Assembly, shoving toward the railing for the best view of the proceedings. Trinity forced her way through, ignoring snarls and threats. She knew she had to show far more confidence than she actually felt.

It worked. Trinity was able to get a good view of the chamber with its inward-curving rows of seats and the wide space between that she guessed was meant for displays of some kind, perhaps even Challenges. Three-quarters of the seats were occupied, so she assumed that Palemon had achieved his goal of alerting most of the members that there would be an unusual event at this meeting. The Bloodlords and Bloodladies formed an ever-shifting sea of white hair and pale features, and the sense of anticipation was as tangible and deadly as daylight on Opir skin.

As she watched and listened, the Opiri fell silent. Trinity swept the chamber with her gaze and found Ares striding into the open area with his staff in hand, bold and fearless as a fairy-tale prince. His black hair and light violet eyes stood out among the other Nightsiders, making him appear like a panther among lambs.

Trinity closed her eyes and took several deep breaths.

"You choose a strange time to join us, Lord Ares," an unfamiliar Opir's voice said, breaking the silence.

Trinity's gaze jerked to the Opir at the center of a group of seven Nightsider men and women sitting behind a table raised on a dais above the Assembly. He was tall, and his clothing reminded Trinity of pictures she'd seen of ancient

Egyptian gods, though modified to complement the usual Opir fashions.

She hated him immediately.

"Imhotep," Ares said, raising his staff as he turned to face the other Opir. "According to law, I can take up my place at any time I choose."

The Council members glanced at each other. Phoibos was among them, his expression neutral. Two of the others were visibly hostile. One of them, a surprisingly broad Nightsider with a bulldog-like expression, glanced at Imhotep and rose when he nodded permission.

"We have heard the rumors," the bulldog said, nearly spitting as he spoke to Ares. "Rumors of treachery on behalf of the serfs, unthinkable alliances no Opir can tolerate."

Trinity nearly gasped aloud. *This* she had not expected. Not when Palemon had yet to make his grand entrance and personally tender his accusations.

Or was he simply using this Opir to set the stage and plant doubts in the minds of the Assembly members, even before his arrival?

"Rumors, Sargon?" Ares said, severing the dreadful coil of her thoughts. "From your usual reliable sources?"

Voices rose among the Assembly, murmurs of anger and of amusement, though Trinity didn't understand Ares's inference. It was impossible to tell if he suspected that he had already been betrayed.

"It will soon be proved that you are a human-loving traitor," Sargon snapped, shifting as if he would circle the table and confront Ares directly. His ally held him back, perhaps realizing that any further insults would lead to a Challenge he was not prepared to meet.

They didn't know that Ares intended to offer only one Challenge today, Trinity thought. *If* he got the chance.

"I await this evidence," Ares said calmly, spreading his arms in a dramatic, mocking gesture.

"It is coming," Imhotep said coldly.

So the leader of the Council had to be one of the Expansionists, Trinity thought, like Sargon and Palemon—the opponents of Pax, the party to which Roxana belonged.

"With Palemon, I presume," Ares said with a slight ironic smile. "One would almost believe his tardiness suggests some reluctance on his part."

"There will be testimony," Imhotep said. "You will be held in judgment by this Council and Assembly."

"Will I?" Ares looked pointedly toward the section of seats that seemed to be populated by the most hostile Opiri. "Where are those among Palemon's brave allies who were to offer Challenge before their master dared to face me?" He bared his teeth. "I stand here before you."

Several of the Opiri he had addressed surged up from their seats. Ares glowered at them, and one by one they sank back down.

"Order," Imhotep said, banging his falcon-headed staff on the floor of the dais. "You have not been given permission to address the Assembly, Lord Ares."

"My honor and rank have been questioned," he said. "And *you* have permitted it, Lord Imhotep."

"Do you question my authority over this Assembly?"

"I question more than that," Ares said. "It is my right to offer Challenge to any member of this august body when it is in session, according to the provisions of our law. I Challenge you, Imhotep, for your place as Lord Chancellor of the Assembly."

Once again voices swelled in argument all around the room. Trinity knew that Imhotep had to be a very powerful Bloodmaster to have won the top seat in the Assembly, but he looked as if he'd bitten into a human throat and swallowed a mouthful of acid instead of blood.

"Unprecedented," one of the Freebloods at the railing whispered. "Imhotep has never been Challenged since he won his place on the Council."

"He is one of the Elders," a woman said. "If he has ever been beaten, it was long before the Awakening."

"They say the same of Ares."

Is that what Imhotep is afraid of? Trinity thought. Palemon had been preparing to Challenge Ares, but only after his enemy had been worn down with lesser Challenges. If Imhotep had been in on the scheme somehow, he must realize now that Palemon's plan hadn't quite worked out.

And the Lord Chancellor clearly wasn't prepared.

"He has no right!" Sargon said, rising again. "One who is accused cannot Challenge!"

"Accused but not convicted," Ares interrupted. "Nothing more can be done until the Challenge is met." He stared at Imhotep. "You may step down without shame, as custom permits. Or you may fight. Choose, Lord Chancellor."

Silence fell in the chambers. Very deliberately, Imhotep walked around the table and descended the steps to the level of the highest row of seats.

"I surrender my position on the Council to Lord Ares," he said heavily.

The uproar following his announcement was almost deafening. Ares himself seemed shocked, though he hid it instantly.

Once again Trinity was left at a loss. Why, if Imhotep had never been defeated and was of the same rank as Ares, had he simply conceded?

The gallery buzzed with speculation and excitement as the Freebloods struggled with the same question. Head down and holding his staff low at his side, the former Chancellor descended to the lowest level and quickly exited the chamber.

After only a moment's hesitation, Ares began to climb

to the dais. Sargon and his ally moved as if to intercept him. But they were forestalled by yet another Council member.

Phoibos, looking nothing at all like the jolly man he had seemed at his party, rose and faced the two Expansionists. "If Palemon is behind these accusations," he said, "we must wait for his arrival before Ares can take his place here." His gaze met each of the Council members in turn. "Are we agreed?"

The Expansionists immediately concurred, while two Councilors, whom Trinity judged as being members of Pax, protested. In the end, another Councilor, perhaps an Independent, joined with the Expansionists, and Ares paused in his ascent. He remained where he was, his staff planted firmly beside him, and the entire chamber fell back into a waiting silence.

It was another excruciating hour before Palemon strode into the room with Hannibal, Medon and two other Bloodlords, followed by a large retinue of Freebloods and vassals. He came to a sudden stop when he saw Ares, and banged his staff on the marble floor.

"Ares," he said, "it is convenient that you are already here. I would have found it tedious to seek you out, though I would have taken some pleasure in sending the Hoplites to drag you in chains from your Household."

Ares clucked his tongue. "I see that Imhotep was remiss in his duties," he said. "I was not aware that insects were permitted to fly freely within these halls."

Palemon started toward him. His allies restrained him, though Trinity could see they were just as eager to sink their teeth into Ares's throat.

Bracing herself, she considered the jump from the gallery to the floor of the chamber. Any dhampir could manage it easily enough.

But Ares wasn't showing signs of weakness, and any

distraction at so crucial a moment could get him killed. He knew what he was doing.

As if he'd sensed her thoughts, Ares's head turned slightly toward the gallery. But he didn't look up. Instead, he ascended the rest of the stairs to the dais, ignoring the heated protests of Sargon and his associate.

"Does the insect do anything more than buzz?" he asked.

"Where is Imhotep?" Palemon demanded.

"A pity Lord Palemon was not present to witness my assumption of the former Chancellor's position," Ares said.

"Traitor!" Palemon snarled. "You had no right! I have evidence that you have been working with the so-called human 'Underground' and intend to smuggle serfs out of Erebus."

The noise in the chamber intensified again. Trinity's heart beat faster.

"I have been told of these rumors," Ares said, still addressing the Assembly. "But I ask where and from whom this 'evidence' was procured."

The Freebloods behind Palemon and his allies separated and Cassandra stepped forward, as stunningly beautiful as ever. She smiled at Ares with vicious triumph.

"This is my Freeblood," Palemon said, placing a possessive hand on Cassandra's shoulder. "She was my agent in Ares's Household, and posed as a member of this Underground. She can testify—"

"She is obviously new made," Phoibos said, looking far from pleased. "She cannot be a reliable witness if she was but recently a serf."

Palemon scowled, as if he had not expected to be called out on his maneuver by someone as soft as Phoibos. Trinity assumed that Palemon had converted Cassandra soon after she'd detached herself from her new "master" at the party.

"I have other witnesses," Palemon said. He signaled

to his allies, who pushed someone forward to stand just behind him. It was Roxana, her long hair tangled and a haunted expression in her dark eyes. She stared at Ares as if she were trying to speak directly into his mind. With her was Garret, who looked very much as Daniel had—bruised and bloodied and almost too weak to stand.

Either they'd simply failed to escape, Trinity thought, or Daniel had reached them and recruited them into delaying Palemon…with horrifying results. Trinity gripped the railing and tensed to jump.

"Lady Roxana was part of these crimes," Palemon said, smiling at Ares. "She confessed to abetting the Underground and admitted your part, as well."

"Because you tortured her!" Trinity cried.

The words spilled out before she knew she was speaking them. Every face in the chamber turned toward her in shock.

"Serf!" Palemon shouted. "A serf in the gallery!"

"No," Ares said, his voice booming over the hum of amazement that followed. "She is my vassal, and has every right to be in this chamber."

"As an observer only!" Sargon exclaimed. "She has no right to speak!"

A rumble of agreement rose from the seats, and the Freebloods in the gallery seemed to close in around Trinity as if they planned to restrain her. And not at all gently.

"Hold your tongue," Ares said to Trinity, meeting her gaze with desperate intensity. She nodded slowly, reminding herself that this was still not the time to make her move.

"Again," Palemon thundered, "you have no rights here, traitor." He shoved at Roxana's back, and Ares strained toward him like a hound about to snap its leash.

"Let Lady Roxana speak!" Phoibos demanded. The

other Council members nodded in agreement, their expressions ranging from worry to gleeful expectation.

"Whatever she told Palemon," a woman from the Assembly said, "it was obviously said under duress."

Roxana glanced once at Garret, who stood slightly behind her. Trinity knew she had made a confession for one reason only, and that haunted look told Trinity that the Bloodmistress had been faced with an impossible choice.

Save Garret and her child, or save Ares.

"She is a Bloodlady," Sargon said. "She may choose to Challenge Palemon at any time if she wishes to refute his claims."

Ares moved to the Lord Chancellor's abandoned chair. "What did you do to her, Palemon?" he asked. "Did you Challenge *her,* or did you set yourself above the law and take her prisoner without consulting the Council?"

"I acted for the good of Erebus!" Palemon snarled. He leaned close to Roxana's ear and she flinched. Once again the Bloodmistress looked at Garret. He gave a barely perceptible nod.

"I will speak," Roxana said, stepping forward. "It is true. I have assisted the human Underground."

Dozens of Opiri leaped to their feet. Others banged their staffs or shouted in anger.

"You see?" Palemon said with a triumphant smile. "She admits her treachery. She attempted to smuggle serfs out of Erebus, including her Favorite." One of Palemon's Freebloods shoved at Garret, who stumbled and fell to his knees. "This one is the leader of the Underground rebels."

Cries of "Death!" echoed through the chamber. Trinity gripped the railing harder, once again preparing to leap over it.

"Tell the Assembly what you confessed to me," Palemon said to Roxana. "Speak quickly, and perhaps you will be cast out of Erebus by night instead of in full sunlight."

"You have no right to pass judgment," Ares said, staring into Palemon's eyes. "Only the Council has that privilege."

"Tell them the rest," Palemon said, gripping Roxana's shoulder.

She moved another step forward. All the doubt and confusion in her expression was gone, and she lifted her head, beautiful and proud.

"I aided the Underground," she said. "I don't regret it. I would do it again. But Ares had no part in this."

It didn't seem possible to Trinity that the uproar could get any louder, but suddenly nearly all the Assembly members were on their feet, arguing, yelling across the space between the two sections of seats.

"She lies!" Palemon shouted. "I have witnesses to her confession!"

"Who?" Ares demanded. "Your allies and Freebloods? Are we to trust their word against that of a Bloodlady of rank and honor?"

Ignoring the Council, Palemon turned directly to the Assembly members. "I have the names of every traitor in the Underground with whom Roxana has had dealings. Give me the right to seek out these treacherous humans, and you will have your proof!"

There were choruses of agreement, but just as many objections as Bloodlords and Bloodmasters expressed outrage at the prospect of their Households being searched.

"Will you give up your right to rule your own Households?" Ares asked, meeting the eyes of a dozen Bloodlords in turn. "Will you allow this Opir and his allies to invade your territory?"

"If you harbor no rebels," Palemon said, "you have no reason to fear such a search. And if they hide among your serfs, you will want them exposed."

"At what cost?" Ares demanded. "What precedent will

this set? What will be the next excuse to soil your Households?"

"Then consider *this* dangerous precedent!" Palemon said, grabbing Roxana by the arm in a cruel grip. "She is with child by a human!"

Trinity flinched and looked at Ares. She could see signs of blood withdrawal in his face, a deepening of the lines between his brows and around his mouth, the slightest trembling in his hand on the staff.

"Now *he* lies!" Roxana said.

"This is the beast who impregnated her," Palemon said, hauling Garret up by the bloodied rags of his shirt. "It will be easy enough to prove with the proper tests. And once it is confirmed, will you still accept her word against mine?"

"She must be tested!" said one of the Opir from the Expansionist section.

"That will take time," Sargon said, "and meanwhile these traitor serfs will hide themselves from our justice. They must be exposed!"

"Let the Council hold Lady Roxana," one of the Independents suggested, "and since these charges have been leveled against Lord Ares as well, let him be—"

Ares banged his staff on the floor, silencing the other Opir's unfinished proposal. "Anyone who seeks to hold Lady Roxana, her property or mine," he said, "must Challenge me now."

No, Trinity thought. But she knew why he'd acted so rashly when he was growing weaker. He had no choice but to brazen it out, or everything would come crumbling down.

And *she* had no more choices, either. Bracing one hand on the railing, she leaped over it and down to the floor. Several Bloodlords started toward her, teeth bared.

But Ares was already there beside her, his gaze sweeping the room, his expression feral in spite of the deepening shadows around his eyes.

"Challenge me now," he said, "or hold your tongues."

No one moved.

"Ares," Trinity whispered, keeping her head down. "You need my blood."

He shook his head, never looking away from those who might threaten her. "It is illegal on the floor of this chamber."

"Can we go outside?"

"If I do, I will yield any hope of—"

"Stop!"

Chapter 24

Imhotep strode into the chamber, looking not the least bit cowed. Behind him were a mob of Bloodlords, every one as grim faced as he was.

Trinity had no doubt that they were Ares's enemies.

"You have no rights here, Imhotep," Ares said, spinning to face the former Lord Chancellor. "You surrendered your—"

"I surrendered my right to *lead* this Assembly," Imhotep said with brittle dignity, "but that does not revoke my right to speak as a member. We have discovered that this vassal—" he gestured toward Trinity "—is not only a dhampir, but also a spy for the Enclave."

It seemed, Trinity thought, that the Assembly had endured too many shocks to summon up the energy for more outrage. When Ares laid a protective hand on her back, she felt his fevered heat penetrate all the way to her bones.

"More unsubstantiated accusations," he said with the calm authority that never ceased to impress her.

"You said you would call Challenge on anyone who attempted to hold you, Lady Roxana or any others who have been deemed traitors," Imhotep said. "I call upon all who accept Palemon's testimony to Challenge Ares now, in succession." He indicated the Opiri who had accompanied him. "These Bloodlords will begin. When Ares loses, as he must—"

"Cowardice!" the woman from the Council shouted.

"How many of you will die before I am defeated?" Ares demanded. But Trinity could see his muscles clench as he tried to maintain the poise of an Opir in perfect health.

"We can't wait," Trinity said under her breath. "You'll be killed, Ares."

He shook his head. She saw the sadness in his eyes, as if he knew he had already lost.

"This is unprecedented," Phoibos said. "Neither you nor Palemon rule this body, Imhotep."

"Then let us put it before the Assembly," the former Chancellor said. "According to custom, any member can call for an immediate vote upon a point of law in question."

The arguments began all over again. But Phoibos, who seemed to have claimed the authority that should have been Ares's, silenced them with a bang of his staff.

"Lord Ares," he said, "You have already placed yourself in an untenable position by daring any in this Assembly to Challenge you. But it is also within your rights to consider if you wish to surrender yourself to the Council for questioning and judgment, where you will be protected from Challenge. Therefore, you are permitted five minutes to make this decision and prepare yourself."

Trinity looked up at Phoibos and knew instantly that he had done Ares a tremendous favor. She had no idea how he might have guessed, but somehow he must know that Ares needed Trinity's blood.

Ares must have realized Phoibos's purpose, as well.

He bowed slightly to the Councilor. "I will be in the antechamber," he said.

"Five minutes," Phoibos reminded him.

Wasting no time, Ares and Trinity strode for the door. But when they were alone, Ares wouldn't look at her.

Laying her hand on his cheek, she turned his face toward hers. "Don't waste any more time, Ares," she said. "You have to take my blood. And then we have to decide how to get out of this."

"There is no getting out of this," he said, his hand trembling as it covered hers. "Even with your blood, I cannot withstand a dozen or more Challenges in succession."

"Then you've been bluffing all along."

"With some success…for a time," he said wryly.

"But the first Challenge takes precedence," she said, holding his gaze. "And you still haven't Challenged Palemon. Why?"

"I will, once you're safely away," he said. "I should never have allowed you to come."

"I did what I had to do," she said.

"You disobeyed me," he said wearily. "And you are the one thing I will not risk."

"You won't have any choice," she said. "And it's not just because I won't go. I don't know Erebus, and there's nowhere I can hide where they won't find me." She inhaled deeply. "Will my blood still be of any use to you if you convert me?"

"What?" he said, clearly struggling to understand her words.

"If you convert me into a Freeblood, how much will my blood change? Can you still get whatever you need to stop the withdrawal symptoms?"

"I don't know," he said, his eyes growing unfocused. "It is not an immediate change. But it will do you no good to—"

"Listen to me, Ares. If I thought it would help to admit

who I am…that I managed to hide what I was, even from you…I'd do it in an instant. But you've told me that'll only make you look weak. So we're back to what I suggested before." She pulled his head down to hers. "Let me fight by your side. Even if I'm only a Freeblood—"

"You will have the right to address the Assembly, but any member who wishes may kill you if your words displease them. That is why so few Freebloods ever venture from the gallery."

"I won't speak unless it's absolutely necessary. But maybe I can do something, even something very small, to help you if Palemon cheats."

"As you did during the Challenge at the Claiming?" He gave her a long, warm smile, and she found the hope she had nearly lost.

"*I* don't mind cheating if that's what it takes to win," she said with an answering grin.

"You will be carefully watched," Ares said. "Your sudden Conversion will suggest some ploy and set my enemies on their guard. And you will still be too weak to fight any but other Freebloods."

"We don't know if anyone's ever converted a dhampir before. I'm already about as strong as most Freebloods, and I may have gone beyond that. Maybe this will make me even more powerful."

"Ah, Trinity," he said. "Do not cling to improbabilities."

"I'll cling to anything my fingers can hang on to," she said. She kissed him, glorying in the feel of his lips. "Please, Ares. I'm going to die if you do anyway. If we have to go down, let's go down fighting. Together."

"You can never be even partly human again," he said, cupping her chin in his palm.

"I'm not afraid."

"You may suffer some small discomfort."

"I'm ready, Ares."

She thought he would refuse, that *he* would cling to some insane hope that he could save her.

But he didn't speak. He bent his head and bit her. This time, she felt something entirely different in his bite, a dynamic warmth that entered her veins and seemed to burn through her body, temporarily blinding and deafening her.

When she regained her senses, she knew she was different. Stronger in a way even *she* hadn't expected. And she saw at once that Ares was stronger, too, the golden color returning to his skin, the lines smoothing away.

But something was missing. A bond she had barely felt before had been severed. She was no longer Ares's vassal. She could go where she chose, do as she chose.

As long as she stayed alive.

"Whatever you do," Ares said, that deep sadness back in his eyes, "act only when you are certain it will be of benefit."

"That I can promise you." She grabbed his hands. "I'll always be yours, Ares. In life or in death."

They kissed again, savoring each other until a Freeblood came to summon them back to the Assembly.

When they were on the floor again, they stood side by side, and Trinity felt the stares of the Opiri as they recognized, by scent or some other unique Nightsider sense, what she had become.

"I have made my decision," Ares said, addressing Phoibos. "By law, a Challenge may encompass any demand, which must be fulfilled by the loser."

"That is so," Phoibos said.

"Also, by law," Ares continued, "an Opir may Challenge an accuser in order to prove his innocence. If he is victorious, all accusations against him and those under his protection must forever be dismissed, never to be raised again."

"That law has not been invoked in more than two thousand years!" Palemon cried.

"Nevertheless, it exists," Ares said without turning. "Lady Roxana, do you accept my protection, with all that it implies?"

Trinity heard the Bloodlady take a sharp breath. "I do, Lord Ares. I and all my dependents, serfs and vassals."

"If you lose," Imhotep said to Ares, "all this will go to the one who defeats you, and all accusations will be judged accurate."

"Yes," Ares said. "That is the law."

"But two Bloodlords have made separate allegations against you and your dependents," Palemon said. "To prove these allegations false, you must fight both and win."

Trinity knew better than to grab Ares, but she was already thinking about what she had to do.

Ares wouldn't like it. He'd stop her if he could. But he wouldn't get the chance.

"Imhotep accused me of being a spy for Aegis," she said, raising her voice above the others. "Therefore, I—"

Suddenly there was a stirring behind Palemon, and Trinity turned. Ares followed her gaze as Palemon's allies pushed another human out in front of them—Daniel, who fell to his knees and sprawled across the floor, looking little better than a corpse.

"This serf abandoned you and came to me," Palemon said. "He betrayed you. And this is particularly interesting, because—"

"He didn't betray anyone," Trinity said, discreetly grabbing Ares's arm as he began to move. "And he certainly didn't go to you because of your highly honorable reputation in this Citadel, Lord Palemon."

Palemon stared at her with open loathing and kicked Daniel in the ribs. The serf rolled on his side, protecting his belly, and Ares started toward Palemon in a blur of motion.

Trinity managed to grab him again and hold on. His muscles were like rock under his velvet sleeve. The strength she had felt growing within her seemed to increase with every passing minute, and she managed to keep her grip on Ares in spite of his violent struggles.

"Let me go," he growled.

"Ares," she said. "You know what will happen if you attack now. You'll be breaking the law of Challenge, and Daniel will suffer for it."

Slowly Ares relaxed, though in his case that meant turning from a killing machine of taut cables and spinning blades into a mere deadly predator again. He stared into Palemon's eyes.

"Let him go," he demanded.

Palemon only smiled. "I think you'll want to hear what I have to say before you act too precipitously," he said. "Do you remember that mortal woman over whom you and I had a small disagreement in the weeks just following the Awakening?"

Ares stiffened. "I remember," he said in a voice icy with hatred. "She wished to stay with me but ran because she feared you too much."

"Oh, yes. I know she loved you and wanted to protect you." He nearly spat. "A human female. But she didn't run far. I caught her, Ares. She was already with child. Yours."

Suddenly Trinity knew what Palemon was about to say. And she knew from the quickening of Ares's heartbeat that he did, too.

"I kept the woman while she was alive, which wasn't long after she birthed your offspring," Palemon said. "I also kept the child as my serf. And because I found it amusing, I sold him to you." He withdrew a long, curved knife from his belt, grabbed Daniel by the hair and put the knife's blade to the serf's throat. "But now he's mine again, and I can kill him at any time I wish."

Ares's shock coursed through Trinity as if it were her own, more painful than the most deadly electric current.

Daniel was his son. A human woman had loved him and tried to protect him—and her child—from Palemon's evil.

"He would be a dhampir if what you say is true," Ares said, suddenly calm again. "He would appear—"

"If he were the offspring of a normal Opir," Palemon said, grinning at Trinity, "he might look as she does under her concealments. But you're hardly *normal,* Ares."

He didn't react to the insult. Trinity saw him meet Daniel's eyes from across the room. The serf shook his head so slightly that Trinity almost missed the gesture.

She looked up at Ares's hard profile. It didn't matter if Ares had loved the woman. That was all in the past. But Ares couldn't move against Palemon now without putting his own son's life at risk.

As the ugly drama played out between the two enemies, someone else was watching, all but forgotten. Roxana, Garret kneeling by her side, met Trinity's gaze. She barely smiled, but there was something in the expression that told Trinity hope hadn't abandoned them yet.

"Choose," Palemon said to Ares. "You are so eager to Challenge in order to prove the innocence of yourself and those you call your dependents. But your offspring left your protection and cannot be included in the Challenge." He pushed the edge of the knife hard enough against Daniel's neck to draw blood. "Challenge me for your innocence, and your son will die. Even if you Challenge for his life and kill me, the accusations will stand. And if you win and do not kill me, you must Challenge me a second time to make the other claim. Then you must face Imhotep to protect your dhampir bitch."

Abruptly he bent his head and sank his teeth into Daniel's throat. An agonized growl rose from deep within Ares's chest.

"Ares," Trinity said.

Slowly he looked at her, his eyes glazed with tears.

"He's still afraid of you," she whispered. "He thinks your greatest weakness is compassion, so if you Challenge for your and Roxana's innocence, you'll be too stricken with grief and rage for Daniel to fight your best. But he'll expect the same if you fight for Daniel and let the others face destruction."

"I must…let my son die," Ares said, his words hardly audible even in the dreadful silence.

"No, Ares. Listen to me. You don't have to go after Palemon now. He's going to wait for you to Challenge *him*. Even if you delay, he won't kill Daniel. He wants a chance to meet you when you're at a disadvantage, and if he can't use emotion, he'll accept a weakened physical state." She pressed very close to Ares, as if she were clinging to him for protection. "You Challenged Imhotep for his seat on the Council, and he just gave up without fighting. But you have the right to Challenge him again, to prove his accusations are false."

His eyes narrowed. "Yes," he said. "But—"

"That's what you have to do. If you beat Imhotep, it's bound to give you a psychological advantage with the Assembly. Especially because we still have one card left to play."

"No, Trinity," he said. "Whatever you're planning…"

"Trust me, Ares. Please."

He held her gaze, and slowly the mad hatred left his eyes. He trusted her judgment. In spite of everything she had done to make him doubt her.

It hurt to know that she had to betray him one more time.

Slowly Ares turned to face Imhotep. "I Challenge you to debilitation," he said, "in denial of your allegations."

"Challenge Imhotep, by all means," Palemon said, pushing Daniel back to the floor. "You will still have to face me afterward, and on the same terms."

"But you'll be facing allegations of misconduct yourself," Trinity said with a smile that displayed the business end of her teeth. "How many in this Assembly know that you've broken both Citadel and Enclave law by breeding humans like cattle, using Ares's son as a stud?"

Several Expansionists rushed toward Trinity. She spun to face them and found Ares standing in front of her.

"You have no right to interfere!" Sargon shouted. "Any member of the Assembly may take her life!"

"Because you're afraid of what I've said?" Trinity asked. "So afraid that you'll silence me before I finish?"

"The human lies," Palemon snapped.

"Do I?" Slowly she removed her contacts and the caps on her teeth, confirming what most of the Opiri must surely have sensed already.

"Your problem is, I'm not human," she said. "I've never been." She glanced at Ares, smiled and faced the Expansionists head on. "There are others here who engage in the practice of breeding humans, against the statutes of the Truce. You risk starting another war…which is exactly what you want. But will it be on your terms?" She looked around the Assembly. "Not all of you are Expansionists. Do you agree that Palemon and his allies should be permitted to break the Truce for the sake of their own greed and amusement, so that they can accrue more wealth and status than those who hold by the laws? Are you ready for a war that could destroy Opiri and humans alike?"

A chorus of "nays" and "ayes" rose over her voice. Ares squeezed her shoulder. She knew he wanted to turn back the clock, refuse to convert her, save her.

But that had always been impossible.

"This Freeblood has no proof!" Palemon cried.

"How do you know?" she taunted. "Maybe there are Aegis spies in your own Household."

"No!" Palemon said. "And if there *were*—"

"If! Are you suggesting it's even remotely possible, Palemon? That you could be weak enough to let spies operate under your nose?"

"Kill her!" Palemon ordered the Expansionists, who still hovered on the edge of attack.

"No, Palemon," she said. "I Challenge you, to prove everything you have said is a lie."

Ares grabbed her and flung her behind him as if he could stop what had already been set in motion. But he knew he could not. A Freeblood could call Challenge on any other Opir, even though it almost always meant certain defeat and a lessening of status that made the Freeblood easy prey for others of his kind.

He had never thought such a notion would enter Trinity's mind.

"No," he said desperately, aware of Trinity's surprising strength as she struggled in his grip. "She is newly made and ignorant. She—"

"I accept," Palemon said lazily. "And because the Freeblood bitch failed to stipulate the nature of the fight, it is my right to choose. This Challenge will be to the death."

"If you kill her," Ares said very softly, "I will make you suffer in ways you cannot imagine."

"I can beat him, Ares," Trinity said, the true light of a warrior in her face. Immediately Ares swung toward Imhotep. "The first Challenge made takes precedence. I Challenged Imhotep before Trinity did Palemon. Therefore, mine must end before the next can take place."

"The Challenge was not accepted!" Palemon said.

"Do you accept, Imhotep?" Ares asked.

He knew that the former Chancellor would have refused if such a refusal would not have branded him a coward. A Council member yielding his seat had long been a customary way of changing leadership without bloodshed. There was no dishonor involved.

But this was very different. To refuse to fight under these circumstances would seal Imhotep's fate. To be disabled would be a humiliation, but it would not end his life or his prospects of maintaining his rank.

That was what Ares was counting on.

"I accept," Imhotep said in a high voice.

"Then I invoke another ancient law," Ares said. "Because you and Palemon have brought forth associated allegations that affect both Trinity and myself, I have the right to request a joint Challenge. I demand that you and Palemon fight both of us, pair against pair."

Trinity made a shocked sound of protest. Imhotep was clearly taken aback, but he would quickly grasp all the implications of Ares's demand. He would believe that Trinity could easily be brought down by either him or Palemon, allowing both the Bloodlords to face Ares as one.

"I make no such agreement!" Palemon shouted, breaking the stunned hush of the Opiri around them. No one in the chamber spoke or moved. But every gaze was focused on Palemon, weighing him as they had weighed Imhotep.

Just as Ares had suspected, Palemon was still afraid to face Ares, even with Imhotep by his side. "I declare Imhotep a coward," Palemon said in the same carrying voice. "He may choose to yield at any time…and he will, rather than face Ares!"

"And you are a coward for accepting the Challenge of a Freeblood you can kill without effort," Imhotep snarled, "because you would rather take revenge than fight Ares yourself!"

The Opiri lunged toward each other. Ares pulled Trinity close again.

"You see?" he said against her ear. "Like most Expansionists, they were allies only for the sake of their common goals, not out of mutual respect or what you would call friendship." He turned back to Palemon. "This chamber reeks of fear. You have always refused to face me in a death match, Palemon. Even at the Claiming, you were grateful that I set the terms at disability."

Palemon looked around the Assembly, at the dozens of Opiri judging him, awaiting his answer.

Then Cassandra stepped up to stand beside him and spoke quietly in his ear, words that Ares heard only as unintelligible murmurs. All at once Palemon smiled.

"I agree," he said.

As the noise of the Assembly's reaction rose to a collective bellow, Trinity grabbed Ares and pulled him aside.

"Don't you know why he backed down?" she asked.

"Why did you Challenge him?" Ares demanded. "You knew I could not allow Palemon to kill you. This is the only way to—"

"Protect me?" She laughed mirthlessly. "I thought you would trust me. I'm stronger than I've ever been. She swiped at her eyes. "Maybe you could face both of them together and win, if that was all there was to it. But you still don't see the whole picture. Palemon knew you wanted to keep me out of this, but once I Challenged him he didn't think beyond what seemed obvious—that he could easily kill me, and you couldn't interfere.

"It's different now. He almost certainly thinks Imhotep will go for me first, leaving Palemon to face you alone. And that's the last thing he wants." She looked into his eyes. "Do I understand correctly that both of them have to win to prove their accusations?"

"Yes. Trinity—"

"And both of us have to win to disprove them."

"It is complex," he said, trying to make sense of her questions. "Because your fight with Imhotep is only to disability, I would still have the right to go after him if he defeated you."

"Then will you let me fight Imhotep, knowing it will give you a chance to take Palemon out once and for all?"

Everything in Ares screamed denial. To let her suffer even the most minor of injuries…

"Yes," he said. "If you will do your best not to engage him more than necessary—"

"No," she said, shaking her head. "You won't. You're no longer thinking completely like an Opir, Ares, even if you believe you are. Palemon hoped you'd be distracted by having to choose between Daniel and the others. He knew you'd be vulnerable with them, but he wasn't quite sure about *me.* No matter how much you seemed to value me, he'd assume you would value your life and status far more.

"But Cassandra knows something he doesn't, something very few Opiri can understand. She just told Palemon that he has all the advantages now, because you'll never be able to focus just on him. You'll constantly be trying to keep me safe because of your feelings for me."

"Cassandra is wrong," Ares said, nearly choking on the lie.

"You once said that blindness afflicts all creatures, Ares," Trinity said with a smile that cut straight to his heart. "But Cassandra can see—she's always seen—that you're never going to behave rationally where I'm concerned."

It took a moment for him to realize what Trinity was saying. She still refused to believe what he had told her, time and again. Yes, at one time he had come very close to feeling what no Opir should. Until Palemon had reawakened them, he had driven the brutal memories of Daniel's mother from his mind, rejecting the knowledge that he had once suffered such a sense of loss.

But Trinity was right. He was truly vulnerable now. More than he had ever been in his long life.

She smiled and touched his lips with her finger. "Don't say anything. Fight Palemon. Kill him. And then, if I'm down, get Imhotep. I'm asking you this because if you—"

He silenced her with a kiss, ignoring all those who watched as if they were animals behind bars in an old-time zoo. She wrapped her arms around him and bit into his lower lip with a strange, feral desperation. Savoring the brief pain, he closed his eyes and held her hard against him.

"There is another way," he said into the warmth of her neck. "You have shown me that we can claim an advantage Palemon and Imhotep will never have." He drew back so that he could see her face. "What I believed was weakness may be our greatest strength. But only if we remain together."

"Yes," she said, smiling with love in her eyes. "You'll trust me, then. Trust both of us."

"I will," he said, stroking her hair tenderly.

"Then I have an idea of how to play on Palemon's assumptions," she said. "Just keep in mind that if I seem to be losing whatever fight I'm in at the time, the situation may be less dire than it appears."

He hesitated, thinking of all the things he so badly wanted to tell her. "The woman from before the War—" he began.

"It doesn't matter," she said.

"If Daniel *is* my son—"

"What are you worried about, Ares? That I won't accept him?"

"If we survive this," he said, his heart expanding to fill his chest with that strange, unfamiliar, nearly overpowering emotion, "everything will change."

"Yes," she said. "Everything."

Ares couldn't read her expression, but he knew she

didn't suspect that—*if* they survived—he would do everything within his power to make sure she left Erebus. She might be a Freeblood, but she could never be a true Opir as he was. And he had duties in Erebus he could not set aside now that he knew what had to be done.

He ran his finger along her jawline. "First," he said, "we must win."

She laid her hands on his shoulders. "I love you, Ares."

"I know." He hesitated, still trying to gather words so foreign to him. "Whatever becomes of us, know that I have never felt for any human or Opir what I feel for you now."

He kissed her again, but it lasted no more than a moment. "Let us waste no more time," Phoibos called from the dais. "We who remain on the Council will still be the ultimate arbiters of what occurs during the Challenge. Remember this, all of you. Fight in honor and in strength."

Trinity nodded to Ares. With a last look at her determined, beautiful face, he awaited the approach of their enemies.

Moving slowly and with suspicious glances at one another, Palemon and Imhotep met in the arena between the rows of seats, standing to face Trinity and Ares.

"The first to fall in disability will be removed from the fight," Phoibos announced. "Whoever remains must continue the Challenge to the death. You may begin."

Chapter 25

This time, there were no elaborate rituals. Each of the three Bloodlords' staffs was set into niches at the edge of the arena. A few seconds of silence followed, and then there was only immediate, relentless savagery. Palemon was on Ares, clawing and biting, while Imhotep went straight for Trinity.

All time ceased. Ares was aware of the fight going on beside him, of Trinity constantly slipping under Imhotep's guard, keeping out of his reach, making him believe she was too weak to close with him directly.

But Ares didn't interfere. He trusted her. He felt her on a level he couldn't explain, and when she let Imhotep strike once, cutting a line of blood through the arm of her tunic, he held himself back from tearing out the former Chancellor's throat.

He turned his rage on Palemon, who had clearly expected him to defend Trinity, and instinctively backed away. She swayed, let Imhotep attack again and dodged away. The moment Trinity was out of his reach again, she charged straight at Palemon from the side.

Startled by the attack, Palemon swung around to engage her. During that brief moment of inattention, Ares lunged and bit deep into Palemon's arm. Trinity stumbled as Palemon lashed out at her with his free arm, and Ares's focus wavered. He felt a shock of pain as his enemy used his long fingernails to slash him deeply across the chest, shredding his shirt and leaving four ugly lacerations that cut almost to his rib cage.

From her position on the ground a few feet away, Trinity shot him an urgent look of warning, and he remembered again. *Trust me.*

Hurling himself at Palemon, he threw every ounce of his strength at his enemy, keeping up a relentless onslaught of fists and teeth and any part of his body he could use as a weapon. He caught a glimpse of Trinity rolling neatly out from under Imhotep as he swept down to grab her by the throat.

She was more than holding her own. She was playing up to Imhotep's certainty that she was merely an inexperienced, newly made Freeblood, forcing him to act the aggressor as she dodged and countered and used the fighting techniques she had learned in the Enclave to turn the Opir's rage and strength against himself.

But she was clearly not content with the role she had assumed. She let Imhotep attack her again, fell, slithered sideways across the floor, sprang to her feet behind him and grabbed him by the back of his neck. He shook her off, but there was surprise in his eyes. Surprise—and fear.

Then Ares was fighting for his life again—fighting more savagely than ever before—because he was battling for more than Trinity and himself, for more than Roxana and his son and Garret and the other serfs who would suffer so terribly.

He was fighting for the future.

He had nearly brought Palemon down when, without warning, the Bloodmaster shrank to the floor and held up his hands as if in a final, futile attempt to save himself. Imhotep abandoned Trinity and rushed at Ares, and Palemon, bleeding profusely but not yet disabled, sprang up to attack Trinity. As Ares beat Imhotep to his knees with a single blow, he saw Palemon swipe at Trinity with those deadly nails, catching her across the shoulder.

She staggered again, falling to her knees, and Ares was about to break his promise to trust her when Imhotep took advantage of his momentary hesitation and grappled with him, biting into his throat. Struggling for air, Ares was unable to see what had become of Trinity. But suddenly she was beside him, slamming her fists into the side of Imhotep's throat. As he released Ares, she ran straight for the nearest staff—Palemon's—and slammed the knife standard against Imhotep's head.

He fell like a stone. Palemon, charging after her, stopped in shock. He collapsed with Ares's teeth tearing out his throat.

Ares rose, wiping the back of his mouth with the ragged sleeve of his shirt. Trinity tossed the staff aside and stood panting, pressing her hand to her shoulder.

Silence gave way to the approving thunder of staffs striking the ground and shouts of astonishment and dismay.

"Lawbreaker!" one of the Expansionists shouted. Sargon and his ally on the Council sprang down from the dais. Phoibos, a dazed look on his face, made no attempt to stop them.

"No weapons are permitted!" Sargon cried. "The Challenge is void!" He gestured to the Expansionists. "Take her!"

"Yes, come," Ares said, baring his teeth as he pulled

a bleeding, panting Trinity into the circle of his arms. "I can still kill many of you before I fall."

"What is the law?" Trinity called, breaking free of Ares with a grimace of pain. "No weapons on the Challenge floor?" She grinned at Sargon. "When has a Bloodlord's staff ever been considered a weapon?"

Ares knew then that Trinity had improvised based entirely on her intuition, believing that she could predict Opir behavior. And perhaps, having known him so well, she could.

"It is no weapon," the woman on the Council affirmed, her voice so quiet that everyone else fell silent to hear her. "No law has been broken. The staffs stand within the boundaries of the floor."

Dozens of Opiri protested, but their cries of anger and denial had a desperate edge. A clear majority of the Assembly and Council would be required to declare an infringement of the laws of Challenge, and the Expansionists did not have the numbers to support their agenda. They left Palemon where he had fallen, lying in a pool of his own blood. Imhotep groaned, alive but too dazed to move.

Trinity's expression was blank, her face leached of color. Ares grabbed at her as she began to sway and swiftly examined her shoulder. He pressed his mouth to it, releasing healing chemicals into her bloodstream.

"Your chest," she said, a little faintly.

"It will heal," he said.

But she bent and pressed her own lips to his torn skin, and he felt the change, knew that she was beginning to lose her humanity…had already begun before the battle started. As he had told her, she could never go back.

She laughed hoarsely at the expression she must have seen on his face. "I was right," she said. "Now we *know* what happens when a dhampir is converted." Her eyes fluttered closed. "All I want to do is fall into a soft bed and—"

"Trinity," Roxana said, suddenly beside them. She embraced Trinity warmly. "I feared—" She broke off as Garret, dried blood on his face and clothing, came to join her.

"You have saved us," he said gravely.

"Don't you know how they did it, Garret?" Roxana said, her lovely face revealing the emotions she could not show with touch.

"I know," Garret said. "It was what you and I always—"

"Look," Trinity interrupted. "Palemon's allies have disappeared."

Ares saw that she was right. Hannibal, Medon, Sargon, even Cassandra…all vanished.

"It seems there will be no more objections to your unconventional method of ending a Challenge," Ares said drily. "But if you—"

He stopped as Daniel approached, limping at the head of an army. Twenty serfs, fifty, a hundred. Vijay and Erin, Levi and Elizabeth and countless more that Ares recognized as belonging to Roxana. And still others he did not know, some hardly more than walking skeletons, others scarred and branded, who must have belonged to Palemon or his cruel allies.

And through the other entrance to the chamber strode six Bloodmasters and Bloodmistresses—all, like Ares, who had remained apart from Opir politics, men and women he hadn't seen in many years. Three were of the eldest, like Ares. Opiri who had nothing to prove.

"Where did they come from?" Trinity asked Roxana.

"We should not speak here," Ares said. "Come with me."

Trinity and the others fell in behind him, and he led them to stand near the serfs, where the humans could best be protected from attack.

"I knew what Ares intended to do today," Lady Roxana said, addressing all of them. "I was trying to get his and my own serfs out of Erebus when Daniel found me and warned me that Palemon planned to accuse Ares in the Assembly. He asked me to delay Palemon as long as possible."

"After he'd already given himself up to Palemon in hopes of making a bargain," Trinity said. "But he escaped and came here to warn Ares about Palemon's intentions. He found me instead, and I told him to go to Roxana."

"And after he warned me," Roxana said, turning Ares, "he rallied your serfs and disappeared again. Some of the serfs visited the Households of Bloodmasters whom I knew to be neutral and opposed to conflict. Your humans, and many of mine, risked their lives to address these Opiri and try to gain their support. Garret and I put ourselves in Palemon's path to…distract him. He—" She reached for her lover's hand, unconcerned with the impression the contact was likely to give the Assembly. "I was forced to give up some information under duress. But I believed I could make it right."

"You did," Trinity said. "Thank you."

"As long as these Bloodmasters and Bloodmistresses continue to take an interest," Roxana said, "and with Palemon and Imhotep defeated, the Expansionists will effectively be neutralized. At least for a time."

"And these other serfs?" Ares asked, looking at Daniel as if he were seeing the valet—his son—for the first time. "Who are they? What did you do?"

"I…" Daniel cleared his throat. "I returned to Palemon's Household, entered secretly and spoke to as many of his serfs as I could find. Some agreed to come to the Assembly to support the charge that Palemon was breeding serfs." He looked with a flash of bitter satisfaction at Palemon's body. "But it seems their presence is no longer required."

Ares glanced at Trinity. She smiled and nodded.

"Look at me, Daniel," Ares said.

The human met his gaze, and for the first time Ares

saw what he had never imagined could exist—something of himself. Not because of Conversion, but in the blood. The same blood that flowed through his own veins.

"Did you know?" he asked.

"I didn't—" Daniel broke off, clearly at a loss. "Not until Palemon...until I went to him, and he told me." He glanced at Trinity and ducked his head. "There is more you should know, my lo—"

"Call me by my name," Ares said.

"Ares," Daniel said with deep sigh. "Before the party, I threatened Trinity with exposure if she didn't arrange to get the Household's Underground members out of the city."

"You *knew* she was not what she claimed to be?"

"Yes," Daniel said. "I also saw how much you cared for her, and she for you. But I couldn't trust her, and I knew the danger to you if any member of the Underground remained in your Household."

So, Ares thought, Daniel had taken it upon himself to both betray and protect his master, completely ignorant of his bloodline. He'd twice been prepared to give himself up to a life of degradation on Ares's behalf.

"I'm sorry," Daniel said. "I should have...taken my own life when I realized that Palemon was—" He flushed, and his lip curled in self-contempt. "When I realized that Palemon was using me to take revenge on you, to mock you. Eventually he would have made it clear to all Erebus that he was breeding serfs of your blood."

Anger nearly overwhelmed Ares, and he briefly considered removing Palemon's head and skewering it on his staff. Trinity took his arm, and he exhaled slowly.

"Palemon is dead," he said. "I take no shame in what he has done. You are no longer my property, but my acknowledged son."

Daniel looked up slowly. "I am still a creature forbidden in Erebus," he said.

"You are my son," Ares repeated. "You are free now, and any who wish to dispute it—" he glanced around the room "—may Challenge me at their convenience."

Trinity felt such a swelling of pride that she could hardly keep from laughing in the faces of the idiotic Opiri with all their arrogance and assumptions of superiority. She was pretty sure it would be a long time before any of them tried to take Ares on again.

She found Daniel looking at her. There was no hostility, no desperation…just something like admiration. Admiration she wasn't at all sure she deserved.

"I am grateful," Daniel said, turning back to his father. "But how can I be free?"

"You will live in my Household as an Opir," Ares said.

"Don't you understand, Ares?" Trinity said gently. "He can't do that when he knows the other humans are still slaves. And—" she swallowed "—neither can I."

Ares looked away, his face expressionless. "Good," he said. "I believe I can arrange for both of you to leave Erebus along with Roxana and Garret and the other endangered serfs."

"And you'll come with us," Trinity said, suddenly afraid of what should have been obvious all along.

"No," he said. "I have gained some status and influence in Erebus. I must use it to guide the Assembly and work against the Expansionists." He met Trinity's gaze again. "You have not completed your mission. But you will know I have done everything within my power to allay the fears of your Enclave."

It hit her hard, knowing that he was right. Knowing that the future she had never quite managed to envision—a future they could share—was impossible.

"You're right," she said, struggling to hide her grief. "You've survived for thousands of years. You can make changes that could last a thousand more. You can work toward establishing laws that will set a standard for the better treatment of humans. If that's what you want to do."

"Of course I wish it," he said, his throat working. "But I cannot free all the serfs in Erebus, Trinity. It would lead to utter chaos and destroy our civilization in a matter of weeks."

"I know. But there are other ways." Her eyes filled with those blasted tears again and she tried to blink them away. "Ways that will allow Garret's and Roxana's child, and others like it, to grow up without stigma, without fear, even in Erebus. That will permit Opiri and humans who care for each other to be accepted for what they are and what they feel. As I feel for you."

He turned away. "Let us waste no more time," he said roughly. "The sooner we get you out, the easier it will be for me to impose my will on the Council and give your Underground a chance to disperse."

Trinity grabbed his hand, lacing her fingers through his. "Do you remember when you said I would never leave you?" she asked.

His gaze jerked back to hers. "That was when you were still my serf. Now you are free, and you have made it very clear why you won't stay."

"Then tell me, Ares. Tell me if you *want* me to stay. Tell me…" She stopped, wondering if he could admit it in the midst of this Assembly when he knew he would have to sacrifice what he had always believed of himself.

Until today, when he had come so very close, when he had almost said—

"Perhaps you will be able to advise me," he said, something behind his eyes snapping shut like a wall between them. "*If* you fully grasp the danger we will be facing. Some Opiri will continue to believe that you are a spy, even though we have refuted Imhotep's claim, and my enemies may attempt to use you against me. I will not permit them to succeed. Do you understand?"

It cut her more deeply than any wound, the realization that he still couldn't speak the words. Might never speak them. And he was intent on making sure she knew he could not protect her.

To drive me away, she thought with a flash of hope. Because he didn't believe he *could* protect her. Not and achieve what he wished for. What they *both* wished for.

And that made her realize all the more that she couldn't leave him. She could still provide that outside perspective he had once wanted from her.

Perhaps that would be enough, to help him achieve his goals. That and her own unbreakable love for him.

"Yes," Trinity said. "I understand."

"Then what are your conditions?"

"Can you give *all* your serfs a choice to leave Erebus or stay with you as free people, running the Household because they regard it as their home?" she asked.

He glanced first at Roxana, and then at Daniel. Trinity could see that Daniel was watching his father's face as intently as she was. Waiting to see just how much Ares was willing to change.

The serfs of Ares's Household were listening, too. Ares swept them with a cold, calculating gaze. They looked back—a little fearful, determined, still clinging to some measure of pride.

"I would stay," Erin said, her voice clear and firm.

Vijay, who stood beside her, nodded slowly. "So would I," he said.

One by one, all the serfs present—Levi, Abbie, Elizabeth, Jonathan and more than a dozen others—nodded in agreement.

"They respect you," Trinity said. "They choose to support you in your work in any way they can, and not only because they believe in it. They believe in *you*."

Ares sighed. "I will continue to require blood," he said to the serfs. "And so will Trinity."

"We know," Abbie said.

No one else spoke, but acceptance was clear in their faces.

"If you do this, Ares," Roxana said, "I will do the same. Garret and I will remain, and I will keep only those serfs willing to stay with me."

"And if you still want me," Daniel said, "I'll stay. But only as I am now. Not Opir, but—" he smiled unevenly "—whatever I am."

"You can acknowledge your Opir half without giving up the other," Trinity said, touching Daniel's shoulder. "That's the balance we dhampires have always had to maintain. Usually we succeed, even though most of us never knew our fathers."

"I understand," Daniel said. "Thank you."

Ares pushed his tangled hair away from his face. "You do realize, all of you, that by doing this I may jeopardize what we hope to achieve."

"Or you may prove yourself stronger than any other Bloodlord or Bloodmaster," Trinity said, "because you can trust your serfs to serve you without the threat of punishment or death."

When Ares looked at her again, the wall was down, and all she could see was raw emotion, so raw that she was unable to interpret it.

"I will do as you ask," he said.

"Thank you," she said, trying to smile. "And I promise you, Ares, I'll never demand anything of you. I'll never speak of my feelings aga—"

He swept down on her like a hunting hawk and caught her lips with his. She sank into his arms, aware of his desire, basking in his tenderness, her heart beating so erratically that she wasn't sure she could stand if she let go of him.

"Oh," Roxana said from a place very far away. "Will you set aside your pride for once, Ares, and let us go on about our business? We have a great deal to do."

Trinity held her breath. Ares's lips brushed her ear.

"I have given you entirely too much power over me, Trinity," he murmured, "from the moment I saw you. I believe…" He gave her a warm, self-deprecating smile. "I loved you even then."

The words were hardly more than a whisper, but they might as well have been a shout. Trinity turned her head into his neck. He pulled her close again and kissed her passionately, making very clear he couldn't wait to get her into bed again.

As if some spell had been broken, the usual agitated, arguing voices rose up from the Bloodlords and Bloodmasters in their seats, and Trinity was reminded that she and her friends were not, in fact, alone. The whole Assembly was on the verge of lapsing into chaos.

"I think you'd better go show them who's boss," she said, rubbing her cheek against Ares's. "Like Roxana said, you have a lot of work to do."

"*We,* Trinity," he said. He took her hand and led her toward the Council dais. "We. For eternity."

* * * * *

NOCTURNE™

Available January 7, 2014

#175 THE VAMPIRE HUNTER
In the Company of Vampires
Michele Hauf

Kaspar Rothstein is determined to find the witch responsible for manufacturing Magic Dust, a substance that can drive vampires insane. When Kaspar rescues a witch from a vampire attack, he instantly falls in love with her bright blue eyes and quirky strength. Until he realizes she may be the very witch he has been searching for....

#176 MOON RISING
Lori Devoti

The vampire-werewolf war has been over for sixty years, but now someone wants to stir it back up. Marc Delacroix, a vampire, and CeCe Parks, a werewolf, must forget their differences and work together to find a lost treasure and solve multiple murders. Along the way, they discover much more about the werewolves, the vampires...and the rebellious longings of their hearts than they ever thought possible.

HNCNM1213

REQUEST YOUR FREE BOOKS!

2 FREE NOVELS FROM THE PARANORMAL ROMANCE COLLECTION PLUS 2 FREE GIFTS!

YES! Please send me 2 FREE novels from the Paranormal Romance Collection and my 2 FREE gifts (gifts are worth about $10). After receiving them, if I don't wish to receive any more books, I can return the shipping statement marked "cancel." If I don't cancel, I will receive 4 brand-new novels every month and be billed just $22.76 in the U.S. or $23.96 in Canada. That's a savings of at least 17% off the cover price of all 4 books. It's quite a bargain! Shipping and handling is just 50¢ per book in the U.S. and 75¢ per book in Canada.* I understand that accepting the 2 free books and gifts places me under no obligation to buy anything. I can always return a shipment and cancel at any time. Even if I never buy another book, the two free books and gifts are mine to keep forever.

237/337 HDN F4YC

Name	(PLEASE PRINT)

Address		Apt. #

City	State/Prov.	Zip/Postal Code

Signature (if under 18, a parent or guardian must sign)

Mail to the Harlequin® Reader Service:
IN U.S.A.: P.O. Box 1867, Buffalo, NY 14240-1867
IN CANADA: P.O. Box 609, Fort Erie, Ontario L2A 5X3

Want to try two free books from another line?
Call 1-800-873-8635 or visit www.ReaderService.com.

* Terms and prices subject to change without notice. Prices do not include applicable taxes. Sales tax applicable in N.Y. Canadian residents will be charged applicable taxes. Offer not valid in Quebec. This offer is limited to one order per household. Not valid for current subscribers to Paranormal Romance Collection or Harlequin® Nocturne™ books. All orders subject to credit approval. Credit or debit balances in a customer's account(s) may be offset by any other outstanding balance owed by or to the customer. Please allow 4 to 6 weeks for delivery. Offer available while quantities last.

Your Privacy—The Harlequin® Reader Service is committed to protecting your privacy. Our Privacy Policy is available online at www.ReaderService.com or upon request from the Harlequin Reader Service.

We make a portion of our mailing list available to reputable third parties that offer products we believe may interest you. If you prefer that we not exchange your name with third parties, or if you wish to clarify or modify your communication preferences, please visit us at www.ReaderService.com/consumerschoice or write to us at Harlequin Reader Service Preference Service, P.O. Box 9062, Buffalo, NY 14269. Include your complete name and address.

SPECIAL EXCERPT FROM

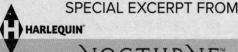

HARLEQUIN®

NOCTURNE™

Two individuals working on opposite sides
band together to enter the dangerous world of
vampires, faeries and secrets.

Read on for a sneak peak of

THE VAMPIRE HUNTER

by Michele Hauf

"Go!" Kaz shouted at the woman who had stumbled upon his
fight against four vampires.

"Impressive." Strangely, she clapped, giving him due reward.
"Like a knight who fights for his mistress's favor."

Kaz arched a brow. Why hadn't she screamed and run? That
was the normal MO for unknowing humans who stumbled
onto a slaying.

Something is wrong with this chick.

As he looked her over, he dashed out his tongue, taking a long
stroll over her black hair, streaked on one side with white. Her
heart-shaped face was shadowed by the night. And that mouth.
All pink and partly open and—he swallowed—kissable.

"Generally," she said, unaware of his distraction, "when the
knight defeats the bad guys, his mistress grants him a favor,
such as a ribbon for him to proudly display."

He rubbed his jaw and chuckled softly. "I'm not much for
ribbons. Guess that means I'll have to take something more
fitting."

Kaz wrapped his hand about her neck and curved his fingers
against her silken hair as he bent to kiss her distracting mouth.

About them, the vampires showed no sign of coming to, yet he remained aware.

Their lips crushed, compelled to one another. Soft and wanting. The burn of her mouth against his flamed his tongue with the sweetest fire. Made him feel alive.

He'd never kissed a woman who felt quite so…right.

When he pulled from the kiss to dart a look back and forth between her blue eyes, he suddenly *knew*. Destined? People didn't just stumble into another's person's life randomly.

Everything happened for a reason.

"Once more?" he asked on an aching tone.

This time when she tilted up her face to meet him, she moaned into the kiss and wrapped both hands about his waist. This woman fit him, as no other woman had fit before. Felt right. Felt different.

Felt dangerous.

"I…" she began. A sweet smile struggled with uncertainty. She shrugged her fingers through her loose sweep of hair. "Suddenly don't know how to walk away from you."

He'd like to wrap her in his arms and take her home with him and leave the world behind. Unfortunately, the real world had begun to groan near his feet.

"What's your name?" she asked.

"Kaspar Rothstein. Kaz to friends and those I tend to kiss. And you?"

"Zoë. Uh, Zoë to friends and those who tend to kiss me."

At that moment, he fell, right into her stunning blue eyes and lush pink smile.

**Don't miss the dramatic conclusion to
THE VAMPIRE HUNTER by Michele Hauf.
Available January 2014,
only from Harlequin® Nocturne™.**